Truth

Roger Deloach

Published by:
CDM Productions
P.O. Box 161401
Duluth, MN. 55816
cdmproductions.net

Printed in the United States of America
Truth

First Edition
10 9 8 7 6 5 4 3 2 1

ISBN 978-0-692-27925-0
Fiction

Dedicated to the unfailing love and unfathomable grace of my Lord Jesus Christ, and to all those who have played a part in introducing me to His truth.

Special thanks to Susie, Ted, Sarah, Joanie and Dan. Your time spent and suggestions made are deeply appreciated.

TRUTH

Part I

Reality

Chapter

1

The fresh smell of summer flowed through the pair of double hung windows as Jess slowly opened his eyes. His gaze fell on the treasure laying next to him... *The most beautiful woman in the world.* He knew he needed to be at his office in less than an hour so he gently rolled to the edge of the bed and sat up. Being as quiet as a country mouse he stood and drowsily staggered to the windows. The lush green meadow of their forty acre hobby farm played host to a doe and two fawns while the sun peaked over the horizon. Jess looked to the left and marveled at the work of art Natasha had made out of a simple vegetable garden. The corn stalks were knee high, and the mixture of other vegetable plants and flowers enticed the eyes. He could almost smell the lavender and sweet alyssum. A glance back at his sleeping beauty stirred his heart... *How is it that I am so lucky to have such a life?*

~~~~~~~~~~

Sunday, May 22, 1955, was an exciting day for the Cradle Roll class at Calvary Lutheran Church in Duluth, Minnesota. The four-year olds believed they were being touched by God Himself when the stoic figure of Pastor Larson placed his hand on their heads to pray a blessing on their lives. Jess Rivers began to squirm under the anointed prayer of God's faithful servant, not because he didn't like what was being done, but because the graduation cap was being pushed down over his eyes from the weight of the pastor's large hand.

Red caps and white gowns temporarily hid the battles and frustrations of the morning's endeavors to arrive at this moment; still, maternal pride compelled Kodak cameras into action when the service ended. Jess wasn't aware of the significance that his mom saw in this day, he was simply willing to hold her hand and let her lead. Life did not yet belong to him.

~

The next white gowns the Cradle Roll kids wore were much larger. The red caps gave way to red carnations. Jess was told that he was confirming his belief in all that he had been taught, although he wasn't quite sure what that meant. What he did know was that he could soon get on with life, having fulfilled the necessary requirements of the church. He had predetermined that he was not going to be among the one or two kids out of the nine standing with him that would continue going to church when this day was over.

Jess had been craving his freedom for some time. His mom promised him that if he finished the confirmation classes she wouldn't force him to go to church anymore. It wasn't that he spent a lot of time there anyway, one hour on Wednesdays after school for confirmation and one hour on Sunday mornings for worship service. He was glad Pastor Larson was careful never to go over the allotted sixty minutes for each, but they were still the longest two hours of his week.

He had dreaded the Sunday morning hour as far back as he could remember; it seemed to drag on forever. Week after week, year after year, he looked down from the balcony on the heads of the pillars of the church, always occupying the same twenty-four inches of pew space that must have been assigned to them when they were born.

Jess wondered how the ladies of the church could spend so much time in that building every week. According to the bulletin they were there for Monday morning Circle meetings, Tuesday morning Bible studies, Wednesday afternoons helping with children's classes, and Thursday afternoons creating quilted masterpieces for those in need. There seemed to be a funeral at least once a month, and the ladies served lunch at every one. His mom lived amongst these church dwelling ladies, but never once did he hear her complain about the time she had to spend on church chores.

The men were even more confusing to Jess. Mr. Johnson, the church treasurer, was an example of his puzzlement. Jess had walked past the church money counter and his neighbor while he was working his paper route; they were talking over the fence that separated their front yards. Jess never heard Mr. Johnson talk that way in church. He was surprised to hear God's name so freely taken in vain. Jess' dad didn't go to church, but Jess never heard him talk that way. His dad was not a religious man, but Jess could see some sense in his dad's claim that, "I can worship God better in His great outdoors than I can in some building man put together."

Pastor Larson had served Calvary Lutheran for as long as Jess could remember, but in all those years he couldn't recall one thing the pastor had talked about in his many sermons. This was not Pastor Larson's fault; Jess learned to tune him out the moment the lanky servant-of-God stepped into the pulpit. There were better things to think about, like the five pound walleye he was sure his dad was pulling into the boat at that very moment.

This church ritual which had been a part of Jess' life was about to be broken. Next week he might very well be out in the boat with his dad netting that walleye. All he had to do was get through one more service and he would be free. Of course he would come back at Christmas and Easter, even his dad did that, but the weekly grind would come to an end with the final amen of this day.

~

The Cradle Roll kids now wore black caps and gowns with white carnations pinned on by doting mothers. The spring of '69 was offering Jess another taste of freedom, but he would not be allowed to savor the joys of this emancipation for long. Jess would begin fulltime employment in two short weeks at Matthews Chevrolet.

Jess had chosen not to further his education, which prompted his dad to serve notice that, "Real life begins now." Living at home would carry a price. Jess was informed that the bedroom he had occupied for the past eighteen years did not really belong to him; he had been a guest in the home owned by his parents. What was once offered freely now would require rent to maintain occupancy.

Matthews Chevrolet was owned by Jeb Matthews, a lifelong friend of Jess' dad. Jess began his part-time employment at the car dealership in the summer of '67, washing used cars and running errands. He purchased his first wheels from the Matthews Used Car Lot, a 1959 Chevrolet Biscayne with a six-cylinder motor and a three-speed manual transmission. Jess wasn't too concerned about what was under the hood. He was more interested in body style. The '59 Chevy offered a feast for his eyes with the lay-down gull-winged fins on the trunk and the teardrop taillights. The car was baby blue and the only customizing he did to it was to swap out the stock hubcaps for Baby Moons. Jess loved Friday and Saturday nights when Natasha was sitting next to him with her head resting on his shoulder as he paraded through town in his '59 Chevy. He was proud to show off both his girls.

Jess' job at Matthews Chevrolet would be a used car salesman trainee. Herman Groves, the used car lot manager, would take Jess under his wings and teach him the ropes. Selling used cars was an art form, and Herman was an accomplished artist when it came to painting a beautiful picture of the worst piece of junk on the lot. "The goal is to move cars," Herman would instruct. "You emphasize the good points about the vehicle. We don't need to tell the buyer what's wrong with the car, he'll discover the problems soon enough on his own." Jess got the feeling that he would have to be an advocate for Herman's mom if she ever came in to purchase a vehicle.

The used-car manager's office smelled of cigar smoke. Herman always seemed to be chewing on a half-smoked Cuban status symbol. He was a patient man, but moved abruptly, never allowing an "opportunity" to pass by the lot unaddressed. His teaching technique was visual. "Son, you can learn best by watching the old pro in action," he would brag. His short stocky frame, balding head, and permanently crooked cigar-clinging lips gave the impression of a lovable cartoon character.

There was another side to Mr. Groves that only exposed itself on Sundays or during church outings: he was a well respected deacon at the First Baptist Church, a roll he had played for twenty of his fifty-five years of life. The congregations of Calvary Lutheran and First Baptist had developed a special relationship, due to the close friendship of the pastors. The congregants shared picnic tables in the summer months and potluck dinners in the winter for all kinds of social events, being careful never to enter each other's doctrinal space. Herman seemed to be everyone's friend and confidant at these gatherings, even though half the people attending had at one time or another purchased one of his lemons. Herman Groves had the gift of persuading people to look past his dealings and embrace his personality.

The summer of '69 was destined to be life-changing for Jess. Maybe it was the fact that he was out of school and had a fulltime job; maybe it was because he began to think seriously about the future. Whatever the reason, his heart gave way to love.

Jess was enamored by Natasha the first time he laid eyes on her in the seventh grade. Something churned in the pit of his stomach, and his face felt so warm that he was sure it was beet red. With his locker door open and his books half in his hands and half on the metal shelf at the top of the locker, Jess slowly twisted to watch Natasha pass by. Embarrassment overtook him when she cast a brief look back to see what had caused the loud noise when his books hit the floor. Their eyes met...and he was frozen in time.

He would never forget that moment, although years later he would have to recount the milestone to Natasha; her memory bank of "love at first sight" was empty.

Being eighteen gave Jess a feeling of manhood. He was aware of the new and exciting phase taking root in his life even though he was still living at home. Natasha had been the only girl who had ever captured his attention. She had ceased being his secret love in the eleventh grade when Jess finally worked up the courage to ask her to a football game. They shared the joys of high school over their junior and senior years. Their future seemed appropriate to consider now that they had graduated.

Jess had always believed he was in love with Natasha, but something was very different during this magical summer. The air was fresher, the sky was bluer, the sun felt warmer, and the mere fragrance of Natasha's hair, as she rested her head on Jess' shoulder, lifted his countenance. In the past Jess was thrilled just to date Natasha, now a metamorphic change occurred revealing he couldn't live without her.

Over the next two years Jess labored diligently, purchased an old farm with forty acres of land, and spent countless hours romancing the love of his life. Jess and Natasha were married July 10, 1971.

~

Jess learned well from his mentors. Even though his dad passed away at a fairly young age, Jess had more than enough time to settle into rituals of worship taught by a father whom he greatly respected. Summer Sundays were, and continued to be, fishing days ever since that final amen on Confirmation Sunday, while fall ushered in the opportunity to worship at the altar of football. Jess had also picked up a few gods of his own, cars being the one which occupied most of his time. He still owned his very first car, the '59 Biscayne was fully restored to showroom condition.

Herman Groves was the professor in business. Jess didn't go as far as becoming a deceiving deacon to help boost sales, but he was transformed into one of the best used-car salesmen Matthews Chevrolet had ever employed, and his reward was taking over the position of Used Car Manager when Herman retired.

Now, years later, Jess ruled over the largest pre-owned car dealership in the state. "Jess' Quality Pre-Owned Cars" became a reality when Jeb Matthews agreed to sell his used car business to his enterprising manager. Of course, times were different; laws dictated ethical methods of selling. No longer could odometers be turned back, or stories be told about cars that weren't true, or tires with bulges simply be turned around so the bulge was out of sight. A used car manager working on commission could make a lot of money with tricks like that in the old days, but today there was a new standard. Jess embraced the changes and built a well respected business that he claimed customers could trust.

Jess now sold cars purchased from auctions, and there were records of the entire life of that vehicle with every purchase. The philosophy of sales was still the same as Herman's; "Sell as many cars as you can no matter what it takes." In today's game that usually meant "helping" with financing. Get the cars off the lot and the money in the bank. If you had to talk the customer into the idea that they could afford the payments knowing the bank would own the car by the end of the first year...well...that was between the bank and the customer, you had done your job.

~~~~~~~~~~

Jess enjoyed the sight of his wife snuggled in the warmth of the comforter that engulfed her, still smitten by her beauty. He was more in love with her today than he had been on their wedding day, thirty-nine years earlier. He harbored but one regret - no little Jess or Natasha to pass this beautiful life on to. Natasha was not bothered by her inability to bear children for she enjoyed the finer things in life.

Jess again looked out the double hung windows he stood in front of, this time at the garage which housed his '59 Chevy as well as his '64 Chevrolet pick-up and his 1960 Corvette. These were his "babies". Natasha's babies were antiques scattered throughout the house, memories of cruises, and the anticipation of overseas trips to come. *None of this would exist if we had children,* he thought. But lately, deep down inside, Jess felt that if he had the opportunity to know the children they might have birthed, he could easily trade all of this away. It was getting late; he now had to hurry to get to his office on time.

A used car salesman knows it's never good to drive a brand new car; Jess made sure that the Corvette he drove daily was at least a year old. He was aware that, even at fifty-nine, he looked good in a Vette. His current ride was bright red, and today he was glad for the power under the hood. The drive to the office normally took about twenty-five minutes, but with a little luck (meaning no cops in sight) he could cut that down to fifteen. The lonely country road was mostly straight and had handled a hundred miles per hour a number of times in the past.

"Hello...Yes, I remember my meeting with Fred this morning. I should be there in ten minutes; I've got the Vette humming."

All it took was one quick look down at the phone to hit the off button... Jess overcorrected, and the red "missile" was airborne. Fear choked his ability to draw a breath as he was overcome by the terror of death...

Chapter

2

The heavenly smell of clover was thick in his nostrils. Jess lifted his head high enough to peer over a field of wildflowers. *Am I dead?* The fact that he could move astounded him. He sat up and stared at what was left of his latest pride and joy, it was unrecognizable. *It must be fifty yards away. How did I land here? How did I get out of the car?* Joy overtook him just to realize he was alive. Without even thinking, "Thank you God," rolled from his lips.

God had never been a part of Jess' adult life even though deep down inside he believed He might be out there somewhere. But at this moment, when Jess was awed by his miraculous escape from the jaws of death, thoughts of God flooded to the forefront of his mind. He slowly stood and walked toward the main pile of wreckage, stepping over parts and pieces of what was, just a few moments earlier, an object of worship. "God, it doesn't seem possible that I can walk away from this." Jess stopped and listened to the silence, everything seemed so still, and then, like a crack of thunder, a voice penetrated his very being, "I AM". Numbness crept up his legs, he felt a blow to his chest, and Jess fell to the ground. The clear blue sky began to blur, the sweet smell of clover faded, and darkness overtook the light...

~

"He's over here!"

"Is he dead?"

"He's breathing, and I don't see any blood."

Jess opened his eyes to a see a man and a woman hovering over him. "Just lie still," the woman said, "we have an ambulance coming."

Confusion now engulfed Jess. *Who are these people? What am I doing on the ground?* He struggled to sit up, but the woman placed her hand on his shoulder and, with very little effort, caused him to surrender. After what seemed to be an eternity, Jess felt a poke in his arm. The paramedic held a clear plastic bag with some kind of line attached to it above his head. He could hear a thunderous sound somewhere behind him. He was on a stretcher within minutes. *Is it a tornado? Am I in a tornado?* The wind was building, and then, with the sound of a door closing, it ceased.

Jess finally put the pieces together. He turned his head to the paramedic and asked, "How bad am I?"

"Well, I'd say you're a miracle man. Your vitals are stable, you don't appear to have any broken bones...there's hardly a scratch on you. If it wasn't for that bump on your head I wouldn't even believe you had been in the car. We're going to get you to the hospital and make sure there's nothing going on internally. I would say you are one blessed man."

Jess remembered the voice - "I AM". Then the cold horrific fear of death that had invaded his consciousness while the Vette was in the air pierced his soul once again. *I'm scared, God. If You're real...take this fear from me.* The feeling persisted...

The pace of activity quickened at the hospital. A dozen medical people swarmed around Jess. Blood was drawn, x-rays were taken, he was poked and prodded, and questions were being asked faster than he could answer them. As quickly as the activity had begun, it ended. Jess found himself in the room with one nurse watching over equipment he had no understanding of. The door opened. "Natasha! Give me your hand. I just want to hold on to you."

"Jess, you scared me! I saw them load up what was left of your Vette when I passed the crash. They told me on the phone you appeared to be OK. I thought they lied to me to get me down here before they told me the truth... Are you OK?"

"They say I am. They're checking stuff, but everybody says it's a miracle I only have a bump on my head. Tash...I think I heard God...."

"You've got a bump on your head alright. Don't get goofy on me."

"No, you don't understand. After the crash I found myself in the field, I stood up and began to walk towards the Vette. Everything got quiet. I heard a voice, a thunderous voice, it said, 'I AM'... I think it was God."

Natasha gave Jess a look of disgust. "Right now let's concentrate on what the doctors have to say when they return."

Jess was aching inside to tell Natasha more about the voice, but he didn't know what else to say. *How do I describe the sound of the words, or the stillness that surrounded them?* The words were meaningless, even though they now seemed to have taken up residence in the depth of his soul. And something else was bothering him; Jess had the distinct impression the words knocked him to the ground. *How do I explain that?*

The doctor's diagnostics found nothing that would prevent Jess from going home. He would be allowed to leave the hospital with Natasha after he signed some papers.

"I'm really stumped, Tash, I don't know how I got out of the Vette. I had my seatbelt on so I couldn't have been thrown from the car."

"How fast were you going?"

"Too fast. Man, I can't figure this out."

A nurse approached Jess with papers in hand; right behind her was a deputy sheriff.

"Mr. Rivers, I need to ask you a few questions." The officer's stern face worried Jess. "What do you recall about the accident?"

"I...I'm not sure." Jess thought hard. "Wait, I remember being on the phone. My secretary called to remind me about an appointment. The next thing I knew I was in the air. I don't remember anything after that until I woke up in the field. I got up and..." Jess decided not to go any further. He wasn't going to get into the "voice of God" thing with a cop. "I don't know, I guess I dropped again and woke up to a woman leaning over me. I was confused, that's for sure."

"Do you want to tell me how fast you were going?"

"Well, I don't really remember." Jess glanced away from the officer's eyes and thought, *That's the last thing I'm going to tell you, you'd arrest me right here.*

"The doctor tells me there's no alcohol in your blood, so you're free to go. There may be some follow-up after we're through with the investigation at the scene. You're a lucky man, Mr. Rivers. Have a safe trip home."

Jess felt a dose of stupidity run through his veins as the deputy left the room. He knew he had dodged a bullet by not being arrested. His actions had been reckless; the high-speed thrill ride to work could have cost him his life. *What if I had killed someone? Thank you, God, for not letting that happen.* There it was again, Jess had now thanked God twice within a matter of hours.

"Did you call Peg, Tash? Does she know what's going on?"

"Yes. She canceled all your appointments for the day and said she would wait to hear from you about tomorrow. She also said that some guy named Luke stopped by and asked to see you. He left a package for you."

"Luke... I don't know any Luke. Let's head home. I think I want to just lie down for a while."

Jess turned down Natasha's offer to let him drive, her smirk betrayed her sarcasm. He leaned back in his seat and stared at his wife. *I should be dead right now. Dead...* When the word passed through his mind, a cold sweat passed through his pores. The fear returned. Jess had hoped God would have answered his prayer by now.

Tracks were laid for the black leather couch in his man-cave as soon as Jess entered the house. This room was his, complete with big screen TV, surround sound, and a fully stocked bar to help dull the pain of loss or celebrate the elation of victory on football Sundays. None of that mattered at the moment. He needed to think, and his beloved couch was the best place for that to happen.

"Tash, if I fall asleep please wake me by four. I'll want to call Peg before she leaves to see how things have gone at the lot."

"I'll be waking you every hour. I'm the 'neurocheck' queen, doctor's orders for the next twenty-four."

"Some nap this will be."

Usually Jess would be out within a minute after his body conformed to the plushy cushions of his favorite piece of furniture, but his mind was still traveling at the speed of light. Front and center was the voice that said, "I AM." The more he replayed the episode, the more questions he had. *I AM what?* He couldn't even think the words without shouting them. *It was the strongest, most commanding voice I have ever heard. It was powerful actually. I don't think I was afraid of it, but I would swear on a stack of Bibles that it knocked me to the ground.* The thought of swearing on a stack of Bibles brought a chuckle to Jess. *Why would I use that expression? I haven't had a Bible in my hands since confirmation class when I was a kid.*

Jess was right, a Bible was not to be found anywhere in his or Natasha's possession. He couldn't remember what happened to his confirmation Bible, and he never cared. Today, though, he kind of wished he had it. *Maybe I could find out what I AM means...if the voice really did belong to God.* A chuckle again rose in Jess' throat. *Can you imagine what Tash would think if she walked in here and found me reading the Bible? She'd have my head examined for sure; convinced this bump was an outward sign of brain damage!*

Natasha and Jess had settled the religion question back in high school. Natasha's parents were Freethinkers; church was never a part of their lives, and Natasha made it very clear that she didn't want church to ever be a part of her life. That was just fine with Jess. He was more than happy to leave the "good" life behind, deciding early on he was not going to be a hypocrite. *Why pretend to be a certain kind of person on Sunday when I want to live my life in a whole different way the other six days of the week?* The young couple even forsook the church on their wedding day, holding the ceremony in Lincoln Park with a Justice of the Peace officiating; the vows put an end to Jess' Christmas and Easter visits.

Natasha also had some present-day reasons for her strong dislike of the church; it was that institution that spawned the protesters in front of the building where she worked. Natasha had been employed part-time at the Women's Center since 1994, and she detested Christians trying to tell women what to do with their bodies. She was acquainted with some women who went to church and still shared her beliefs, but they were more into compassion than the dictatorial rules of the Bible.

Jess rolled over on his left side and looked around at the stuff that kept the walls from being seen. With the success of his business he had not wanted for anything. If he desired the latest in high tech equipment he just went out and bought it. Proof of that ability was everywhere.

He was amazed when an old Bible story he learned as a kid came to mind. *How did that go? Something about being a fool and that, "...this very night your life will be required of you".* The thought of death once again brought a cold sweat to the surface.

What's wrong with me? I could've died, but I didn't. I should be happy, not full of fear.

~

"Jess...Jess"

Jess could feel his shoulder being pushed around. "What time is it?"

"Four o'clock"

"Man, I've got a headache now."

"I'll get you something. Do you hurt anyplace else?"

"No, just my head."

"You do remember that you wanted to call Peg?"

"Yes...I remember."

"I called your mom right after you laid down. I didn't want her to hear about this from anyone else. She wants you to call her when you feel up to it."

"I'll give her a call tonight after supper."

"I also got quite a few phone calls asking about you. Some of them said they saw the car and couldn't believe you lived through the crash. Fred was the first to call."

Jess was warmed by the concern of his friends. He slowly rose from the couch and made his way to his other favorite piece of furniture in the house, the chair behind his desk. "Thank you, Tash." Jess washed the pills down with a long cold drink of water. He had Peg on the phone with a push of a button. "Peg, it's me. Just checking in to see how things went today."

"Oh, Jess, I'm so glad to hear you're OK. They dropped your Vette off at the garage here; that shattered mess has been quite the attraction. It's a miracle you're alive, everybody thinks it's a miracle."

"I only saw what was left from a distance. I didn't get much of a look at it, but what I saw made me shudder. How was business today?"

"We had more people in here than I've ever seen in one day, but they weren't looking at cars to buy, they were all looking at the one that will never be on the road again. We did sell that '08 Monte and the '06 Ford van, though."

"Wednesday's have always been slow. We'll get'm tomorrow. Did you reschedule my appointment with Fred?"

"No, I didn't know how you would be feeling so I wanted to wait to hear from you."

"That's fine. I'll be there tomorrow sometime, not sure exactly when. I'm going to take my time coming in."

"Jess..."

"Yes?"

"Drive carefully."

"You got it, Peg. See you in the morning."

Supper was surprisingly silent. Jess seemed preoccupied, and Natasha gave him space.

~

"Hi mom, it's me."

"Oh son, are you all right?"

"Yes, just a bump on my head; and you know how thick my skull is."

"What happened? Did you fall asleep?"

"No, I just wasn't paying attention. Mom...I want to ask you something."

"What son? You can ask me anything."

"Have you...have you ever heard God speak to you?"

Silence overtook the short conversation. Jess could detect just the slightest spark of joy in his mom's voice when she finally answered. "Yes...I have, and I have prayed for years that you would too."

"Thanks mom...I...I gotta go. I just wanted you to know that I'm OK. I'll stop by and see you soon. Bye."

Jess was almost sorry he asked the question. He had successfully terminated any conversation with his mother about God years earlier. Now he knew those conversations would begin again.

~

Just over twenty-four hours earlier Jess was standing in front of the window in their bedroom, grateful for the life he had. Now he was sitting on the edge of their bed, wondering if it had all been a dream. He slept well, even with Natasha's hourly nudges, but something was different this morning. *It's funny how a brush with death will put a different perspective on things. God, I feel so empty. Did something die?... God? Why am I even talking to You? I don't know who You are...or IF You are.* A dark presence came over Jess, a feeling of oppression. What he wanted more than anything was for Natasha to turn over and pull him close. He felt like a little kid scared of the dark, even though the morning's light chased sinister shadows from the room. *This isn't me! I've got to shake this! Why am I so afraid!*

The Vette was a basket-case at the shop so Jess took his pickup truck out of the garage and headed down the road. He wondered how he would feel when he came to the site of the crash. He had traveled six miles so far and not exceeded thirty miles per hour. He pulled to the shoulder about a block from where he thought the Vette had left the road. Even though the sun was shining and the skies were blue, Jess could feel his spirit sinking into blackness. "God, I don't understand this. I felt nothing but wonder when I heard Your voice, but since then I feel nothing but fear. If it really was You, why does the fear keep growing?"

Jess slipped the truck in gear and crept ahead, remaining on the shoulder of the road. He came to a stop where the police paint-lines indicated the last place the Vette tires were on the ground. He exited the truck and slowly began to walk to where he thought he might have been when he heard the voice. The grass was pressed to the ground like a deer had bedded there the night before. He couldn't be sure, but this had to be close. "God, speak to me again. I know I heard You. Let me know I'm not going crazy." Nothing but silence.

"I'm not going crazy! THIS is crazy! Why am I standing in the middle of a field trying to talk to a God I don't even know exists?"

Fear struck again and Jess took off running. Panting, and in a cold sweat, he jumped in the truck, shifted into drive, and sent rocks flying from the rear tires. "There is no way I can explain finding myself out of the car and in the field if You didn't have something to do with it! Why don't You speak to me?"

Jess pulled into his parking spot, got out of the truck, and slowly walked toward the sales building. He didn't know where they had parked his Vette, but he did know he did not want to see it right then.

A thunderous sound of applause ignited when Jess stepped through the door. Every one of his employees stood in the showroom clapping and wearing huge grins. Tears came to Jess' eyes. Choked up and unable to speak, he gave a wave of his hand and took refuge in the sanctuary of his office. He was surprised at his emotions. *I know I am only in this office again, God, because of You. Somehow...and for some reason...You got me out of the Vette before it hit the ground. I was belted in...there was no other way. I don't want to think I am so blind that I don't know a miracle when I see one. If You would just talk to me again, let me know You're there.*

Jess plopped into his desk chair emotionally exhausted. In front of him was a package wrapped in brown paper. A note was taped to the top.

Jess,

I thought after all these years you might want to have this.

Luke

Luke... Who is Luke? Jess opened the package and stared in disbelief. In his hand was something he had not seen since Confirmation Sunday... "My Bible!"

Chapter

3

"I can't tell you how good it is to see you sitting there in one piece," Fred Carlson pulled up his usual chair and sat across the desk from Jess. "Are you really OK? I mean, I saw the Vette...how on earth are you walking around?"

"Angels, I think."

Fred and Jess had been best friends since childhood. Decades of fishing trips and football Sundays littered their past. Their wives became inseparable from their first introduction, assuring couples' dates and shared vacations for years to come.

Business increased the bond between the two friends. Fred was a respected accountant in the Duluth area, and Jess depended on his expertise. Jess' office was the only place serious conversations ever occurred between them, and those conversations only involved the bottom line. Work hard/play hard was a common ethic; one never interfered with the other.

Fred noticed the Bible Jess was gripping in his hands. "Wow, you must be shook. Don't tell me you found religion."

"Hmm...religion hadn't crossed my mind...but I sure have been thinking about God the last twenty-four hours."

"Whoa, this is getting too deep for me already. You think you're going to feel good enough to hit the lake on Sunday?"

"Huh?... Oh, sure...I'll be fine."

Fred pushed his chair back and quickly retreated, relieved to have changed the subject without missing a beat. "Call me when you feel up to going over the month's accounts... Jess!... Call me?"

"Yah, sure... I'll have Peg call your office and set things up." Jess' thoughts were far from business. *Who is Luke...and how did he have my Bible?*

The remainder of the business day was filled with interruptions. Friends stopped by to proclaim their joy upon hearing the miraculous news of Jess' deliverance from the jaws of death. He wondered why so many people believed a miracle had happened when he knew most of them had no belief in a "miracle-maker". He entertained the notion that the spiritual aspect of these conversations might be more about superstition than about a God who had saved his life.

~

Jess opened the front door and smelled the tantalizing aroma of his favorite meal. One glance at the dining room told him that Natasha was up to something special. The burgundy tablecloth, white china, and candelabras appeared only for occasions of celebration.

"Welcome home, Love."

"Tahitian Chicken!"

Putting her arms around Jess' neck, Natasha whispered, "We're celebrating, celebrating that my husband has come home."

Jess loved home. He especially loved the fact that Natasha was his home. There had always been a lingering feeling deep down inside that he loved her far more than she could ever love him. He was grateful that she would love him at all, believing she could live without him just fine, but he could not live without her. Natasha had never given Jess any reason for suspicion in their relationship, but there was an awkward knowledge that haunted him; revealing she could have married someone better, and that he didn't really deserve her. Moments like this forced that haunting feeling to rest in peace.

"How was your day?"

"Disorganized. I couldn't get anything done, too many people stopping by to check out the 'miracle man'."

"It has to make you happy that so many people care."

"I was pretty choked up to see the reception I got when I walked into the showroom. I couldn't even talk. I almost ran to my office just so I wouldn't start bawling, and you know that's not me. I think there were some who came in more curious about what was left of the Vette than what was left of me."

"Did you look at the Vette?"

"No...I never got a chance to walk back to the garage."

"Are you afraid to look at it?"

Jess savored the marriage of ginger and pineapple he had just placed in his mouth, hoping the pause would erase Natasha's question. "...I don't know...it's like a light goes off when I think about the crash. I should still be in that car. I don't know how I got out. I'm spooked by the feeling that if I go look at it...somehow...it'll reach out and grab hold of me, pull me in, and strap me into the seat that should never have released me."

"Oh, honey, you know that's just your mind playing tricks on you. The truth is you survived a terrible crash, and you're lucky to be alive. Be happy about that. Don't look for something dark in it."

"I am happy to be alive...but something died...I know something has died. I just can't put my finger on it. I look around at things and I... I don't know... I feel like I'm in mourning over something, and I just can't shake the feeling."

"Jess, you're starting to worry me. Give it some time. Don't think about it so much. You'll be back to your old self in a few days. Once you get out on the lake with Fred the accident will be a distant memory."

"I hope so... I sure do love you, Tash."

~

Sleep was elusive. With eyes open, Jess viewed objects of beauty; the bedroom Natasha had so skillfully decorated with romance in mind, the soft light of a full moon shining through double hung windows exposing joys of their home life together. With eyes closed, Jess regressed to the morning of the crash, airborne and in fear. *"God, please don't let me have nightmares."*

"Tash...are you awake?"

"Half awake."

"You know that package Peg said some guy named Luke left for me?"

"What about it?"

"It was my Bible...from confirmation."

"Really... I hope you didn't bring it home."

~

Morning dawned through grey skies, rain pelted the windshield, and gloom filled the cab of Jess' pick-up. It was Friday, the second morning after the crash. Jess' mind was still preoccupied with the event that seemed to have altered his life in some unknown way. He was heading into work early to prepare paperwork for Fred; capitalizing on the chore to arrive at the lot before anyone else, deciding not to avoid the Vette any longer.

Jess drove around to the back of the garage, parked his truck, and entered through the service door. Complete darkness turned to light with the flip of one switch. All ten stalls were inhabited, assuring a busy day ahead for his service center; a sister-business to the car lot. Way back in the right-hand corner of the garage sat the remains. The crumpled mess bore no resemblance to the work of art it once was. Jess approached with the determination needed to face what he believed to be the cause of lingering fears deep within.

"Not much left of you, is there." Jess lightly kicked the fractured nosepiece and then cautiously walked to the driver's side of the mutilated machine. The smell of battery acid and antifreeze permeated his nostrils. He timidly leaned over the driver's seat and grabbed hold of the seatbelt. *That's not what I wanted to find.* A hard yank confirmed it was still latched. *If it was unlatched I could see how I might have flown out of the car. Could somebody have latched it after the accident? Why would they do that? Would the cops have latched it?* His one hope of an explanation was disintegrating. He possibly could accept flying out of the car, landing in the grass, and being OK. He couldn't accept flying out of the car with the seatbelt still securely latched. The first scenario might be explained by being extremely lucky, the second only by a miracle. He decided to call the sheriff's office in search of any explanation.

On his way to the sales building Jess realized that fear had not overtaken him during his reunion with the Vette. This was unsettling. *God, I thought I could end it right there, but it's deeper than a piece of machinery, isn't it. What has happened to me? When I think of things that used to make me happy, they seem mundane. And here I am talking to You like I know You...and like You know me. Where did this come from? I've never talked to You. I've never really believed in You. But ever since I heard You say those words – "I AM" – I can't get You out of my mind. And yet, You seem so far away...out of reach...or am I so far away?*

Man, if people could hear what's going on in my head they would think I'm nuts. This is all because you thought you were going to die, isn't it, Jess. No...it's because I know I should be dead! Part of me IS dead!

How did You get me out of that seat with the belt still latched? Silence... The fear swelled in Jess' stomach, pushing its way upward through his throat.

~

"Is Officer Berkman available?"

"Let me see if I can catch him before he heads out on patrol. Who's calling?"

"Jess Rivers."

"One moment, Mr. Rivers."

... "This is Officer Berkman."

"Good morning, this is Jess Rivers. I was involved in an accident a couple of days ago that you handled."

"Yes, I know who you are."

"I have a question that I'm wondering if you could answer for me."

"Go ahead."

"When you investigated my accident...did you happen to check the seatbelt on the driver's side?"

"I really can't discuss the investigation until it's complete."

"Can you at least tell me if the seatbelt was still latched at the scene?"

"It was."

"I AM."

"What! What did you say?"

"I said it was."

"No...no, I mean after that."

"That's all I said, Mr. Rivers. I really need to get out on patrol if you have no other questions."

"Uh, yes...I mean, thank you. Goodbye."

Am I hearing things? God, was that You? This is getting crazy. I've got to pull myself together. I've got a business to run. I can't go around hearing voices!

Jess filled his day with paperwork. His Bible, which was still on his desk as he entered his office, found a new home on the shelf behind him.

~

"Jess, Fred's in the Garage hooking up the boat." Natasha's voice found its way out of the kitchen, down the hallway, and into the bedroom. "Breakfast will be ready in ten minutes."

"OK, I'll go out and let Fred know."

Jess was not against Sunday morning rituals as long as they were welcomed ones. The Sunday morning church rituals of his youth couldn't hold a candle to the ones he enjoyed now. For the last thirty-nine years the smells of coffee and bacon woke him on summer Sunday mornings; his wife preparing a feast to send him off with his best friend to the lake of their choice.

"Hey, Fred, Tash says breakfast is on the table."

"You know, it doesn't seem fair."

"What doesn't seem fair?"

"All these years Tash has made us breakfast, and Julie sleeps in on Sunday mornings."

"Ah, Tash loves it, you know that. Besides, as soon as we're gone she has the day to herself. I think she's just making sure we get out of here."

Breakfast was a time to relive fishing trips of the past and to place bets on who's going to catch the biggest walleye on the trip ahead. With their hunger abated, the two anglers were ready to cast off.

Fred made his way to the refrigerator Jess kept in the garage. "Where's the beer, Jess?"

"Oh man, I forgot to pick some up last night."

"You forgot to get the beer? You've been getting the beer for over thirty years. How could you forget the beer?"

"I don't know. I had other things on my mind I guess."

"Jess, 'other things' don't take priority over getting the beer. Are you all right? You're not having memory lapses from that bump on the head you got last week, are you?"

Jess had decided on Saturday that he was going to enjoy his Sunday fishing without thinking or talking about the accident. "That's got nothing to do with it, I just forgot. We'll pick some up on the way."

"OK, but maybe I better drive in case you can't remember the way to Boulder Lake."

"Not funny." Jess jumped behind the wheel of his pickup and waited for Fred to load the cooler.

Jess and Fred were completely comfortable in each other's company. Conversation was not forced and silence was not awkward. This morning, however, Fred sensed a battle waging amongst Jess' occasional bursts bragging of catches gone by.

"You've got something heavy on your mind, Jess."

"I'm trying not to have."

"Hey, I know I cut you off the other day in the office. I'm sorry. We just...well, we never talk about things like God. It's kind of like it's off limits."

"Off limits?"

"Yah...you know...not manly. There are certain things inside you just don't talk about, especially with another guy."

"Are you saying inside you think about God?"

"Well...sure...not all the time, but I have thoughts."

"What kind of thoughts?"

"Oh man, this isn't the conversation I wanted to have this morning."

"You brought it up."

"Yah...well...there are times when I sit in the boat, quiet times, times when you probably think I'm napping. I look around at how beautiful things are, and I wonder... I wonder how all this could be a mere accident."

"An accident?"

"Don't get me wrong, I'm not smart enough to argue with scientists, but there are some simple things that just don't make sense to me...about how they say all this came to be I mean...and it makes me wonder."

Conversations always paused when the time arrived to put the boat in the water. Fred jumped out of the cab and trotted to the dock. Jess had backed his boat and trailer into Boulder Lake so many times through the years that he could do it with his eyes closed. Each man knew his responsibility and accomplished his task with military precision.

With the launch maneuver complete, and the boat afloat on calm waters reflecting warm rays of sunlight, both fishermen readied their poles to cast for smallmouth bass.

"Wow! That was quick! First cast! It's going to be an active day." Fred reeled in a ten inch smallmouth. His prediction was premature, though, as cast after cast produced only satisfaction of a cast well done.

"What do you wonder, Fred?"

"...I wonder how people think all this could come into existence without someone planning it out."

"You don't buy the Big Bang thing, huh?"

"Listen to us, in decades of fishing together we're finally having a deep conversation."

"I thought you didn't want to have deep conversations?"

"I didn't...but I'm getting older...things change I guess."

Jess flashed his best smirk at Fred and gushed, "You mean to tell me you want to bond, man!"

"Don't get sappy."

"I'm sorry."

"...Have you ever wondered about a squirrel falling out of a tree, dead, having all kinds of things fall on top of it over thousands, and maybe millions of years, and forming a fossil?"

"A squirrel? That's a deep thought." Jess coughed up his first genuine laugh since the accident.

Fred's look of displeasure put Jess on notice. "...It couldn't have happened that way."

"Why not?"

"It would have decayed. The little critter never would have lasted long enough to become a fossil."

"Now that is deep."

"Don't you see? That's what they've told us."

"Who?'

"Everybody! In school, on the news, in movies, it's everywhere you look."

"You've lost me now. I don't ever remember hearing about a squirrel falling from a tree."

"You're missing the point. The squirrel is my thought, how fossils are formed is what I'm talking about. Thousands, billions of years? Heck, that squirrel would have been gone in no time at all. Something else would have had a good lunch, and the rest would have decayed long before it could fossilize. The fossils exist, but they had to have been formed before decay set in. In other words, that squirrel had to have been buried very quickly to form a fossil, almost instantly."

"Ok, so what's your point?"

"They lied to us. From little kids we've been taught something that makes no sense...you know...the whole evolution thing. And I think they know it, but they don't want to admit it."

"Why would they do that?"

"Because they don't want to admit somebody...like God...did all this."

"You surprise me, Fred. It takes me almost getting killed in my Vette to think about God, and you think about Him because a squirrel falls out of a tree?"

"I know, it's crazy. I just wonder how many other things I've thought all my life were true...really aren't true."

Both men knew the conversation reached its end for the time being. Along with that knowledge was an awareness of a new relationship birthed on the waters of Boulder Lake.

"Hey, Jess."

"Huh?"

"What's said in the boat stays in the boat! Throw me a beer."

~

Monday morning offered no new fish escapades to share with the guys in the service center. Still, Jess stayed true to his summer Monday morning ritual of starting his week with a cup of coffee to wash down any fish stories the guys in the shop served up. By eight-thirty he walked through the front door of the sales building and headed for his office.

"Mornin' Peg."

"Good morning, Jess. There's a gentleman waiting to see you, Mr. McGrady. He stopped by last week, but missed you because it was the day of your accident. I told him he could wait in your office.

Jess entered his office to find a spry elderly man rise quickly from a chair and extend his hand. "Hello Jess, I'm Luke."

TRUTH

Chapter

4

Jess was caught off guard. He stumbled through a "good to meet you" and invited his unexpected visitor to be reseated. Jess couldn't help but fix his gaze on Mr. McGrady as he found his way to the chair behind his desk.

"Excuse me, have we met?"

"Yes. It was a number of years ago. We spent the afternoon fishing together, you, your dad, and me."

"My dad?"

"You couldn't have been more than sixteen, maybe seventeen years old. I was fishing from shore on Fish Lake at High Banks I think they called it. You and your dad were trolling by when you got your line snagged. Your boat wasn't far off so I struck up a conversation with your dad about how fishing was, and out of the kindness of his heart he asked if I wanted to do some trolling with the two of you."

"I remember! You pulled in an eight pound walleye!"

"That's right."

"Yes...sure I remember. I couldn't believe you gave us the fish!"

"Well, I don't care much for fish, but I love to catch 'em."

Jess leaned back in his chair in complete amazement. The story brought back the memory like it was yesterday.

Luke leaned forward with his hands on his knees, "I just stopped by to see if you got the package I left for you last week."

Jess shot back, "Yes, I did... How did you get my Bible?"

Luke received the question as an invitation to settle back in his chair. "I've been working at Calvary Lutheran Church, doing odd jobs. You see, I travel around a lot, always have. Work a job here and there, and then move on. The last time I was in Duluth was when we fished together."

"No family?"

"Nope, just me and my traveling shoes. I'm a drifter I suppose. Anyhow, I was cleaning in the library when I found your Bible. There it was, behind a shelf that I don't think had been moved in years. The Bible was loaded with dust, but when I cleaned it off it looked like it was brand new, you know, like a page had never been turned."

"Pastor Larson gave us all Bibles on Confirmation Sunday. I remember him handing it to me, but I don't remember ever seeing it again after that. I must have left it on the pew I guess."

"Well, when I saw the name in gold letters at the bottom of the cover, my mind went right back to that day of fishing with you and your dad. I remember names, especially when they're connected with times I love remembering. I looked you up in the phonebook, and...well...that was it."

"Why would you even think of bringing it to me? I would have just cleaned it off and put it on the shelf."

"I'm a praying man, Jess, and there are certain things I believe in. One of them is that people change. You might not have been interested in that book as a teenager, but through the years things can happen that'll make you think. It's good to have the book that holds the answers." Luke glanced over Jess' shoulder then peered straight into his eyes, "I hope it doesn't fall behind that bookshelf. I jotted down a verse for you to look up; it's written there just inside the front cover. Like I said, I'm a praying man, and sometimes God says things to me. He told me you'd be interested in that verse. Maybe it'll get you started."

Luke's words startled Jess. "God told you something about me?"

Jess' quizzical look stimulated a chuckle from deep within the kindly old man. "Did you think God doesn't know what you're thinking? Oh my, look at the time. Pastor Miller will be wondering what happened to me." Luke rose from the chair and leaned over the desk with his hand once more extended, "It's been good seeing you again, Jess. God Bless." With a smile and a handshake the old man was out the door.

"Thanks!" Jess stood and appeared a bit dazed by the abrupt departure. Thirty seconds elapsed before he found his seat again. He swiveled his chair around, took hold of the Bible, and placed it on his lap. He pondered the idea of God knowing what he was thinking. He opened his Bible for the first time and read the inscription on page one:

PRESENTED TO JESS RIVERS

ON MAY 22, 1966

BY CALVARY LUTHERAN CHURCH

Beneath the inscription was a note from Luke:

Dear Jess,

God knows all your thoughts, all your desires, all your needs. He told me you needed an answer to a question and then gave me this verse to give to you. Exodus 3:14.

God Bless,

Luke

How do I work this thing? Jess flipped through the first few pages and found the index. Exodus, page 80; noticing chapter and verse numbers, he quickly found chapter 3, verse 14; "And God said to Moses, 'I AM WHO I AM'; and He said, 'Thus you shall say to the sons of Israel, I AM sent you to me.'" Jess felt the air leave his lungs and pressure seemed to be pushing down on his shoulders. The fear returned. *How did he know? How did he know that's what I heard? God, did You really tell him? Do You do things like that?*

Morning hours at work usually passed quickly for Jess, but on this morning time crept along at a snail's pace. His ability to concentrate on the jobs at hand was impeded by thoughts of God talking to someone else about him; not to mention the idea that there really is a God who talks at all. *God, I'm beginning to believe You're not just some thought in my mind, and that You really do exist. But what do I do with You? I'm sure I heard You speak... You must have spoken to Luke or he wouldn't have known to give me that verse in the Bible. But the fear, God, what about the fear? If You are real, why don't You take the fear away? Every time an attack comes I feel like death is all around me, like I'm going to be swallowed up.*

The miraculous escape from death rushed back into Jess' memory. The moment the Vette had left the ground Jess knew he was in death's grip, a grip so tight it wouldn't let him breathe. Waking up in the field was beyond understanding then and now. *Why can't I put this thing behind me? Why do I feel like something died? Why do I feel like death still has an icy hold on me?*

Jess reached for the phone book in his desk drawer and thumbed through to find the number for Calvary Lutheran Church. "Hello, is Luke McGrady available? I mean, I understand he's working there."

"Yes, Luke is here. Hold on and I'll get him for you."

Why am I calling him? I don't even know why I'm calling him.

"Hello, this is Luke."

"Luke...Jess Rivers."

"Well, hello Jess, I was expecting your call."

He was what? "Expecting my call? Whhh... why would you be expecting a call from me?"

"I was sure you would read that scripture and want to talk about it."

"I do, but..." Jess was dumbfounded by Luke's reception of his phone call. "Could we meet for lunch? Can you get away for lunch?"

"Why sure. Where do you want to meet?"

"There's a Perkins on fortieth, right off the freeway. Can you meet me there at twelve-thirty?"

"Sure, I'll be there."

Jess hung up the phone, held his hands palms up, and looked back and forth at them. They were wet with sweat. The agony of nervousness began to swell inside his stomach; *I just set up an appointment to talk about God with somebody I don't even know. What am I doing?*

Jess arrived early and asked for the booth in the farthest corner of the restaurant. There were no people seated within five booths in either direction. *All I need is for somebody I know to come in and hear me talking about God.*

Luke walked through the door at 12:30 on the dot. He was a willowy figure, just over six feet tall. He scurried in with just a hint of joy in his step. A waitress directed Luke's attention to the corner booth.

"Hi Luke...um...thanks for coming."

"My pleasure, Jess. Nothing I like better than company for lunch."

Jess could understand how easy it was for his dad to have invited this man to fish with them so many years earlier, he seemed the type of guy who could befriend anyone in a very short time. "I called you because...well, you bringing my Bible to me and writing what you wrote...it just...well, it just left me with some questions."

Luke picked up a menu, opened it, and began to scan for the lunch special. "I don't doubt that any. I would have questions too if somebody gave me a verse that took the breath right out of me."

Jess abruptly moved his attention from his menu to Luke. "How did you know that? That I felt like the air came right out of me?"

"I've found that God gives me just the right amount of knowledge about a person He is leading me to. He wants you to know He's real, Jess."

"Leading you to? God led you to me?" The thought that Luke might be a nut case crossed Jess' mind. *But he knows things, he might be a nut case, but somehow he knows things.* "What else do you know about me?"

"That's all for now."

Their waitress interrupted their conversation, "What can I get for you fellas today?"

"I see the Reuben is on special. I'll have that; just water to drink please." Luke handed his menu to the waitress and fixed his eyes on Jess as if to say, "It's your turn."

Jess' mind was still reeling from Luke's revelation. "I'll...um...oh, I'll have the same." Jess returned his full attention to Luke when the waitress left. "Do you really believe God led you to me?"

"Twice now, once decades ago in the fishing boat, and the second time last week when He had me find your Bible. I always wondered when He was going to show me the purpose of our first meeting, but I knew He'd get around to it someday. And now, I see."

"Luke, I've got more questions now than when you first walked in. Why do you think God led you to me in the fishing boat years ago? What has that got to do with today?"

"He created a bond, one that made you feel comfortable enough to give me a call today to meet for lunch. When you think about it, you have to admit that having been fishing together, me, you, and your dad, made it easier for you to call me. Actually, God's been working on you your whole life. He's been planting seeds for years, and He knows when those seeds are ripe for harvest. Once you come to be His, you'll look back and see a lot of the seeds He's planted."

Jess' mind was spinning. *Come to be His? I don't even know what this guy is talking about.* "Luke, I'm sorry, but I'm lost here. I wanted to meet with you to ask you about the Bible verse, and now I've got twenty more questions. I don't know what you mean by 'coming to be His'. I don't even know who 'He' is!"

"I guess I get a little excited and get ahead of myself when I see God putting the pieces together. What's the biggest question you have in your head?"

"Here you go fellas, a Reuben apiece. Let me know if I can get you anything else. Enjoy!"

Jess hesitated until the waitress was out of earshot. "Man, I don't know. I've collected so many questions over the past week that I don't know where to start... I guess if I have to start someplace it would be...who is God?"

"That's the big one."

"I had a car accident last week."

"I heard about that."

"I'm only telling you this because of the Bible and the verse. Somehow you know, but I haven't told anybody about this except Natasha, my wife, and I know she wouldn't tell a soul. She didn't even want to talk about it with me. Anyway, my car went off the road, crashed big time, I was going a little fast. Somehow I was thrown from the car and landed in the field. I woke up to the smell of clover. I couldn't believe I wasn't hurt, I thought I might be dead. I stood up and began walking towards the car when I noticed how quiet and still everything was, no birds, no wind, nothing. Out of nowhere came this voice, strong, firm, commanding. It said, 'I AM'. I felt like it went right into me, not through me, into me, like it penetrated right through my skin. Then I felt a thud in my chest, like somebody threw something at me. It knocked me right down to the ground. Everything got blurry, and then I woke up to a woman leaning over me telling me to be still."

Jess examined the face of this man who was sitting across the table in the booth. *How ironic. I think this guy might be a nut case, and I'm looking at him to see if he might think I'm crazy.*

Luke reached in his shirt pocket, pulled out a little book, and started turning pages. Jess could read the words on the front of it: "The New Testament". His face felt hot and he knew he was turning red. He scanned the occupied booths nearest theirs to see if anyone was looking. "Are you going to read something from that...right here...in the restaurant?"

"Sure, I think you'll find it quite interesting. John 18:6; 'When therefore He said to them, "I am He", they drew back and fell to the ground.'

"You probably don't know anything about the account of Jesus being arrested right before He was crucified, but what happened was this. Judas betrayed Jesus and led the arresting party to where He was spending the night. The Bible says that along with Judas there was a Roman cohort and officers from the chief priests and Pharisees. Now we don't know exactly how many men that was, but a Roman cohort was normally about six hundred men. These were Roman soldiers, fierce, armed men; ready to do battle if necessary. This is the party that came to arrest a preacher who had eleven of His followers with him.

"I reckon they figured Jesus and His followers were going to run, and that they would have to chase them. So they must have been surprised when Jesus stood up to them and asked, "Whom do you seek?" They said, "Jesus the Nazarene". Jesus answered them by saying, "I am He". Then the verse tells us that they drew back, and fell to the ground. The power of His word simply knocked them over. Jesus was letting them know that if they were going to arrest Him, it would only be because He allowed it. He was telling them who was in charge, and that they could not stand against Him. You see, He was about to lay His life down for us. No one was going to take from Him what He was freely willing to give.

"I think you experienced the same blast of breath that knocked down those who came to arrest Jesus. Jess, God wants you to know that He is real, and you cannot stand against Him."

"So...are you saying Jesus is God?"

"Oh yes, Jesus is God."

"But, how can that be when he was a man?"

"It's all in the Bible, Jess. The answers to these questions are in there. I can't begin to explain everything to you over one lunch hour, but I know one thing for sure, you'll not find the answers in any other book. That's why it's important not to let your Bible gather dust behind some bookshelf."

"What about I AM, what does that mean?"

"When God said to Moses 'I AM WHO I AM', he was saying that He is self-sufficient. He needs nothing outside Himself. He is, always has been, and always will be."

"Boy that's a step of faith."

"You've hit the nail right on the head. It takes faith to believe that God is eternal. We know nothing about Him other than what He tells us, and that isn't much compared to who He fully is. But it is evident that He's real. Romans 1:20, says; 'For since the creation of the world His invisible attributes, His eternal power and divine nature, have been clearly seen, being understood through what has been made, so that they are without excuse.'

"God tells us to just look around. The evidence of His existence is everywhere. We can come up with all kinds of ideas about how all this came into being without God, but we'll have no excuse for not believing what God said when we stand before Him."

Jess' conversation with Fred the day before immediately came to mind. *Maybe Fred's got something there. I wonder if he knows about this verse in the Bible? Naw...Fred and the Bible? I don't think so.*

"I know God's word is true because I know God. The Bible is the standard that I measure everything by. When I come across scripture I don't understand I ask the Holy Spirit to explain it to me. When I read things that seem to conflict with what man believes I believe the word of God. I don't judge God's word by man's philosophies; I judge man's philosophies by God's word."

"Luke, how do you come to know God?"

"You seek after Him. You don't let dust pile up on your Bible. You open your heart and ask Him to reveal Himself to you. You'll get to know God by being in His word."

The conversation continued between bites until Luke snatched a glance at his watch. "Jess, I'm sorry, but I have to get back to the church. Pastor Miller gave me a job that has to be done this afternoon."

"I've got so many more questions. Can we meet again?"

"Of course we can. Do you want to meet here for lunch again tomorrow?"

"Yes! I'll be here at twelve-thirty."

Luke set the money for his meal on the table and headed for the door. Jess sat for a moment, trying to comprehend all that had just happened. *You are real, aren't you God, or Jesus, or I AM. I don't even know what to call You, but You've got my attention. I want to know who You are... How do I ever explain this to Tash?*

Chapter

5

"Jess, Natasha's on line three."

"Thanks, Peg. Hi Tash, what's up?"

"Julie just called and wanted to know if we would like to meet her and Fred for supper."

"That's fine with me, where do they want to eat?"

"She suggested the steakhouse down by the canal."

"Sounds good. Do you want to meet me there, or are you gonna come by the lot here?"

"I'll meet you there at six if I can get through the protesters."

"Protesters again?"

"They've been out front all day. It's some prayer thing I guess. If they only knew there's nobody up there listening they wouldn't waste their time."

A split second decision was made by Jess that this would not be the night to bring his Bible home.

"Are you going to be OK?"

"Yah, it's a pretty wimpy bunch. All they're doing is praying. They won't get in my face."

Six o'clock, I'm really going to have to hustle to make that. Jess' afternoon was smothered by paperwork. Business had picked up and every car sold brought work to his desk. What he really wanted to do was sit down with his Bible and see if he could make any sense of it. *I've lived my whole life and never once had a desire to open a Bible. Now I want to push this paperwork off my desk and do just that. This is a strange feeling, God. One I never thought I would have.*

Jess left work with just enough time to reach the steakhouse by six. Dinner with Fred and Julie usually meant an hour for eating and another couple of hours at a sports bar, talking and having a few drinks. The two couples thoroughly enjoyed each other's company.

The sweet smell of clover flowed through the open window of Jess' truck as he drove past the front lawn of the sales building. Instantly his mind reverted to the moment of awakening in the field after his accident. Silence cut through the noise around him and stillness overcame his entire being. Then, as quickly as it came, it left, and fear overwhelmed its void.

This fear seemed darker than any other, enormously oppressive. Jess jerked the steering wheel to the right and abruptly stopped on the shoulder of the road. Urgency attacked his spirit. "God, help me!" Jess whipped his truck around and sped back to his office. Once in, he only slowed long enough to close the door behind him. His hand reached out for his Bible as if it was being guided by some invisible force. He opened it, and his eyes fell on words that ran through him like a rushing river. "Peace I leave with you; My peace I give to you; not as the world gives, do I give to you. Let not your heart be troubled, nor let it be fearful." Jess dropped into the chair at his desk, let his face fall into his hands, and wept.

"Jesus..." Jess felt utter remorse when the name passed his lips. How many times in his life had he used this name without any thought to whom it belonged? "Jesus, I'm so sorry." Tears pooled in his eyes until they spilled onto the words that had come to life. "I'm a fool...a complete fool to have ignored you. I've heard you calling before...I know I have...but I didn't want to answer. I want to answer now...oh how I want to answer." Peace flooded the room. Jess lifted his head, fully expecting to see someone, or something. Then, the same peace that seemed to engulf his body penetrated the hardened shell around his heart.

The ring from Jess' cell phone clashed with the peace that now surrounded him. Five rings pierced the calm before he reached in his pocket to put an end to the intrusion. Natasha's number appeared on the screen. *Jesus, I don't want to leave this place. I want to sit right here with You. I want to know what this book will say to me...but Natasha won't understand... What do I tell her?*

Jess attempted to gather his emotions and pushed a button on his cell phone to dial Natasha back.

"Jess, it's six-thirty, is everything OK?"

"Ah...yes...everything's fine, just had some things to take care of here."

"You don't sound fine. What's wrong?"

"Nothing... I'll be there in a few minutes." Jess didn't wait for Natasha to reply. He closed his phone, wiped tears from his face, and headed out the door; leaving his Bible open on his desk.

~

An anxious threesome welcomed Jess. It was apparent they expected an explanation that carried with it some unhappy news.

Jess was aware that his masked conversation with Natasha was unable to hide the outpouring of emotion he had experienced.

"Jess, what's going on? You sounded terrible on the phone."

"Nothing, Tash...really, nothing. I just lost track of the time." Jess worried that the redness of his eyes would betray his denials.

Fred pounced, "Did you get some bad news?"

"Look guys, everything is OK. Can we just order? I'm hungry."

Unconvinced, the three retreated, halfheartedly entering into other topics of conversation. Just over an hour later the party occupied a table at their favorite sports bar.

"Hi, your usual first round?" The cocktail waitress was more than familiar with the drinking habits of these repeat customers.

A nod of agreement followed from everyone but Jess, "Nothing for me right now."

Six eyes turned to Jess in disbelief. It was well known that after a long day Jess enjoyed nothing more than to be relaxed by the numbing effects of a few drinks.

Apprehension settled over Natasha; sensitivities warning her not to push. Fred's senses were not so acute. "Look buddy, something's really got you bothered. Tell us about it. We're here for you."

Jess looked at Fred with eyes that said, "Back off, now's not the time." The message was received, and the evening continued with Jess drifting in and out of his own world of thoughts.

Jess desperately wanted to talk to Natasha when the evening ended. He yearned to tell her that Jesus had filled his heart with peace and that the fear, the choking fear of death, was gone. *How can I explain it to her?* Jess knew all too well what Natasha thought about God. She hated the thought that some all-knowing being wanted to control her life. She hated the self-righteous people who claimed to know the truth and demanded she know it too. Husband and wife climbed into bed in silence; Jess afraid to speak the truth, and Natasha afraid to push for answers.

~

Peace I leave with you; My peace I give to you; not as the world gives, do I give to you. Let not your heart be troubled, nor let it be fearful. The words that unleashed a storm of tears the evening before rolled over and over in Jess' mind. *Jesus, let me wake up to these words every morning.*

Jess placed his bare feet on a wood floor drenched in streams of sunlight. He knew the day ahead would be different from any other he had inhabited. He stepped to the window and feasted on beauty that had been hidden from formerly blind eyes. *Fred's right, how can anyone believe this all happened by accident?*

Breakfast was a banana grabbed on the way through the kitchen. Jess stopped and leaned against the fender of his truck to enjoy the warm southerly breeze against his face. The smell of clover permeated the air. Fear was nowhere to be found. He turned and looked toward the windows that separated him from the woman he loved. "Jesus, speak to her, prepare her for what You've done to me."

Jess arrived at his office early, settled into the chair behind his desk, and fixed his attention on the open book in front of him. *Where do I begin, Jesus?* He flipped a few pages back and noticed the name John at the top of the page with the number 11 after it. Scanning down, he came to a sentence numbered 25: Jesus said to her, "I am the resurrection and the life; he who believes in Me shall live even if he dies."

Wow! Jesus, would I really have lived if I had died in the accident? ...Or would death have grabbed me...and not let go...because I didn't believe in You? Is that why I was so full of fear then, but I'm not now? If I faced death today, like I did last week, would it be different? Jess talked to Jesus for over half an hour until he was interrupted by Peg knocking on his half open office door.

"Come in. Good morning Peg."

"Jess, I've got..." Peg froze in mid-sentence. "Are you...reading the Bible?"

"Oh...um...just looking it over. This is what was in the package Luke McGrady left for me last week. It's really very interesting. You...ah can look at it too...later...if you want." Jess stumbled over his words in embarrassment.

"No, that's all right, I'll pass. Does Natasha know you have this?"

"Ah, yes, I told her about it."

"Does she know you're reading it?"

"Peg, please, let's keep this quiet for now. OK?"

"Sure, Jess, I didn't see a thing. Here are the papers for the Impala that was sold last night." Peg plopped the papers on the desk and, wearing a sarcastic smirk, backed out of the office.

Jess knew he could count on Peg to keep his secret. She had been his secretary since the day he opened for business, never betraying his trust. He closed his Bible and placed it in the desk drawer. *Lunch is four hours away. Man, do I have questions for Luke now!*

Luke was prompt once again; at twelve-thirty sharp he joined Jess in their booth.

"Luke, things have happened, things have really happened."

"Things?"

"Well, not things, I don't know what to call it, but I have to tell you!" Between ordering, receiving their food, and eating, Jess relived the events of the evening before as he shared with Luke about the peace that swallowed up the fear. Luke listened in blissful silence, feeding off the joy and embracing Jess' every word. Absent were Jess' glances to see who might be listening.

"You have come to be His, and He will hold you close and teach you if you'll let Him."

"I want to let Him. I'm not sure how to let Him, but I do want to let Him. Luke, you know I've got lots of questions, but there's something that has been kind of following me around since the accident."

"I'm listening."

"I know I survived the crash, by some miracle I survived, but I still have a feeling something inside me has died, and I'm mourning the loss. Last night Tash and I were out with Fred and Julie. I didn't want to be there. I didn't want to leave my office. All I wanted to do was sit and bask in that peace...that wonderful peace. When Tash called to see why I was late, it was an intrusion. I knew I had to go meet them. I knew I couldn't tell them anything about this yet. All night long I sat like a bump on a log. I had no fun. I didn't even want to have a drink! It just wasn't like me. I've always enjoyed nights out. But last night, with that feeling like something has died, I couldn't enjoy anything."

When Luke reached in his shirt pocket Jess knew what he was after, but this time Jess welcomed what was to come.

"I'm going to read James 4:9; 'Be miserable and mourn and weep; let your laughter be turned into mourning, and your joy to gloom.' Jess, what's died is the love."

"The love?"

"Love of things that used to make you happy, things that fill the void when you don't know God. Your joy was found in things that were a substitute for God, and they kept you from Him. The things that made you happy had no eternal value, and yet you gathered as much as you could. God calls every person by name and every person has the opportunity to come to Him or turn away. When you turned away you became consumed with what you wanted; cars, nights out with friends, fishing trips…Natasha."

"Natasha?"

"Yes, even Natasha. It's not that these things were evil in themselves; it's what you used them for that was evil. You used them to drown out the voice of God. But God's voice is stronger. He will shout at you if necessary. This time you listened, sat at the foot of the cross, and told Jesus how sorry you were. He forgave you and filled you with the presence of His Holy Spirit. Now the things that have kept you from answering God's voice are seen in the light of Him, and they are seen for what they are; stumbling blocks that have tripped you up. You don't see the joy in them anymore because they are the very things that have kept you from the joy you now know in Jesus. So, let your former joys turn to gloom and mourn over what used to make you laugh because they have kept you from your Savior. What has died is the love of the world, because you have experienced the love of Jesus Christ."

Jess' heart felt as though it had been plucked from his chest. "I don't understand this. I can see where my drinking and fishing and things like that might have kept me from listening to God, but Natasha?"

"Especially Natasha."

"But how?" The thought of exchanging Natasha's love for God's love was agonizing. Jess couldn't absorb it. He couldn't comprehend that God would even ask him to do something like that.

"You have always worshiped her, Jess. You have always put her above anything God has asked of you."

"You don't know that. You don't even know me."

"God knows you."

"Are you saying that God wants me to give up Natasha? That I can't love Him if I love her?"

"I'm saying that God wants us to give up the things that keep us from Him, no matter what they are. Understand that the things that once made us happy were really destroying us, because they were keeping us from belonging to the One who created us. The more you come to know Him, the more you will see how much He loves you. He wants you to trust Him."

"Luke, in such a short time I've learned so much from you, but not this...no, not this. On this you're wrong. I can love Natasha and God too."

"Jess, keep the ears of your spirit open to hear God's voice. Don't let worldly love keep you from Him any longer. I'm not suggesting that you move away from Natasha, I'm telling you to move closer to God. When you do, you will understand why He asks of you the things He asks." Luke rose from the booth, laid money down for his meal, and left.

Jess' mind was reeling. *What was that all about?* He fumbled through his pockets for money to put on the table and then scrambled around people on his way out like a linebacker hunting the quarterback in a football game. His intention was to catch up to Luke and continue a conversation he didn't think was over.

Where is he? He couldn't have disappeared that fast! Jess scanned the parking lot. He didn't know what Luke drove, or even if he drove. *I really don't know anything about this guy. Where does he get off telling me Tash has kept me from God. He doesn't know Tash. And the idea that I can't love God and Tash, I don't get it! Jesus, this is out of Luke's head, isn't it? This isn't You saying this? I know You wouldn't ask me not to love Natasha. She's my wife. It's just some crazy talk from a crazy old man.*

Jesus, I know so little about You, but I know You love me, that's for sure. You saved my life, I mean you saved my life for eternity. I see that now. I remember as a kid hearing about why You died. I'm not as ignorant of You as I think I am. I didn't understand as I do now, but I remember.

Suddenly, people's stares began to register in Jess' consciousness as he realized his private conversation with God was attracting a small crowd. *Oh great, I hope these people don't come in to buy a car!*

The rest of the week passed without any more lunch meetings. Jess called Calvary Lutheran several times trying to reach Luke, leaving messages to no avail. He prayed that Luke had not left his life for good; he needed to talk to him. The more Jess thought about their last conversation, the more he believed he misunderstood what Luke was saying. He wanted to set things straight.

~

Silence now occupied most of Natasha and Jess' time together. All Jess wanted to talk about were the truths God was showing him from reading his Bible and he knew Natasha would cut him off as soon as he opened his mouth. Natasha didn't understand what was going on with Jess, but believed she was doing him a favor by not intruding on his contemplations. Her mind wrestled elsewhere. Each workday planted her in the presence of those praying predators, thieves wanting to steal the rights of women who didn't agree with them.

~

Saturday night meant a run to the liquor store for beer. Jess felt awkward just entering the building. His life had changed so much over the past week that he felt he was walking into enemy territory.

"That's not much beer for two thirsty guys in a boat all day", the clerk was surprised at Jess' reduced purchase.

"Oh...we're trying to cut back, I guess." Jess knew he thirsted for other things. Fred, on the other hand, would expect a day of sucking down his favorite brew. Even so, Jess looked forward to his Sunday morning ritual with Fred, but not for the usual reasons. He wanted to test the waters of the new relationship he caught a glimpse of the week before. He was going to fish for more than walleye.

Chapter

6

The lifetime fishing buddies had their boat in the water by eight in the morning. Jess made a last minute decision to go to Fish Lake instead of Boulder. Fred didn't much care where they went, as long as the fish were biting and the beer was flowing. A light chop from a west wind ruled over the main body of the lake, while walleye played hit and run with tantalizing trolling rigs. By the end of the first hour, three walleye, each over four pounds, searched for a way out of the live-well.

"What a start to the day!" Fred's demeanor boasted of the fact that he had hooked the largest walleye.

"Yah, we haven't had a morning like this in a while. Those will be good eating."

"Jess, you mind if I ask you something?"

"Have I ever minded?"

"Julie talked to Tash yesterday and she said you've been awful quiet all week. I've been worried about you. When we were out the other night you looked pretty shook about something. What's been on your mind? Is there anything wrong?"

Jess didn't think an entrance into the kind of conversation he wanted to have that day would be so easy. He was sure he would have to work at reeling Fred in. "No, nothing's wrong...as a matter of fact...I guess you could say something is finally right."

"What do you mean, finally right?"

"You better sit down Fred. I don't want you falling out of the boat." Jess decided to jump right in. *After all, what's said in the boat stays in the boat.* "I wasn't shook that night at dinner, I was drained."

"Drained of what?"

"Emotionally drained, I guess. I'm sure you couldn't help but see how red my eyes were."

"Yah, I thought you had been on a binge without me." Fred mustered half a chuckle before he saw how serious Jess' expression was.

"That crash is what shook me up. I felt like my heart stopped when I was in the air. I still can't account for how I got out of the car."

"You were thrown out, and you had a lucky landing. What's the mystery to that?"

"Fred! I was going a hundred miles an hour. I had my seatbelt on! Do you really believe I flew out of the car and had a lucky landing? Even if I did fly out of the car, I would have hit the ground at a speed that should have killed me. I hardly had a mark on me!"

"Woooo...that's no walleye! It feels like a pretty good-size northern to me." Fred fought the fish for almost ten minutes before it surfaced. Normally, Jess would be excited for his friend, but this fish put a halt to the conversation.

"I bet he tips the scale at ten pounds." Jess' halfhearted enthusiasm disclosed his desire to rush the process along in order to return to more important matters.

The scale proved Jess to be close. The slimy mass weighed in at nearly eleven pounds. Fred curled the fish and placed it in the second live well. "I don't want that monster in with those walleye!" He then turned to the side of the boat, dropped anchor, splashed his hands in the water to clean off the slime, and reached for a beer. "I think I better rest for a while."

"You've been pretty active for an old man."

"Hey, I know you want to talk, so let's take a break and just sit for a while."

Jess was ready to ask Fred what had happened to him, he had never been so accommodating. "Are you sure you don't want to talk and fish at the same time?"

"You know, we have four beautiful fish in the live-wells. We've got to give those poor guys over there a chance." Fred's head gave a nod toward two men in a boat about fifty yards away.

"Thanks, Fred. Well...surviving that crash the way I did got me thinking an awful lot about God. We're not kids anymore you know, and after that crash I realized for the first time that I'm not immortal. One day I'm going to die."

"You didn't really think you were immortal? Everybody knows they're going to bite the dust sometime."

"I've come to think that we really don't know that. I mean...we know it, but it's always happening to the other guy. I know this sounds stupid, but we're always going to someone else's funeral, never our own."

"That bump on your head still bothering you, son?"

"I'm serious, Fred. Think about it. You don't wake up in the morning and think this could be your last time getting out of bed, or the last time you ever shave, or you may not get a chance to eat supper tonight because you might be dead. We don't think like that. There's always tomorrow. We think tomorrow will always be there for us. I've heard people talk about the end of the world, being worried about it. They don't stop to think that the end of the world for them could be after their very next breath.

"No, I really don't think we understand how mortal these bodies are unless death confronts us somehow; cancer, heart attack, or maybe an accident. If you fell over the side of the boat, bumped your head enough to be disoriented underwater so that you couldn't find the surface, fear would choke the thought of life right out of you. I was there. I was right at the edge... Man, I think I was leaning over the edge. I knew I was in the last split second of my life. My heart was pounding so hard that it sounded like a bass drum in my ears, and then it felt like it stopped. My throat was so tight that I couldn't draw a breath."

"But you made it through. You lived."

"So does that make me immortal now? No...and not all of me made it through. Part of me did die, Luke helped me see that." Jess paused and allowed Luke's words to pass through his mind. The love of worldly things that kept him from Jesus was dead, except for one, but he refused to believe Natasha was one of those things.

"Luke? Who's Luke?"

"Oh, he's a guy I've been talking to about God. God led him to me."

"God LED him to you? Jess, you're sounding like one of those fanatical preachers on TV."

"You've been watching preachers on TV?"

"Purely for entertainment."

"Well, the fear of death stuck with me until last Monday evening, right before I came to the steakhouse. Jesus filled me with His peace, Fred. I was so overwhelmed with His peace that I cried like a baby. I've never felt anything so beautiful in my life. At first, though, I felt so ashamed...ashamed of who I was, and then...it was like a river of rushing water washed over me, leaving this peace...this wonderful peace."

The sounds of waves licking the sides of the boat were the only sounds to be heard until Jess finally ventured forward again, "I know it sounds so...so 'spiritual', but it was so real, Fred. And it's still real today. I know that Jesus is my Savior. I know that when I die, I'm going to live...forever!"

Fred sat motionless. The look on his face explained the awkward lull. "I'm speechless, Jess, I'm absolutely speechless. This is the last thing I ever expected to hear from you."

"Believe me, it's the last thing I ever expected to say, especially to YOU!"

"You haven't told Tash this yet, have you?"

"No."

"How do you think she's going to handle it? You know what she thinks of those right-wing zealots."

"Do you think I'm a right-wing zealot?"

"Well, not yet I guess. But you better be careful, or you could become one."

"What about you? Just last week you were talking about how everybody lied to you about how all this was made. Remember the squirrel falling out of the tree? Weren't you saying that you believe in God?"

"God, yes, but this Jesus thing I'm not so sure about. Seems to me it gets pretty fanatical when you start saying Jesus is God. I mean, maybe He's one of them, I don't know. I think God's more like all of them put together."

Jess remembered a verse he had read Friday morning. He had been sneaking into work early just to have the opportunity to read his Bible without Natasha knowing. He would first read John 14:27, about the peace Jesus had given him, then he went to the beginning of the book of John and began to read through it. The verse that he remembered now was John 14:6, "I am the way, the truth, and the life; no one comes to the Father, but through Me." *If that's true, Fred is completely wrong.*

"Well, according to the Bible, Jesus IS the only One."

"See, fanatical. That's what I mean. You've got to be careful with this stuff. When you say things like that people are going to look at you differently. Next thing you know, the bottom line gets hurt. I've come to think that believing in God is a good thing. Like I said, all this couldn't have happened by accident. But don't take it so far as to say somebody else is wrong, that's when it gets fanatical. I know Natasha, and I would never deliberately talk to her about God. She's got her own belief. Her belief is that she doesn't believe, but that's OK. We have a great friendship, the four of us, and it's because we don't get into that kind of stuff as a foursome. We just go out and enjoy ourselves."

Fred could see the fallen look on Jess' face. "Hey, buddy! We're friends, best friends. I'm glad that after all these years we can finally talk like this, just the two of us I mean. And you know why we can? Because what's said in the boat stays in the boat!" Fred reached for another beer, pulled up anchor, and said, "Come on, there's fish out there just begging to get caught!"

Jess turned on the electric trolling motor and threw his line in the water. His motions had now become mechanical, being stunned by the direction the conversation of the morning had taken. He scanned the shoreline hoping that, by some miracle, Luke had decided to go fishing.

The rest of the day welcomed only superficial talk, while Jess' heart ached for something more. Sunday evening at home was not much better. Conversations with Natasha only covered the basics. *Where is Luke, I really need to talk to Luke!*

~

Peace I leave with you; My peace I give to you; not as the world gives, do I give to you. Let not your heart be troubled, nor let it be fearful. These words once again began Jess' day, and ministered to a man who was now feeling more and more separated from those around him. *Maybe mom would understand all of this. She said she's been praying for me.*

~

Helen Rivers' frail body hid the history of its life of service. Being the mother of one child, she had ample time to attack any cause that moved her. Her servant-hood at Calvary Lutheran was legendary, and her work outside the church with the PTA and Cub Scouts during Jess' elementary school years was award-winning. Jess' childhood activities were filled with motherly involvement. His teen years, though, revealed the lack of relationship between mother and son. Respect was always enforced by Jess' dad, but communication was a gulf that only grew wider with time.

Jess was unaware of regrets that burdened his mother's heart. He had been faithful to dutiful visits that respect required, but never more than twice a month. Two weeks had almost passed since the accident, and he had not yet made good on his promise to visit her. Jess' decision to fulfill that promise after work was not born out of concern for his mother, but rather out of a desire to talk to anyone he thought might understand this new life he seemed to have.

A knock on the door of Helen's assisted-living apartment was a welcome sound, as this was not the time for a scheduled visit from the building's staff. Jess waited patiently, knowing the time it took for his mom to get up out of her chair and come to the door, relying on her walker for stability.

"Jess! Come in, come in! It's so good to see you!"

"Hi mom, I'm sorry it's been a while since I've been here."

"I know, you lead a busy life. How are you? Are you OK, son, from your accident I mean?"

"Yes, mom, I'm just fine. You know Tash would have called if there was anything wrong."

Helen did know that, there was no other reason she would call. The mother-in-law/daughter-in-law relationship had been nonexistent since the day of the secular wedding. Helen tried to establish some sort of bond a number of times through the years, but a wall of cold unwillingness from Natasha always derailed the effort.

Jess was in no mood for small talk. He waited for his mom to struggle back into her chair and asked, "Mom, when I called you after the accident and asked if God had ever spoken to you, you said you have been praying for me to hear His voice. What did you mean by that? How did you think God would speak to me?"

Helen's body was weak, but her spirit was strong, and the words from her son set her spirit to flight. She had been praying for Jess for over fifteen years, ever since God had revealed to her the difference between being religious and coming to Him in repentance to receive His gift of salvation. Her heart had hungered for this very moment, and she prayed God would give her the words to bridge the gulf between her son and herself.

Helen reached for her Bible on the end table next to her chair. As if holding a treasure tightly with both hands, she began to share words lovingly familiar to her own mind. She shared with confidence, having seen the hand of God topple the wall that had kept those words from being spoken. "Jess, some years ago God helped me see how I failed you. I was everything you needed growing up, except your mother. I talked at you all the time, but I was too busy to talk with you. I know your dad was a great companion for you until the day he died, but I also know that he didn't talk with you either. We both let you grow up on your own; finding your own answers to the questions every person has about life. The truth is, we didn't know those answers, so we kept ourselves hidden away to avoid hearing the questions. Like so many parents, we figured you would find your way as we did, even though we still felt lost ourselves."

"Mom, I never looked at you and dad as being lost. You were always strong and sure of yourselves, knowing where you were going."

"Oh sure we were, in the world around us, but not in our hearts, not in our souls. We could give you great advice about how to get a job, how to buy a house, but we knew very little about how to love others as ourselves, how to put others before ourselves. I finally allowed God to break through my shell fifteen years ago, and I have been praying for this conversation every day since. God spoke to my heart and told me that this day would come. He assured me my prayers would not be in vain."

"How mom, how did He tell you? How do you hear Him?"

"He speaks to my heart when I listen."

"But how do you know it's His voice?"

"Because I know it from this," Helen held up her Bible, clutched in both hands.

Jess moved from the couch where he had found refuge and knelt next to his mother's chair. He noticed for the first time how tired and worn out she appeared. *This is my mom, and I've abandoned her.* "I've come to be His, Mom. I've heard His voice, and I know who He is."

Jess sat with his mom and shared the events of the past two weeks. Tears filled the gulf until Jess was finally able to dive in and swim across.

Chapter

7

Late meals at the Rivers' hobby farm were not unusual; Natasha had a reason for waiting to eat until her husband came home from visiting his mom. She had been patient long enough. At this meal there would be conversation. For Jess' part, he possessed a wholehearted desire to share with his wife; his apprehension lay in her anticipated response. After almost two weeks of building up inward conversations, the bubble was about to burst.

The front wooden screen door slammed; Natasha yelled out, "I'm in the kitchen, Jess. We can eat on the back porch."

Jess washed his hands in the half bath on his way, consciously stalling to formulate an opening line.

"Grab your plate, hon, everything else is on the table."

Jess could smell hamburgers and knew they would be accompanied by corn-on-the-cob and potato salad, a favorite summer banquet at their comfortable country home. The back porch offered an inviting view of Natasha's ravishing gardens. The aroma of lavender and sweet alyssum mixed with the smell of grilled beef and fried onions. Jess had mused many times in the past that if heaven had a smell, this would be it. He was grateful that God had arranged such ambiance to share his heart with the woman he loved.

The first bite of hamburger hadn't been swallowed before Natasha threw a zinger. "So, have you heard the voice of God again?"

"What?" His response was muffled as it passed by the half chewed food in his mouth. *Is she being funny, or serious?* He swallowed hard and asked again, "What do you mean?"

"In the hospital, you told me you thought you heard the voice of God, remember? I was just wondering if you've heard it again."

It was apparent Natasha was in a no nonsense mood. Jess wasn't prepared for this kind of conversation. He had gone over soft, loving approaches in his mind, fully expecting that he would be initiating the discourse. "Ah...yes...I have."

"That's what I was afraid of. I knew there was something on your mind that you didn't want to talk to me about. God was the only thing I could think of."

"I've wanted to talk to you for two weeks, but I didn't know how. And certainly, this is not how I wanted the conversation to start."

"What's wrong with this conversation?"

"It's harsh, Tash, your tone is harsh. I want to have a conversation, not an argument."

"Were you going to serve God up to me with flowers?"

"Now you're being mean."

The ambiance was gone. Both Jess and Natasha reverted to their previous inward conversations. Food displaced words as an excuse for silence, and the cool evening breeze delivered an unwanted stench from the garbage can next to the porch.

Natasha was the first to give in. "Jess, I'm sorry. I've been giving you space, but you've been ignoring me for two weeks. You've hardly said two words to me. It's like you did die in that accident and I'm a widow."

The words cut through Jess like a knife. His heart screamed out, *It's not true!* Luke's words, *"Especially Natasha"*, echoed through his mind, fostering a fleeting glimpse of a truth not yet seen. With a will to suppress the unknown, Jess took Natasha by the hand and confessed his heart. "Tash, I love you. I love you more than anything in my life, I always have..." He stopped short of saying, "I always will". There seemed to be an alien battle of voices going on in his head, one uttering, *"Tell her the truth, Jess"*, the other roaring, *"You'll lose her if you do!"*

"Jess, I know that, but something seems so different. You seem so distant, almost detached. And if it's this voice of God thing that's doing it, I want to talk it out."

"It's not a 'thing' Tash...it's...it's God. I've come to know God." Jess knew immediately his words were not the right words. He stated a fact instead of sharing his heart. *Jesus, give me time. I don't want to scare her off. She'll run if I tell her everything.*

"What do you mean you've come to know God? What does that mean?"

"I mean...I know He's real."

"Jess, this kind of thing happens to people when they have a brush with death. They get scared and they think believing in God will take that fear away."

"But He did, Tash. He not only took my fear away, He gave me peace."

"That's great, Jess. If you have to have something like that to get you over what happened, that's fine. But don't let it stop you from talking to me; don't let it come between us. I know you had a heck of a scare, but don't let what happened change our lives. We've got a great life here, let's get back to it."

Jess tried to stuff the truth into the recesses of his mind, but the truth was boundless, unable to be confined. *Our lives have already changed because my life has changed.* These words struggled to be voiced, but fell victim in battle. Courage seemed to seep through his pores until he was held captive by the fear of being rejected by the woman he cherished, losing the love he had never believed he deserved. Jess remembered asking Jesus to prepare Natasha for what He had done to him. *Why didn't You soften her heart? Why didn't You get her ready for this? Why?*

Knowing full well where this conversation with Natasha would lead if he persisted, Jess drew back. "I'm sorry, Tash. We do have a good life here. I don't want to lose that." He knew that was a lie, he knew he was already living a new life. How he wanted to spend his time had changed, what he wanted to talk about had changed. He had fallen head first into the depth of God's love, and was sickened by the thought of retreating once again to the shallowness offered by the world.

"Then let's just do it. Let's just forget this accident ever happened and get back to where we were. If you want to believe somewhere in your mind that God is real, then go ahead. Just don't let it come between us, don't let it change the life we love."

Jess took a bite of potato salad, seasoned with secrets only Natasha held. Flavored memories flooded his mind, so much of this life he did still love. The sweet smelling ambiance returned, and Jess convinced himself that Natasha needed time. *I can't push her. I need to live with her, love her, and slowly show her the love God has shown me.* On the surface he knew this was a good plan, but there was a discomfort deep inside. The battle being waged was not between a husband and wife; it was between the spirit of this world and the Spirit of God. The consideration of spiritual compromise had been introduced, a concept foreign and unrecognizable to a soldier so young.

~

"Line one, Jess."

"Thanks, Peg." Jess was feeling the affects of a night of restlessness. He also felt the pangs of spiritual hunger, regretting not having arrived at work early enough to read his Bible. "Hello."

"Good morning, Jess, this is Luke."

"Luke! Where have you been? I've been calling the church and leaving messages. Didn't you get them?"

"Oh sure I got them, they're real good about giving messages around here."

"Well then...why didn't you call me?"

"You needed some time."

"Time for what?"

"Oh, I think you know."

Jess wasn't sure he did know, but he was aware that he wasn't upset at Luke any longer. The way their last conversation ended left him feeling defensive and a bit angry. Now he longed for reconciliation and the opportunity to be mentored. "Luke, can we meet today? I really want to talk to you."

"I'll be there at twelve-thirty."

"Thanks. Thank you very much."

In just over a week Jess had come to crave Christian fellowship without even knowing what Christian fellowship was. The time spent with his mother on Monday evening was more precious to him than any other time spent together throughout their entire lives. The time spent with Luke shed new light on the reality of life itself.

Ordering lunch was just a formality, neither cared if they ate or not. In Jess' mind food only slowed the conversation. There were many things he wanted to talk about, but there was one subject he decided was off limits, Natasha. He would work that out on his own.

A man who appeared to be in his late thirties stepped up to the booth just as Jess was ready to ask his first question. Luke was obviously acquainted with this trespasser. Jess had come to consider this time spent with Luke over lunch as his own private little world, a very important private little world, and he was unwilling to share it.

"Hello Pastor Herman." Luke stood and reached out to shake the trespasser's hand.

"Hi Luke, good to see you."

"Can you join us?"

Join us? Luke, don't invite him to sit down! Jess felt the presence of a thief come to steal time that didn't belong to him.

"I can for a while. I'm supposed to meet John Bishop here, but I just got a call from him saying he's going to be late. I can sit until he comes." Pastor Herman slid into the seat on Luke's side of the booth.

"Pastor, I would like you to meet my friend, Jess Rivers."

"Good to meet you, Jess."

Jess shook Pastor Herman's hand with reluctance and returned, "It's good to meet you too." But in his mind he was saying, *Hey, can't you see we're talking here!*

Luke saved Jess from accidentally blurting out something impolite by quickly jumping back into the conversation, "Pastor Herman is pastor of Duluth Christian Fellowship, a church I've been visiting on Friday nights since I've come to town."

"You have church on Friday nights?" Jess was unaware such things took place.

"We meet on Friday night, Sunday morning, and Sunday night for worship services, and on Wednesday night we meet for Bible studies."

This must be where the fanatics go that Fred was talking about. Jess' attitude towards Pastor Herman's intrusion seemed to flood him with unwelcome memories of encounters with Christians. *Jesus, forgive me for being angry with this man, I don't even know him.*

"Herman.... You don't hear that name very often anymore." Jess tried to inject something civil into the fray unfolding in his mind.

"A family heirloom I'm afraid, one that I refused to pass down to my son. I didn't believe the world needed a Herman John Groves the fourth!"

"Herman Groves?" Jess immediately savored the sweet smell of the Cuban cigars that filled the air of his youthful employment. "My old boss' name was Herman Groves, sold used cars for Matthews Chevrolet."

"That was my grandpa!"

Instantly a bond replaced the antagonism inside Jess. "I remember meeting you when you were a little kid. How is your dad doing?"

"Just fine, he and mom still live in Denver. That's where we moved when we left Duluth. I always wanted to come back here, though, and had the opportunity when the church where I was an associate pastor agreed to sponsor a church plant here."

A church plant? This was not a concept that Jess understood, but he allowed it to pass in order to continue the exchange. "I knew your grandpa pretty well. He taught me everything I know about the used car business...and maybe some things I shouldn't know."

"Yes, I understand grandpa had quite a reputation. We didn't know that as kids, though, to us he was a lovable guy."

"He was lovable to everybody, that's how he sold so many cars!"

The chuckles brought on by memories shared planted a devious thought in Jess' mind; *I wonder if this pastor sells religion in the same way his grandpa sold used cars?* He was surprised at his own skepticism and wondered if his views from the past would always be the filter through which he would scrutinize "church people".

"What are you preaching on Friday night, Pastor?" Luke seemed in no hurry to resume a two way dialogue.

"What it really means to be a disciple of Christ, an area that needs a lot of attention in all of our lives."

"Jess is a brand new Christian, maybe I can get him to come along with me. How about it Jess, you interested in some wonderful fellowship?"

"Me?...um...I don't know, I..." Jess was racking his brain for an excuse not to go, simply because he didn't want to face Natasha about the visit. "I'd have to check with Tash to see if she has plans for us on Friday."

"Well, go ahead and do that, you can let me know later." Luke was expecting an answer, even if it was a delayed answer. Jess had hoped the question would have passed without a real response required.

"There's John, he's not as late as he figured he would be. Thanks for the conversation guys. And Jess, it would be great if you could join us on Friday night, we'd love to have you. Service starts at seven sharp." With a wave of his hand, Pastor Herman was off.

"He's a great speaker. I sure hope you can come Friday night."

"I don't know, Luke, I would have some heavy explaining to do if I told Natasha I was going to church. I don't think she would be ready for that yet."

"Are you ready?"

"I'm not sure. I haven't been to church in decades. I can't even get Natasha to go to a funeral if it's in a church."

"Is that what's kept you from going, Jess, because Natasha won't go?"

"No!... No, I wanted out when I was in junior high school. That was my decision. I did enjoy going with my mom and dad on Christmas and Easter, though; there was something special about those times."

"Why did you stop going to those services?"

"To keep peace in our new home. The first Christmas we were married Natasha made it very clear there'd be none of that." Jess sat silent. Luke's words, *"Especially Natasha",* opened the door a little wider. *That was clever, Luke, but I don't want to go there.*

Jess mulled over a question as he played with his food. "Luke, what did he mean by really being a disciple of Christ? Aren't you His disciple if you believe in Him?"

"No, there's a big difference. Believing God exists is one thing, following what He teaches is quite another. When you become a disciple of Christ He wants you to completely die to self. You have a free will, but you freely give it up to follow His will."

"So there are rules to this whole thing."

"There's God's Law, but you're looking at this all wrong. It's not like this is a game and you have to follow certain rules to play, it's a restoration. God made man in perfect union with Himself. He walked with Adam and Eve in the garden. They were allowed in His presence. When they disobeyed Him they fell into judgment, and the relationship between God and his creation changed.

"God gave us His Law as a witness, a witness to His righteousness and our unrighteousness. Without His gift of the Law we would have no understanding of our sin. Our sin against God would remain, but it wouldn't be known to us. He points out our sin so that we understand our need for redemption. Jesus died on the cross to pay the penalty for every law we have broken; He is our Redeemer. God's desire is to restore us to the relationship He intended. That's what happened to you in your office, Jess. God confronted you with your unrighteousness and you came to your Redeemer through tears of repentance."

Jess permitted his mind to revisit the peace that permeated the shell of his heart after his tears had softened its crust.

"Something else happened to you that evening in your office, you became a brand new creation; old things passed away. You don't see things as you used to because you're looking at them through brand new eyes. You have begun to be transformed from living in the world to living in the presence of God. Once in His presence, the things of the world don't hold the value they used to. Their value has been diminished compared to the joy of being in the presence of the God of all creation!"

"This is what you meant before about weeping and mourning over the things that used to make me happy, knowing now how they were the very things that were keeping me from being in His presence."

"Yes, Jess, yes! The door of your heart is opening to Him more every day; don't allow anything from the world to slam it shut again. So, what do you think, will you come to church with me on Friday?"

"Luke, you know I've still got the problem of explaining it to Natasha."

"Sometimes when you're not quite ready to let go of things, God will help by removing an obstacle so that you're able to follow

His leading. Would you be willing to go if God handled that for you?"

"What are you talking about?" Jess' stomach churned at the thought of God removing Natasha from his life so that he would follow His lead.

"Your phone's ringing, Jess."

Jess' ears were deafened by the battle waging in his heart, he retreated just enough to notice Natasha's number on the screen. "Hello Tash."

"Hi Jess," each party entered the conversation sheepishly, having thought long and hard about the words exchanged the night before. "How's your day going?"

Once again Jess knew he couldn't share the things he really wanted to say, so he offered a generic, "Fine, I guess."

"Say, Julie called and wanted to know if I would go to The Cities with her on Friday, she wants to do some shopping at the Mega Mall. We would probably stay overnight and hit a couple of antique stores on Saturday morning before heading home. Do you mind if I go?"

"Ah...no, not at all, I know how much you girls love to shop." As Jess closed his phone he whispered, "I hear You Lord," and then surrendered to the man across the table. "I suppose you'd like me to pick you up?"

Chapter

8

Friday arrived cloaked in anxiety. Jess didn't know what to expect from a Friday night church service. *I sure hope they aren't like those Holy Rollers Fred saw on TV.* Jess left the house at 6:15 to give himself time to pick up Luke from the old Sherman Hotel in the West End. He found Luke sitting on a bench with two other men in front of the run down building.

"Hi Jess, these are friends of mine, Carl and Joseph. You don't mind if they hitch a ride to the meeting tonight, do you? They've been going with me for the past few weeks."

The men were welcome, but the odor was not. Jess turned the air conditioning off and opened all four windows. He was test driving a fully loaded two year old Chevrolet Impala from the lot as a possible replacement for his mangled Vette. *I'll never get the smell out of here.* He was ashamed of his thought as soon as it entered his mind. *These two guys obviously have nothing, and I'm more worried about this car.* He glanced over at Luke who was in a chatty conversation with both men. *This guy sure keeps busy for You, doesn't he, Jesus.*

"I've got to get out more. I never knew this place was here," Jess pulled up in front of a rescued store front in the Spirit Valley business district. He dropped his passengers off and informed Luke he would be in after he found a place to park. When he did return he was almost pushed through the door by a stream of people entering. He maneuvered against a wall to scan the room in search of the man who had roped him into coming to this unknown territory. Luke was waving his arms from the second row of burgundy padded chairs. *Not up front, Luke. Have some compassion on me!* He hesitantly made his way to the chair being saved for him, all the while begging God to allow him to hide in the back row.

"Do we have to sit this close?"

"Too late now." Luke was right; the place was full by the time Jess turned around to look.

Church has sure changed since I've been last. No stained glass windows, no hard pews. Where's the organ?

Pastor Herman was true to his word; he stepped up front at seven sharp. "I want to welcome everyone to this place where we are going to spend some time praising, worshiping, and hearing from God's word. Please be seated and join me in prayer... Jesus, thank You for giving us life, new life in You, and for allowing us to gather in this place to bow before You in praise and worship. Lord, speak to us tonight, open every ear and every heart to receive what You desire to give through Your word. In Your name we pray. Amen!"

Words to the hymn "How Great Thou Art" appeared on the wall, music began to play, and people stood to sing. Jess noticed the musicians off to the right of the sanctuary; guitars, key board, drums, violins - *This is not my mama's church. I would have to get used to this if I made a habit of coming here.* Some songs were familiar, others he had never heard.

When the music stopped, Pastor Herman reappeared up front with the same zeal he witnessed his grandpa display when he saw a potential customer take his first step onto the car lot. "Please be seated." He allowed a minute to pass for the musicians to find their seats.

"Before I share what God has laid on my heart for tonight's message, I would like to invite John Bishop to come and update us on the prayer vigil taking place at the Women's Center downtown. John."

Devastation devoured Jess' heart. *I'm encamped with the enemy! What will Natasha do if she ever finds out I'm sitting with the very antagonists of her soul?* Jess was not a crusader, he steered clear of any involvement in the cause that defined his wife. He viewed her work to help maintain the right for women to have an abortion in the same way he viewed his passion for fishing and football; something they both loved to do, but didn't expect the other to take part in. Actually, it was more a trade-off, allowing each to dive head long into their passion without the other complaining.

Jess was now angry at Luke for seating them up front. Getting up and walking out would be embarrassing. He would have to endure his confinement and hope Natasha would never hear of his betrayal.

"Thank you, Pastor. We have had a wonderful week! People have been praying in front of the Women's Center every minute of the day and night all week long. But the most wonderful news is...a teenage mother decided to allow her baby to live after talking with Sally and Joanie. We will be helping her through her pregnancy and counseling with her and her parents about the decision of whether to keep the baby or consider adoption. The young mom's name is Amanda, so please pray for her. This is a very needy family. There may be times when we call on some of you to help get Amanda to doctor appointments, provide maternity clothes, and help financially. Please pray that God will prepare your hearts to help when the need arises. Thank you."

Jess' anger softened. All he had ever heard from Natasha was how thoughtless and selfish these "vultures" were; preying on young women to advance their cause, not caring about what happens after they save the "baby".

"Thank you, John. People, please pray daily for Amanda. Just because she made this decision this week doesn't mean she won't have doubts next week. She is carrying a precious life inside her, and it is going to take courage for her to stand against the peer pressure that surrounds her. John and I met last week and talked about this very problem.

"Young girls like Amanda are being bombarded with lies daily. They are told that this life inside of them is not a baby, but a piece of tissue that is easily removed. They are rarely told the truth about what happens in an abortion; how the baby is cut or sucked to pieces, or how it is burned to death with saline solution. They are told it is a simple medical procedure. They are never told that the baby writhes in pain as its limbs are being ripped or cut away. You who know me understand my passion for this issue. For those of you who don't, let me explain.

"I've not been a Christian all my life, as a matter of fact I came to know Jesus as my Savior when I was twenty-seven years old.

Before that, I lived a very secular life. My wife, Martha, and I...yes, she was named after her grandmother as I was named after my grandpa..." Jess found himself laughing along with the rest of the congregation, "fell in love in high school, at least we thought it was love. It was actually self-centered desire. We had our share of premarital sex and ended up facing a pregnancy neither one of us wanted or were ready for. We believed 'the lie' and Martha had an abortion.

"Even though we experienced a dead feeling inside of us after the abortion, especially Martha, it wasn't until years later that we realized what we had done. Seeing pictures of aborted babies, and learning about abortion procedures, brought on despair. It had become inconceivable to us that WE were complicit as our baby squirmed and recoiled to evade the instruments of death.

"I know for some of you this is hard to hear because you have been in that same place. But this is reality, and we need to stop pretending we don't know what goes on once the tools of abortion are hidden within the womb that was created to nurture life.

"Martha and I repented and asked to be forgiven for allowing our unprotected baby to face the violence it was subjected to. Nothing we can do will ever change what's been done. Only the forgiveness of our gracious God enables us to live on.

"We understand why young girls walk into that Center; we understand their worries and their fears. Some of them are there of their own volition, others because they have been pressured or bullied into the decision to have an abortion. So please pray for Amanda. Pray that her concern is for her baby. Pray that no matter what got her to this place, her love for her baby motivates her actions. Jesus told us that the second greatest commandment is to love others as ourselves. Pray that Amanda will love her baby as herself and do everything in her power to nourish new life."

Jess sat motionless. He had never considered that some of the people Natasha railed against as "religious do-gooders" might actually have at one time walked into that building themselves. This was a different perspective on Christians. *Jesus, Luke said that old things would pass away. Is this one of those old things? Are You changing how I think?*

A time of corporate prayer consumed the next twenty minutes. Jess' eyes were wide open, apprehensive about what might happen next. His spirit quieted down when Pastor Herman stepped behind the pulpit with Bible in hand. *This must be the sermon, maybe we're close to the end.*

"Let's pray. Father, it's easy to hear Your word and apply it to others, it's quite another thing to hear Your word and apply it to our own lives. Speak to our hearts, God. Give us the wisdom to understand the necessity of surrendering our will to Your will in our daily living. Amen.

"Do you consider yourself a disciple of Jesus Christ, a follower of the King of kings and Lord of lords? Please turn with me to Matthew 7:13-23; 'Enter by the narrow gate; for the gate is wide, and the way is broad that leads to destruction, and many are those who will enter by it. For the gate is small, and the way is narrow that leads to life, and few are those who find it. Beware of the false prophets, who come to you in sheep's clothing, but inwardly are ravenous wolves. You will know them by their fruits. Grapes are not gathered from thorn bushes, nor figs from thistles, are they?

Even so, every good tree bears good fruit; but the rotten tree bears bad fruit. A good tree cannot produce bad fruit, nor can a rotten tree produce good fruit. Every tree that does not bear good fruit is cut down and thrown into the fire. So then, you will know them by their fruits. Not everyone who says to Me, "Lord, Lord," will enter the kingdom of heaven; but he who does the will of My Father who is in heaven. Many will say to me on that day, "Lord, Lord, did we not prophesy in Your name, and in Your name cast out demons, and in Your name perform many miracles?" And then I will declare to them, I never knew you; Depart from Me, you who practice lawlessness.'

"Brothers and sisters, there's a heavy burden on my heart for the church. By the church I mean those of us who claim to be disciples of Christ. In many ways we are allowing ourselves to be led astray by false prophets, prophets who appear to be sheep, but are really ravenous wolves that have infiltrated the flock to destroy and devour from within. Their goal is to divert us from the narrow gate that leads to life, and entice us toward the wide gate which leads to destruction. Who are these ravenous wolves? They are agents of deception, cunning demons who delight in distracting us from the word of God.

"Now, I know we would all like to believe we could recognize a ravenous wolf when we see one. The truth is they cannot be seen with physical eyes. Ravenous wolves can only be discerned with spiritual eyes, opened by the Holy Spirit through scripture.

"For an example, physical eyes view a homosexual as someone who has accepted an alternative sexual orientation. While spiritual eyes, opened by the Holy Spirit through scripture, recognize someone who has succumbed to a ravenous wolf tearing at the truth of God's word with teeth sharpened by compromise. Physical eyes enjoy watching today's TV shows and movies in the name of entertainment. Spiritual eyes, opened by the Holy Spirit through scripture, recognize the ravenous wolf behind the scripts, mocking the word of God.

"Today's church is being easily fooled by these agents of deception because we have taken our eyes off of the word of God and allowed them to stray, unchecked, into the dark culture of sin that surrounds us. So many who claim to be disciples of Christ define righteousness through the philosophies of man instead of accepting God's truth from scripture. Once we begin to go down that slippery slope we lose our footing, and all righteousness becomes questionable under the cover of darkness.

"In John 8:12 Jesus said; 'I am the light of the world; he who follows Me shall not walk in the darkness, but shall have the light of life.' If we are disciples of Christ, we will not be fooled by the philosophies of man, because they will be revealed for what they truly are by the light of Christ.

"Paul tells us in Ephesians 5:6-10; 'Let no one deceive you with empty words, for because of these things the wrath of God comes upon the sons of disobedience. Therefore do not be partakers with them; for you were formerly darkness, but now you are light in the Lord; walk as children of light (for the fruit of the light consists in all goodness and righteousness and truth), trying to learn what is pleasing to the Lord.' But sadly...so many in the church are setting aside what is pleasing to the Lord in a misguided attempt to be accepted by those who love the culture of the day.

"Within so many churches the immorality of premarital sex is not challenged, we allow those who are living together to teach Sunday school. The immorality of homosexuality is not a topic of discussion any more; the discussion now centers on what those who practice this sin will be allowed to do in the body of Christ. Evolution, a theory of how everything came into being without the Creator and the need for the Redeemer, is accepted in whole or in part by most people claiming to be Christians. The idea that one god encompasses all religions is prevalent, proclaiming many ways to eternal life. These are just a few examples of compromising the word of God.

"You say, 'But Pastor, I don't believe these things.' I used to say that too, until God pointed out to me my passive acceptance of these issues in my everyday walk. We're bullied by political correctness and tolerance. We believe that showing what the world proclaims as compassion is more important than standing on the word of God. We wouldn't dare refer to scripture in conversations for fear of being called fanatical.

"And what about our personal lives? We can party out loud with our friends at our favorite sports bar, but are embarrassed to bow our heads in silence at a restaurant to give thanks for God's provisions. We allow our sons to play video games that are full of violence and wonder where their disrespect comes from. We allow our daughters to dress in the scanty fashions of the day, tempting male eyes to go where they shouldn't go, and then wonder why our daughters get pregnant.

"Yes, the church is in trouble because it has turned from God to follow man. The church has stopped preaching the need for repentance from sin and has fallen into the cultural trap of justifying and being tolerant of sin. How do we expect the world to see the light of Christ when we, His church, desire to walk in darkness?

"God calls us to righteousness, to be set apart, to walk as children of the light. We read in Roman's 6:7-8; 'Do not be deceived, God is not mocked; for whatever a man sows, this he will also reap. For the one who sows to his own flesh will from the flesh reap corruption, but the one who sows to the Spirit shall from the Spirit reap eternal life.'

"To what do we sow? Do we dress with holiness in mind? Do we turn away from TV programs and movies that bring glory and honor to unrighteousness? What do we do and think in our secret times, when no one is around? Does our heart crave God's righteousness, or does it practice sin in the presence of the prince of darkness? Will we be among those to whom Jesus says, 'I never knew you; Depart from Me, you who practice lawlessness.'

"Oh church, my heart aches for us to see the truth in this. My heart aches for us to understand how serious God is about following Him...about being His disciple.

"If you find that you're sowing in the wrong place, repent. If you find you are practicing sin, repent. A disciple of Christ does the will of the Father. Is a disciple of Christ perfect? No. Is a disciple of Christ repentant - resulting in being forgiven, washed clean, sanctified, and made holy by the precious blood of Jesus? YES!

"Church, we need to stand firm on the word of God. We cannot compromise on His truth. We cannot fall prey to the ravenous wolves who seek to devour us with cunning lies from Satan.

"Are you a disciple of Christ? If so, you are not one just because you say you're one. You are one because you seek after His truth above all else. You are one because you do the will of the Father. You are a disciple of Christ because you sow to the Spirit, and not to your own flesh.

"Get in God's word. Know His truth and stand firm on it. We, by that I mean all who have accepted the offer of salvation through our Savior Jesus Christ, are the Church which God desires to gather unto Himself...one disciple at a time.

"Father, bring us to repentance in the areas of our lives where we have turned away from Your word. Show us how to rely on Your strength to do Your will by walking in Your truth. Amen."

Most of the people in the building stood to sing, some walked forward and seemed to form several huddles, a few headed for the exits. Jess wasn't sure if the service was over or not, so he waited for his cue from Luke, who at the moment appeared to be praying with Carl.

I never heard a sermon like that from Pastor Larson. Of course, Pastor Larson may have preached a sermon like that, but Jess would never have known, as he never listened to the lanky servant-of-God. He did listen to Pastor Herman, though, and was quite surprised at the content of his message. *Now I've got more questions for Luke!* What weighed most heavily on Jess' mind was what Pastor Herman shared about abortion.

"Carl gave his heart to Jesus tonight!" Luke was beaming as he approached Jess with the good news. Jess could see tears running down Carl's cheeks as he succumbed to the urge to put his arm around Carl's shoulders. He didn't know what to say or do, but he was genuinely happy for him, so he gave him a squeeze.

Joseph kept his distance all the way to the car. Just as Jess was reaching for the door handle he heard his name being called out. He turned around and found himself face to face with Fred who was in the passenger's seat of the pick-up truck which had stopped alongside him.

"Hey Jess, what are you up to?"

"Oh, hi Fred...just giving these guys a ride home."

Carl jumped into the impromptu chat with radiant joy, "We've been to church, and I accepted Jesus!"

Oh man, did you have to say that?

"You've been to church, Jess?" Fred questioned with a menacing look.

"I'll see you Sunday morning, Fred. Don't tell Julie because you know she'll tell Natasha."

Jess was not acquainted with Fred's chauffeur, but hoped the bond of discretion amongst the brotherhood of men would prevail.

Chapter

9

Natasha would not be home until at least early afternoon. This would allow Jess the liberty to pursue an otherwise unthinkable option to the start of the weekend; Saturday morning breakfast with Luke.

~

"That was some service last night, Luke, not at all like I remember church."

"Well, church services like you remember still exist. Style does not define worship. What's important is that you come to God in reverence, desiring to know His truth."

"Guitars, drums, keyboard, violins, they all surprised me. Church music to me has always meant an organ had to be played."

"Some people think drums and guitars don't belong in church, but there was a time when people thought an organ didn't belong in church. It's not the instruments you bring before the Lord that matter; it's the heart you bring."

"I have to tell you something that scares me a little."

"What's that?"

"It has to do with what Pastor Herman said about abortion, it kind of puts me in a spot."

"How so?"

"Well...what he said was pretty graphic. What do you know about abortion, Luke? Does the baby really feel pain?"

"I think you know the answer to that."

"Yah...maybe I do. If Pastor Herman is right, then they must feel pain. I've never heard anyone talk about what happens in an abortion. I've always thought the doctor just went in and scraped some tissue. Does a baby really go through what Pastor Herman talked about, being cut up, or sucked apart?"

"It's amazing what one human being will do to another, isn't it, Jess?"

"Yes, it really is." *Natasha must know this. She must know what they're doing. How can she fight for that? How can she know it and still say it's all right?* "My wife works at the Women's Center."

"Oh, I see, that's the spot you're in."

"She hates these people. If she finds out I spent the evening listening to them...she'll think I've betrayed her. But it's worse than that. What I heard does have me thinking, and that makes me wonder if I actually AM betraying her."

"Coming to the truth doesn't constitute betrayal. It simply means you have walked out of the darkness and into the light. Once that happens you can help others do the same."

"You mean Natasha? Oh man, you don't know Natasha. This is like a religion to her. I mean, she doesn't believe in religion, but if she did, this would be hers."

"So what are you going to do? Are you going to talk to her about this?"

"I don't know. I've never entered into that space in her life. I've just let her do her thing." Jess paused and then said, "We've never had kids. Natasha wasn't able to, but secretly I always wanted to. I just never talked about it because I didn't want to cause Natasha any pain...due to her inability. I can't comprehend someone allowing that to happen to their own baby."

Jess finished his breakfast before he was ready to speak again. "I was impressed last night with Pastor Herman's ability to hold my attention. That has to be the first sermon in my life I have fully listened to. He was pretty hard on the church though, wasn't he?"

"He told the truth."

"Maybe, but he made it sound awfully hard to be a disciple of Christ. No TV, no movies, no sports bars."

"I didn't hear that. I heard no desire for unrighteousness. We've had this conversation before, have you forgotten? 'Let your laughter be turned into mourning, and your joy to gloom.' He was talking about the things that keep us from God... I sense a little defensiveness in this part of the conversation, Jess. Is there something from the old life you're having trouble giving over to Him?"

"I don't know, maybe there is. I haven't forgotten our conversation, there are so many things that I look at differently now. Maybe it's beginning to scare me."

"Change can be scary."

"That's just it. Is God going to change something around every corner? What's the next thing he's going to tell me I have to give up?"

"Jess, has God told you to give up anything? Has He said, 'Give me that, you can't have it anymore?' Or do you see things more clearly because you're walking in the light and not the darkness? What have you given up that you have not had a desire to give up?

Has God said, 'I demand you give that to Me?' Or has He asked, 'are you willing to give that to Me?' You have a free will. You can say no."

Jess was startled by Luke's last statement, "I can say no? What do you mean, I can say no? I can say no to God?"

"Sure you can, that's what having a free will is about. God won't force us to do anything we don't want to do. Look around you, people say no all the time."

Jess' mind was befuddled, "You mean to tell me that it's OK to say no to God?"

"I didn't say it was OK, I said you have the freedom. You can say, 'No God, not that,' and walk away hugging that possession as tightly as you want."

"But God will do something, right? Like strike me dead with a bolt of lightning."

"You've been watching too many movies, Jess. No, if that's how He worked, we all would have been dead long ago. What He does is show us the truth; He shows us the destructive nature of our decisions.

"Pastor Herman mentioned 'practicing sin' in his message last night. There is a difference between falling to sin and practicing sin. When we fall to temptation we know what we did was wrong, we have a conscience. That conscience is God showing us the destructiveness of our thoughts or actions and makes clear the transgression in light of His righteousness. At those moments He calls us to repentance, to see the error of our ways, to turn from sin and come to Him. Those who do are forgiven, because Jesus paid the price on the cross for all transgressions. For those who don't, their hearts begin to harden against the truth. When we say no enough times we begin to come up with excuses, and then reasons for believing that what we once knew was wrong...we now see as right. We justify our actions in order to continue fulfilling our desire. We are no longer falling to sin, we are embracing sin and practicing it with a conscience that was first dulled and is now dead. When this happens, God honors our decision to say no and turns us over to the lusts of our heart. In short, we have heard the truth, but have believed the lie." Luke paused to allow Jess time to soak in what was being shared.

"We can say no to God, Jess, but there are consequences. When we embrace that sin and practice it with a conscience dead to righteousness, it becomes our identity. We are not what God longs for us to be, a remorseful sinner, forgiven, and saved by His grace; we are a liar, an adulterer, a murderer, a cheat, a homosexual, a rebel; we have become our sin. We are separated from God by our unrighteousness, when we proclaim that unrighteousness to be righteous we are calling God a liar."

"That's some pretty heavy stuff."

"Sin is heavy. It weighs us down and, in the end, destroys us. God loves us so much that He took on our sins and carried them on the cross. Jess, God has given us the freedom to say no, but His greatest desire is that we say yes. Yes to His offer of salvation, so that we can stand in His presence. Yes to His plan for our lives, because He sees all things and knows all things. Yes to trusting that He causes all things to work together for good to those who love Him."

"I want to say yes, but I'm afraid there will be something that He'll want that I won't be able to give up."

"Why wouldn't you be able to give something to God?"

"Because...it would tear my whole life apart."

Luke could see the anguish in Jess' eyes, "He's already asked you, hasn't He."

Silence ruled the moment. Jess realized he was standing on the edge of the very cliff he had been trying to avoid. "Yes...and I'm afraid of what will happen if I give her to Him."

"Do you mean Natasha? Do you think God is asking you to give Him Natasha?"

"Yes."

"No, Jess, He's not asking that. You can't give Natasha to Him; she's not yours to give."

"I don't understand."

"What He is asking you to give to Him is your love for Natasha, the love that stands between Him and you. It's the love that has influenced you to turn a deaf ear to Him ever since you met her. He has called your name in the past, but answering Him would not fit into the life you desired with Natasha. No, it's not Natasha He wants from you; it's your heart that He wants from you. He's asking you to turn away from all the gods you worship and worship Him only."

"But isn't that the same thing? How can I allow God to change my life and not have Natasha know about it? She would hate what's happening to me. Look what's happened just since last night. God has opened my eyes to something that's a huge part of who she is. What do I do with that? How do I ignore that?"

"I don't hear you talking about a love for Natasha, Jess, I hear you talking about your love of yourself. Your concern should be for her need of salvation, not for your possible loss of happiness. Would you want to keep Natasha from any opportunity that might bring her to Christ because you're afraid you will lose her if she rejects Him?"

"She will reject Him, I know her, she'll say no to God and to me!"

Luke reached across the table, put his hand on Jess' forearm, and bowed his head. "Father, I pray that You give Jess the wisdom and strength he needs to listen to Your direction. I pray he doesn't allow selfish desire to win out over love for others. I pray that You bring Jess' heart to the place of being willing to lay down his life for Natasha. Amen."

~

The drive home was interrupted by an unscheduled stop at the crash site. Jess was drawn to the birthplace of his problem like metal to a magnet. The midmorning sun was warm on his face, and the balm, rising from plant life as he meandered through the field, soothed the turmoil hidden in his soul.

"Why do things have to be so complicated, God? Why pull me toward You if it's only going to push me away from Tash? Why do I feel like I have to choose between her and You? Can't I accept the reality of You and just go on living my life?" Jess plopped down on a rock and slowly brushed his hand back and forth across the tops of the tall grass. "I love her, Jesus... I can see the truth in what Luke says. He's right; I have stayed away from You because of Tash. I never wanted to rock the boat by even suggesting we go to a Christmas Eve service." Jess nervously smiled at the irony rising to awareness, "Now, You want me to sink the ship by telling her You're my Savior... Can I trust You, God, to prepare Natasha this time...to help her understand what all this is about? I'll talk to her, but don't let me lose her." Jess' prayer was a conditional surrender.

The rest of the way home Jess mulled over several scenarios of access to Natasha's heart, none of which produced any amount of hope. The fragrant breeze flowing through the open driver's door window seemed to speak to Him, *"Ease it in; just ease it into a pleasant conversation."* It was the most lame of any scenario which had passed through his mind, but it was noncommittal. There would be no exact point of entry, making it the most acceptable, allowing Jess to say yes to God at his convenience.

Jess parked his truck in the driveway, went inside the house to change clothes, and headed for his garage. He had not spent any time in his favorite hideaway since the accident. Cleaning his "kids" and exercising them down a paved country road on a beautiful summer day was his definition of pure leisure.

The garage was as much a child to Jess as the mechanical occupants it sheltered. The rustic wooden exterior boasted antique oil, tire, food, and drink signs, while two antique gas pumps welcomed visitors to this step back in time. The office offered treasured childhood memories of time spent in penny candy stores, of buying Nesbitt Orange Pop from bottle-clanking pop coolers, and of building plastic model car kits with neighborhood friends. The garage stalls were home to the apples of his eye. A time machine could not have produced a better collection of days gone by. Cherished nostalgia swallowed any troubles that walked through the door.

Hours passed quickly in this private world. Stepping outside, Jess noticed Natasha's car turning into the driveway. A smile from this undercover homebody solicited a wave from the driver of the approaching 2009 Mustang. Natasha knew nothing about cars, but recognized style when she saw it, even if it was not from her husband's favorite car manufacturer. She never grasped the torment of a Chevy man seeing a Ford parked in front of his garage.

"Welcome home, hon, how was your trip?"

"It was wonderful! Julie makes me laugh more than anyone I know. We were so loud we almost got kicked out of the mall."

Natasha exited her car and took in the full picture of the man waiting to give a hug. "Why don't you change out of those dirty coveralls before you embrace me, the last thing I want to do is put my arms around a greasy old rag." Jess looked down at the front of his coveralls... *Hmmm, they look pretty clean to me.*

"Have you had lunch yet?" Natasha threw the question back at Jess as she headed for the house.

"No, I ate a late breakfast."

"I'll make us an early supper. Julie and I ate late this morning too."

Jess turned and walked back into solitude. He would have another hour before Natasha was unpacked enough from her shopping spree to expect him in.

~

Stories of shopping escapades filled the supper hour. Jess was amazed he hadn't been called to the cities to bail out the wild women after hearing of their post sports bar shenanigans. Natasha had always possessed an unrestrained knack for fun after a few drinks. Jess couldn't help but laugh at his wife's descriptions of the antics the two tipsy women employed in an effort to steal enough Lego blocks away from kids to build the "world's tallest castle" in Lego Land at the Mall of America. He thoroughly enjoyed the company of his wife, but enjoyed it most when she was bubbling over with laughter. The contagious episodes lifted his spirit from any sort of melancholy.

"How 'bout we go for a walk, it's going to be a beautiful evening."

"That sounds great, let's just get the kitchen picked up first."

The experienced couple effortlessly moved through the motions. Within minutes they were out the door and in the meadow, walking hand-in-hand.

"How was your day, Jess?"

"Oh, lazy, I had breakfast with a friend and then came home and played in the garage."

"Who'd you have breakfast with?"

Jess couldn't believe he even brought up his meeting with Luke. *That was stupid... Maybe this is my smooth entry already?... Maybe not.* "Just a guy I met at the lot. He knew my dad so it was fun talking to him." *That wasn't a lie. Not the whole truth, but not a lie.* He waited to see if he had satisfied the query.

"It sure was good to get away with Julie. We had some good talks."

Jess breathed a sigh of relief. "About what?"

"About our husbands, what else?"

"Maybe what's said on the trip should stay on the trip." They both laughed as they scampered down a short hill.

Small talk continued in an almost flirtatious manner. This was the closest they had been since the accident. Jess slipped his arm around Natasha's shoulder and eased her close to his side. "I love you, Tash."

"I love you too, Jess."

A warm embrace became a loving kiss; the two walked on, shoulder to shoulder.

TRUTH

Chapter

10

Sizzling bacon and perking coffee enticed Jess to the kitchen. The cook reminded him of the flirtatious woman he was with the night before. The two exchanged knowing looks; silently leaving Fred out of the playful banter. For the first time in thirty-nine years Jess was sorry he was going fishing.

"What lake are we going to today?" Fred's words, spoken through eggs and toast, were ignored. "Jess...hey, Jess! What planet are you on this morning?"

"I'm sorry, Fred. Ah, I thought we might try Rice Lake, we haven't been there for quite a while."

"Fine with me. You remembered the beer, right?"

Jess nodded his head as he outmaneuvered Fred for the last piece of bacon.

"I can't believe I have to ask about the beer," Fred shook his head in lighthearted sarcasm.

~

Both lines were in the water before the expected question rolled off Fred's lips, "So...how was church?"

"Do you really want to know, or are you going to have a little fun with this?"

"I really want to know... Really!"

"OK, well, it was interesting. Nothing at all like I expected. They had a band instead of an organist, and people really got into the music. You know who the pastor is? Herman Groves the third."

"You've got to be kidding. Are they keeping a close eye on the collection plate?"

"I don't think he's like his grandpa at all, there doesn't seem to be any con in him. To old Herman the church was just another pool of potential customers, but I think Pastor Herman takes this stuff seriously."

"Are you going back?"

"I don't know how I can, not yet anyway. I've got to be honest with Natasha about it first; I can't sneak around and go behind her back."

"She's going to pop a cork when she finds out you've already been."

"Probably, but I'll tell you what she'll really blow her stack about; these are the people that have been holding prayer meetings in front of the Women's Center."

"What! Are you crazy? Sitting down with those people! Are you trying to end your marriage?"

"Please, don't even joke about that. I didn't know it was them until after I was already there." Jess stopped and took measure of his friend. *Do I dare say it; do I dare let my thoughts outside of my head?* "I, ah...I was surprised at what they said, about why they do it I mean."

"You mean why they antagonize your wife?"

"They aren't going there to do that, they don't even know her. They really care about what's going on, not just the babies, but about the moms too."

"One night and you've been brainwashed already."

Did it sound that bad? Did it sound like I've already taken up the cause? "I haven't been brainwashed, but I have to say I heard some things I hadn't heard before. Things that have made me think."

"Forget it, Jess. What has it got to do with you anyway? You're not having a baby. Thinking about this stuff will just stir up trouble at home. You don't want that."

Jess drew back and thought he would change the subject. "Why haven't you and Julie ever had kids, Fred?"

"We've never wanted them. We made a decision years ago that we wanted to have the kind of life we have. Look at me. What kind of a dad do you think I would have made? A pretty poor one, I'll tell you that."

"Was Julie able, or did you get fixed to make sure it didn't happen?"

"Man, you're getting personal."

"I'm sorry, I shouldn't have asked that."

Fred grew uncharacteristically quiet, making several casts before setting his pole down and looking at Jess as though he wanted to get something off his chest. "What I just said isn't true... I'm going to tell you something that I've never told a living soul. When Julie and I were in college we fooled around some, you know, we were in love and couldn't wait. Julie got pregnant. We knew it would kill her folks if they found out about it. Plus, they wanted her to finish college more than anything in the world; you remember how they made us wait to get married until after Julie graduated. Well...we decided to handle the problem before they ever guessed what was going on."

"Julie had an abortion?"

"Yes...and something went wrong. I don't know anything about it medically, but something went wrong. A few years later when we tried to have kids we found out that she couldn't. It's not that we didn't want to have kids...it was just the hand that was dealt us. The doctor was some kind of quack. I've always believed this was one of the reasons Julie and Natasha hit it off so well right away. You know how strong Natasha's been on the subject forever. Well, Julie had just been through all this and was angry at the botched abortion. She didn't know she wasn't ever going to be able to have kids, but she was mad enough at how things went that she wanted to see quacks like her butcher out of business and safe abortions offered everywhere. She moved away from the fight after a few years. I think she just wanted to forget it ever happened, but I know it formed a bond between her and Natasha that's still there today."

"What about you, have you ever thought about who that baby might have been?" Jess couldn't help ask the question, but it was not in an effort to cause his friend remorse. He was simply curious to hear how Fred has handled this through the years.

"It wasn't a baby, Jess. It never had time to become a baby."

Fishing suddenly became priority, and the rest of the day was spent complaining about the lack of action. At four p.m. they cut the day short and headed for home.

~

Natasha was in her garden when the fishermen pulled in the driveway. Jess loved coming home to the sight of his wife in bib overalls and straw hat, on her knees, nurturing beets, carrots, beans, and squash for future feasts in his kingdom. By six they were in the outer courts of his castle savoring the tastes from last season's harvest.

"Fishing was lousy today. I don't think we had four strikes between us and we didn't land any of those."

"What do you do all day in that boat when the fish aren't biting?"

"Talk about our wives, what else?"

"I know, 'What's said in the boat...'"

Jess was amused by the understanding that had gone on for years, but now wanted to break all the rules. "I learned something from Fred today."

"What was that?"

Jess took a bite of home grown broccoli and wondered how dangerous his next move was going to be. "Did you know that Julie was pregnant before they were married?"

Natasha hesitated for only a moment, and then dove in, "Of course I knew. Julie and I have shared just about everything through the years."

"So you know she had an abortion."

"Yes."

Jess wasn't sure where he wanted to go with this line of questioning, but it certainly was capable of opening the discussion of just what Natasha knew about this seemingly barbaric practice. "I suppose you also know that something happened that left her unable to ever have kids." The tone of this question left Jess feeling like he had just crossed a line.

"You sound like you're accusing me of something. Julie told me all of that when I first met her. Are you feeling left out?"

"Left out? No! I..." *This isn't where I wanted to go.* "I was just surprised, that's all. I always thought they didn't want kids, but they did... I think that would be pretty hard, knowing that something you did kept you from ever having kids."

"It wasn't something Julie did. It was something that doctor did. Julie is just the kind of person I work at the Center for. Unsafe abortions just shouldn't exist. We've come a long way since then, but if those religious radicals get their way we could go back to those barbaric days." Natasha was now using a venomous tone, surprising Jess with how fast it possessed her.

Time had come to back off and allow peace to settle over his thirty-nine year old compromised monarchy. Jess had discovered early in marriage where the line of perceived encroachment was, and besides, the evening was too beautiful to waste on an argument.

~

"Peg, do you have the papers in order for my meeting with Fred?"

"Yup, sure do. I'll run them into you in a second."

It had been a good start to the week. Jess had left the house early to have extra time to read his Bible. He was reading through each Gospel, astonished at his hunger to know more. *Jesus, I feel strong this morning, like I can face the world and not deny You. Luke would get a kick out of my confidence.*

"Good morning, Jess." The door flew open, exposing his accountant's eagerness. "Are you ready for me?"

"Yes, come on in."

"Peg handed me these papers on my way in, she said we needed them."

The two businessmen put on their game face and went right to work. Three hours passed before they even thought about taking a break. "I need some coffee, how about you, Fred?"

"Sure, I'll take some."

Jess headed out the door to the show room. *Maybe Peg's got some doughnuts hidden out here someplace.* His search turned up two chocolate éclairs just begging to be eaten.

Leaning back in his chair with treat in hand, Fred came out of left field with, "Julie was surprised you hadn't known about our situation. She figured you and Natasha must have talked about it back then."

"No, we never did."

"Course, I was just as surprised to hear Julie tell me about Natasha's abortion, so you can't fault me for not sharing things with you. I guess we all felt that stuff was too personal in our younger days, at least for us guys to talk about." If Fred would have been looking across the desk instead of at his éclair, he would have seen the bombshell he had just laid in his friend's lap.

Jess sat shell-shocked, eyes wide open, body motionless, as if not knowing whether the bomb had already exploded or if the impact was yet to come. "What are you talking about, Natasha's abortion, when did she have an abortion?"

Now Fred was shell-shocked. The blood drained from his face, horrified at what he had just done. "Jess...you never knew? ...Man, I'm sorry, all I know is what Julie said."

"What did she say, Fred? What did Julie tell you?"

Fred pushed down on the arms of his chair to bolt him out of his seat as quickly as possible. "Maybe we better finish this stuff up tomorrow...to give you some time..."

"Sit down, Fred! I want to know what Julie told you!"

Fred dropped back down in his chair, buried his face in his hands, and drew a deep breath. After several seconds had elapsed, he allowed his hands to slowly slide down his face while lifting his head. "She just said that Natasha got an abortion six months after you guys were married. Julie went with her to help in case anything went wrong... I didn't know that you didn't know... How did you not know?"

Words were frozen in Jess' mind, not a sentence would form; confusion kept understanding at bay. He began to focus on anger, but he wasn't sure if the anger was born of the abortion or the secret. Fred recognized his opportunity to escape and made his way out the door. Jess remained in place, wearing a cold hard stare into nothingness.

The rest of the day was next to impossible to get through, but that was nothing compared to the thought of going home and facing Natasha with this new knowledge. An unfamiliar heaviness of deceit now burdened his heart.

~

Seeing the house as he turned in the driveway was always a welcome sight, except on this night. The building now appeared as a foreboding vault, holding a secret that Jess was sure would change his life forever. Too many thoughts flashed through his mind to settle on one, too many questions to know for sure which he would ask first. *How did she get pregnant if she wasn't able to get pregnant? Why did she have an abortion? Why wouldn't she tell me? Is it possible that it wasn't my baby? Was I so dense I didn't know what was going on?*

Jess parked the car in front of the house and sat there, unable to reach for the door handle. *Maybe I shouldn't say anything. Maybe I should pretend I don't know... Julie will tell her that I know. Besides, I'll never be able to look her in the eyes and not wonder.* Jess opened the door, got out of the car, and began the painful walk toward his wife.

Natasha was perched on the couch in the living room as if she was waiting up for her man who didn't come home when he was supposed to. The look on her face was one he didn't recognize, her fists clenched in her lap. The image portrayed a scorned wife about to face a cheating husband. *Julie must have called her. But what does she have to be mad at me about? How can she be mad at me for this?*

Jess sat down on the couch with no clue how to start. Before he could get a word out, Natasha pounced, "Why did you go there, Jess? Why did you go THERE of all places?"

Jess looked at Natasha as though she was from another world, "What are you talking about?" He couldn't fit her rage or her question into his frame of mind.

"I'm talking about that church! That arrogant, judgmental, self-righteous, damn church! How could you have gone there?"

Jess was beyond speechless. Words babbled their way to his mind, but nothing fit the stunned state he found himself in. Being upset about going to that church now seemed so insignificant compared to the repulsive revelation he harbored within. "I don't want to talk about that right now, Tash."

"Well I do! Don't you know the people at that church are the people that have been down our throats for the past three years?"

"I SAID I DON'T WANT TO TALK ABOUT IT RIGHT NOW!" The unexpected outburst from her husband caused Natasha to retreat. Jess couldn't remember the last time he shouted at Natasha. His stomach tied in a knot, and his head ached from pressure.

As angry as Natasha was, she discerned that Jess was reeling from something other than her confrontation. "What's wrong, Jess, did something happen at work?"

"No!"

"Is it your mom? Did your mom die?"

"NO, NO, NO!" Jess realized his anger was about to explode. He pushed himself up from the couch, turned, and burst through the front door, heading to his garage. Rage like this was completely unfamiliar to him. In thirty-nine years of marriage he had not screamed at his wife. *Why did that happen now? I've got to calm down, I've got to be able to sit down and talk to Tash.*

~

Jess locked his garage door two hours later and aimed his sites on the house. Natasha's garden drew him off target, offering a respite with reminders of his love for her. Natasha was waiting on the front porch swing.

"Is this seat taken?" A soft tone replaced the harshness that had earlier overtaken Jess' voice.

Natasha smiled and patted the empty space on the swing with her hand. Jess welcomed the invitation and joined her in a gentle sway on what they had always considered their loveseat.

"I'm sorry, Jess. I should have talked to you, not yelled at you. But there's something else on your mind, something a lot worse than going to church. I'm almost afraid to ask what it is. I've never seen you like that, ever."

"Yes, there is something on my mind, but let's handle the church thing first. I didn't know who those people were until after I was there."

"Why did you go in the first place?"

"I was invited by Herman Groves' grandson."

"His grandson?"

"Yes, I was introduced to him by a friend. He's the pastor of that church...and I was curious. You were going with Julie to The Cities, so I thought I would check it out." Jess told himself that his explanation was good enough for now. Natasha didn't have to know just yet how God seemed to work the whole thing out. "How did you find out I was there?"

"Gail, who I work with at the Center, told me. Her husband was out with Fred that night, and he said they saw you coming out of the place."

"Hmmm, busted."

"Why don't we let this slide for now, we can talk about it later. What's got you so upset, Jess?"

"I...I don't know any gentle way to work into this, so I'm just going to say it... I know about your abortion."

Natasha's color changed in an instant; tears welled up in her eyes. She leaned over on Jess' shoulder and began to weep uncontrollably.

Chapter

11

A torrent of tears rained from Natasha for over an hour. Jess slowly rocked the swing, softly stroking his wife's hair. Finally the deluge ceased, and words began to flow.

"I'm so very sorry, Jess... I was stupid not to tell you... I've held this secret inside for so long. You don't know how many times I wanted to tell you."

Jess continued to lovingly stroke Natasha's hair, signaling he was there to listen for as long as she wanted to talk.

"We were so young, with so many dreams. How I got pregnant, I don't know. We were so careful. It never should have happened. I didn't want kids. I never wanted kids... I just wanted it to always be you and me."

Natasha's head remained on Jess' shoulder; she hadn't the courage to look him in the eyes. "It's the only secret I have ever kept from you in our entire marriage...this whole thing."

This whole thing? Is there more? Somehow Jess knew the other shoe was about to drop.

"I was selfish... I regret being so selfish. Through the years I've consoled myself, knowing that together we would have come to the same decision. Neither one of us wanted kids. You had so many dreams... While you and Fred were on that three week fishing trip to Canada in our first year of marriage...I had my tubes tied so there wouldn't be any more accidents."

The loving strokes came to an end. Jess' arm slowly recoiled as his mind deciphered the full meaning of his wife's confession.

Natasha reluctantly raised heavy eyes; weighed down with years of deception. "You thought I was having 'woman' problems during that couple of months, and I just let you think that. I lied to you, Jess... I told you the doctor said I couldn't get pregnant... Ohhhh, Jess, I'm sorry. This lie has haunted me our whole marriage. We have a good marriage. Everything has turned out the way we wanted... Please forgive me, please forgive me for not telling you the truth."

Bewilderment overtook compassion. *She's sorry and this upset for telling me a lie? She's not sorry or at all upset about killing our baby?* Jess turned his head and stared into the sky. He couldn't bear to look at her, not right then. *I need time. I need time to think this through.* He once again slipped his arm around Natasha's shoulder as she returned her head to its resting place. The light strokes resumed, but not with love.

Over two hours had now passed since Jess had revealed his knowledge of the abortion. A one way conversation occupied only ten minutes of that time, Jess had yet to utter a word. Finally he retracted his numb arm and informed Natasha he needed some time alone.

Jess walked deep into the meadow, turned and viewed Camelot. His entire adult life had been spent building his beloved kingdom. He yearned for the return of the peace that once ruled over this happy domain.

Why is the abortion so much more repulsive to me than the lie? Had she told me this before I went to church would I feel the same way? Am I willing to accept something, from someone I don't even know, as truth when that truth will divide my house from within? Self-serving doubts surfaced as the nausea of the thought of losing the love of his life began to boil in his stomach. *I don't really know that it is truth... Natasha doesn't accept it as truth.* Jess fought against the urge to allow God into this dialogue of digression.

The meadow had received a man torn by choices; choices which Jess believed had been forced upon him. He knew he could deal with the lie. His marriage could survive this revelation, even though his wife had selfishly decided his potential for fatherhood. But could his marriage survive the killing of his child when his wife didn't even believe there was a child? How could he ever look at her the same if he believed she had allowed the "instruments of death" access to torture and murder his baby? How could she look at him with love knowing he harbored such a belief?

Confrontation on this issue of abortion, ingrained so deep in Natasha's heart, will drive a wedge between us that might never be removed. No...NO!... Too much is being asked of me.

An hour after he entered, the meadow released him as a man resolute in preserving the life he loved. Risking a life without Natasha was not an option. Spiritual compromise was now fully manifest to this soldier in retreat.

~

Jess arrived at the restaurant ten minutes late. For the first time since they began meeting for lunch, Luke was waiting for him.

"Hi Luke, sorry I'm late."

"That's OK. I'm actually pretty free today. It seems I've run out of nooks and crannies to clean at the church. If I don't find another job in town I'll most likely be moving on."

"Moving on?" Jess was startled at how he received this as good news; a nagging notion from his decision the night before hounded him with the idea of ending these spiritual meals. A change of perspective, born of his resolve, left him more concerned about Natasha's discovery of these mentoring meetings than what he could glean from them. "Where to next?"

"Not sure, never am."

Jess seized on an abrupt desire for small talk. All hope for such a conversation evaporated the second Luke reached in his shirt pocket and exposed the word of God.

"Jess, God has shown me that this will be our last meeting for some time, your wish, not His. I am to share with you one more truth before I leave."

Luke's boldness was received in turmoil. *Why does he have to stir things up? I made a decision to protect my marriage. That's a good thing!*

"God knows your heart; therefore He knows your motives. You want to believe you're acting in Natasha's best interest, but you're not thinking of her at all, you're only thinking of yourself. Show her the same love God has shown you. Don't try to preserve a life that's doomed to perish. Lay your life down for the cause of Christ."

Run, run, run! Get out of here, Jess. Just get up and leave! Jess' mind could not persuade his legs to move. He seemed frozen in place, bound to the booth by an unseen force.

"I'm going to read you something from Mark 10:17-22: And as He was setting out on a journey, a man ran up to Him and knelt before Him, and began asking Him, 'Good Teacher, what shall I do to inherit eternal life?' And Jesus said to him, 'Why do you call me good? No one is good except God alone. You know the commandments, DO NOT MURDER, DO NOT COMMIT ADULTRY, DO NOT STEAL, DO NOT BEAR FALSE WITNESS, Do not defraud, HONOR YOUR FATHER AND MOTHER' And he said to Him, 'Teacher, I have kept all these things from my youth up.' And looking at him, Jesus felt a love for him, and said to him, 'One thing you lack: go and sell all you possess, and give it to the poor, and you shall have treasure in heaven; and come, follow Me.' But at these words his face fell, and he went away grieved, for he was one who owned much property.

"This man of wealth recognized Jesus as the Good Teacher, God himself. He was not confused as to who God was or what God had commanded of him. He kept God's commandments and was willing to obey...up to a point. It's easy for us to love God, until He asks us to deny ourselves. The scriptures tell us this man owned much property, and his love for that property kept him from the treasure in heaven.

"Jess, God is asking you to lay your life down, to exchange your kingdom that will perish for your inheritance in His Kingdom that will never perish. He is asking you to follow Him, to be His disciple, to forsake all else for His sake. Put your trust in Him, Jess, not in your own understanding."

Luke stood and left the restaurant without giving Jess an opportunity to respond. The freedom to run was restored, but Jess remained seated; willing to watch his friend pass from sight.

~

The sharpness of God's truth gradually dulled in Jess' heart as his Bible collected dust on a shelf for over a year. Old habits returned. He slowly remembered the joy of being numbed by sports-bar-spirits after a hard day's work, and the Saturday night beer run for a Sunday morning fishing trip once again net enough for two. Most important was that Jess' relationship with Natasha was stronger than ever, having deposed all rivals. Jess found his way back to Camelot.

Yes, all was well in his kingdom, except in the corner room of his heart where he had suppressed the knowledge gained during his month long diversion following the accident. But light streaming from that room became dimmer each day as the door was slowly being forced shut.

~

"Jess, I'm heading into town. Are you sure you don't want to come with me? You could spend some time with Fred and then meet us girls for lunch."

"I'm sure. I've been looking forward to spending the day in my garage. Tell Fred to drive out if he's got nothing else to do."

Jess had his morning planned; clean and wax the '59 Chevy and the '64 pick up. If Fred happened to stop by after lunch, they could each take one for a run. Saturdays like this were exactly the kind of days Jess lived for. *It'll be in the high seventies today, blue sky, sun shining; there couldn't be a more perfect day. Thank you, God.* Jess' enthusiasm to give thanks was due more to the beauty of the day than to the One who created all that made the day possible. A hint of guilt brushed his slowly dying conscience for even offering such thanks. He still believed God had proven His reality, but came to understand the necessity of applying this belief in a practical way. Fanaticism was not how he wanted to live his life, nor was the division it would cause welcome. He was sure he had struck a good balance, *believe what I want...but keep it to myself.*

Jess stopped for an early lunch. He gathered up the sandwich and veggies that Natasha had made for him and headed out to the bench in the middle of his wife's garden. This was his favorite summer lunch spot when Natasha was gone, feeling her presence in the handiwork she left behind.

Half his sandwich was eaten when a car turned into the driveway. *I better not bite into this other half, Fred might be hungry.* It was only on a beautiful summer day that Jess would feel content enough to be willing to sacrifice half his lunch. "Are you hungry, Fred?"

Fred didn't answer.

"Hey, you look terrible. You better sit down. What on earth is wrong? Did you have a fight with Julie?"

"Jess...there's been an accident."

"The girls?" Jess' face turned pale.

"Not the girls, Jess...it's...it's Natasha." Fred hardly got the words out before he broke down.

Jess could feel the knife plunge into his heart, "Whh...what are you saying, Fred?" Agony almost didn't let the question surface.

Between short gasps of tear-stained breaths, Fred managed to get out, "She's gone, Jess...she's gone..."

Blank eyes stared at Fred as a stillness of disbelief flooded Jess' soul. Then, an explosion of emotion ripped through his body, destroying the beauty around him. With a scream of "NOOOOO", Jess buried his face in hands that fiercely tried to shield him from the news. He bolted from the garden to find refuge in the house, far away from the torment of being in the presence of the messenger. A half hour later he reemerged to find Fred sitting on the steps of the back porch, waiting to help his friend face what lie ahead. "Take me to her." With trepidation the two men set out on the eternal thirty minute drive. Jess, in fear of hearing the details, pried the words from his lips, "What happened?"

"She was hit by a car... She parked and got out to cross the street... She stepped right in front of it, she never saw it coming. I...I saw it, Jess... I was there. I was dropping Julie off to meet her, and we were waiting in the car on the other side of the street... I'm sure she never knew...there was no time to feel pain."

Jess began to sob uncontrollably as he envisioned the horror that put an end to the life he loved. *This can't be true, it just can't be true!* He argued with himself as if his forceful denial could change the events of the day.

At the hospital, the two friends were led to a room in the basement. The hard floor and concrete walls offered no comfort. The sheet-covered body stretched out on a table in front of them was what remained of Jess' joy in life. An attendant spoke in a consoling voice, words that passed through Jess' mind without comprehension. The sheet was pulled back, and Jess drew a breath that refused to exhale. Gone was her beauty. Gone was the softness of her presence. An expression of fear was frozen on the battered and swollen face he didn't recognize. *You were wrong Fred! She knew, she knew!*

Jess tried to cram his thoughts into oblivion. What she might have known in that last second of life scared him to death. *I never told her. I was afraid to tell her.* Convulsions overtook his ability to stand. He sank to his knees with regret, but within seconds regret turned to anger. Pounding the tiled floor with clinched fists, Jess cried out, "Why, God? WHY?"

~

Alone, tired, and wrought with sorrow, Jess stood in the bedroom that held so many reminders of a life shared with the woman he loved. Staring at the empty bed only produced heartache. Jess turned to Natasha's closet, took her favorite dress from its hanger, and laid it out on her side of the bed. He crawled in next to the dress, wrapped his arm around it, and pulled it close. Three hours later, sleep conquered anguish.

~

Jess picked lupines from Natasha's garden. "Your grave will look as beautiful as your garden, Tash." He looked up as if he was expecting a response from the white puffy clouds serenely floating across blue skies. "This is just the kind of day we love, hon."

Setting aside his Chevy loyalty, Jess settled into Natasha's Mustang for the drive to the cemetery. The memorial service was held at graveside, short and simple, with words shared by friends and family. Jess was honoring Natasha's wishes. Only once had she ever mentioned what she wanted for a funeral, and this was it; no church, no speaker, no rites, just goodbyes.

One by one people peeled away to stand and visit by their cars. Jess looked at his mom, supported by her walker with Fred and Julie standing on each side. He understood her tears; they were not for the loss of a daughter-in-law she hardly knew, they were for what she believed lay ahead for a lost soul. Jess turned away, unwilling to allow such thoughts to burden his memory of the most beautiful part of his life. His eyes became glued to the lupines adorning the casket while he imagined Natasha's loving arms around him. He could no longer hold back the tears. His legs gave way.

Jess was alone now. He sobbed uncontrollably as he kneeled next to the coffin with his head buried in his arms, clutching the hard metal capsule that separated him from the love of his life. Time seemed to evaporate; he would stay there forever, never leaving her side, talking to her, holding her...

"Jess...Jess."

The voice heard between his long hard breaths was familiar. Jess lifted his head and looked up with eyes squinting to see a figure obscured by the bright sunlight cascading from behind.

"She's gone, Jess. She can't hear you. She can't look down from somewhere and smile. You will never again hear her voice, or feel the warmth of her body as she holds you in her arms." Luke's voice was calmly assertive.

"Why are you here? Go away and leave me alone."

"Was it worth it, Jess? Would you have done things differently if you had known you only had a year left with her? Or are you happy you had that year together, sharing in the life you both loved so much?"

Jess begged in agony for Luke to go away. He once again laid his head as close to Natasha as he could.

"What about Natasha? What did she gain from that final year spent with her husband? One more year of worldly happiness? Was that brief period of happiness worth ignoring the reality that God so graciously brought to light? This is reality, Jess; this life passes away, and you enter eternity either in God's presence or out of God's presence. You lied to Natasha, Jess. You lied to her because you didn't tell her the truth."

Jess was now screaming at Luke, begging him to leave, but Luke's words quietly pierced the tumultuous wall Jess tried to use as a shield.

"If you had it to do over again would you tell her the truth or live the same lie, selfishly clinging to what you love above all else? Would you be willing to sacrifice your happiness to provide Natasha one more opportunity to accept the gift of salvation leading to eternal life with her Savior, or would the thought of being rejected by her in this world once again rule over your compassion for her very soul? Now that you have her no more, was your happiness worth the tradeoff? Natasha is facing reality without her Savior, for it is appointed unto man once to die, and then comes judgment."

"Why are you doing this to me? WHY!" Jess rose to his feet in defiance. "SHUT UP! JUST SHUT UP AND GET OUT OF HERE!" He turned and saw that everyone had gone; Luke was the only one with him in the cemetery. Anger and fear told him to run, run away from this man who wouldn't shut up. His legs carried him faster than he believed possible, but Luke's affirming voice was on his heels.

"You can't run from reality, Jess. God's truth is present whether you acknowledge it or not. No matter what games you play in life, no matter what rules you make up to live by, God's truth stands and will not be shaken by cunning lies from the father of lies."

Jess was losing control. He felt his legs go out from under him. He was falling, falling into an abyss, well aware of fear's intent to choke him into unconsciousness. His arms flailed upward in an attempt to grab hold of anything to stop his descent. The ground came at him with the speed of light...

~~~~~~~~~~

"Jess...can you hear me? Jess.... I saw his head move. I know I saw it move!"

"Natasha? Natasha!" The pain was acute and the claustrophobic presence was agonizing. Jess was yelling inside his head, but knew his words were not reaching his lips. Confusion overpowered his mind. He struggled to move his arms, tormented by not being able to thrust them forward and punch through this force that had him bound.

"Jess... His eyes are moving, under his lids, they're moving."

"If there appears to be too much pain we will have to put him back under."

Jess could hear the voices slip away; numbness and a sense of relief set in as the muscles in his body relaxed...

~

A dagger of light penetrated the slit in Jess' left eye. He quickly closed it and then realized he had the ability to peer into the world outside his body. Slowly, with blinking motions, he attempted to view what was beyond. A blurred figure was close enough to touch, if he could only lift his arms. His eyes, half open, stared in disbelief. *This is a dream... God, why are You allowing me to see her?* Natasha's face was as beautiful as it was when he looked upon it snuggled by the down comforter the morning all this began.

"Jess, I love you, Jess"

Jesus, PLEASE Jesus, take this dream from me. Jess desired the haunting feeling to pass, while at the same time his eyes yearned to look upon Natasha, his ears coveted the words she spoke. All slipped away and he was at rest once again...

~

The blinds were closed, but warm streaks of sunlight seeped through the cracks. Jess was awakened by gentle words from His Savior, words that ministered to the depth of his soul; *"Peace I leave with you; My peace I give to you; not as the world gives, do I give to you. Let not your heart be troubled, nor let it be fearful."* He fixed his eyes on the apparatus that was making the beeping noise. The door opened, and a nurse walked quickly to the machine. The beeping ceased. Jess' puzzled gaze was met by the nurse's warm eyes.

"Your wife just stepped out to get some breakfast. I'll call down to the cafeteria and have someone send her right up. She'll be overjoyed to see you awake."

My wife? Does she mean Natasha? Lord, I don't understand. Am I dreaming?

Struggling through pain to make the words come out, Jess whispered, "Why am I here?"

"You had a car accident. Your friends have said something about trying to make your Vette fly. I don't know all the details, but you're a miracle man, that's for sure. Your wife will fill in the gaps for you."

My wife... The thought flooded Jess' heart with joy. *Oh Lord, please let it be true. Please let her be alive! Please let THIS not be a dream!*

Jess' mind struggled to understand. His heart seized upon longings deep within. His love for Natasha was overwhelming; his love for Jesus penetrated his very soul. *Jesus, the only thing I know that's real right now is You. I will not surrender that knowledge for any earthly dream or desire. Please give me strength!*

The door to Jess' room opened, and in walked the most alluring gift the world could offer him.

"Natasha!"

Part II
Transformed

Chapter
12

"...I didn't sleep much last night. I found myself swallowed up in a life I couldn't believe was mine. I screamed at God, asking why...why has this happened to me. I agonized over how I was going to explain this to you. I plotted scenarios to conceal the truth. When the sun forced its way through the cracks in the bedroom blinds, I knew I was out of time. Within a couple of hours I would be standing here...unable to hide any longer."

The congregation of The Victorious Church on the outskirts of Minneapolis sat motionless, sensing a storm was about to disrupt the emotional high they loved to envelop themselves in on Sunday mornings. Never before had they seen their beloved pastor tremble as he spoke. They knew him as a strong "Man of God" who could be counted on for counsel in how to overcome any of life's struggles. Now, here he was, opening the word-of-faith morning gathering in a state of devastation.

"I've been living a lie. I've preached to you Sunday after Sunday that having a victorious life in Christ meant having a loving family, the perfect job, a beautiful house, a mega-church to attend. I've implied that people would look at you with envy and want to know how they too could have such a life. This would give you opportunity, I would convincingly coax, to tell them what God could do for them.

"I've told you that God created us to live in a state of happiness; that He wants to bless us with prosperity and keep us from every earthly affliction. I've taught that you can make a positive confession with your mouth and speak these 'victories' into existence...but it's not true...and I have known this for some time."

An uncomfortable stir moved through the crowd as if they were trying to figure out how to shield themselves from invisible walls crumbling around them.

"I have all the material things that I said were an outward sign of walking in victory, but my life is a mess. Last night my worst fear came to pass...Jennifer left me for another man. She packed her clothes and left a life that she said I had crammed down her throat. Our outwardly beautiful existence has been a sham... This morning I am resigning as pastor of The Victorious Church."

Pastor Jacob Hamilton stepped off the stage, walked down the center isle, and headed to the room that, up to a few moments earlier, had been for him the seat of power. He opened the door to the office of the senior pastor, made his way to his desk, and fell into his chair. Jacob buried his head in his arms and released pent up emotions that had accumulated over the past several years.

A stunned associate pastor stared at the doors his boss had utilized to escape the three thousand seat sanctuary. Sean Parkman eventually mustered the strength to break the shock-induced trance and began to scan the congregation as if assessing damage after a raid by enemy forces. Calculating thoughts forced him to center stage.

"Our pastor needs our prayers this morning. Please stand and pray with me. God, we claim victory over this attack on our church and our pastor. Amen. All services will be canceled this morning so we, as a staff, can attend to the needs at hand. As you leave, speak words of victory over the work of Satan."

Pastor Sean took advantage of the exit near the stage to avoid the mass exodus of the wounded. He burst into the senior pastor's office in search of his prey. Pastor Jacob sat motionless, his chair now turned toward the window. He watched as his flock reluctantly found their way to their cars.

"Jacob! What were you thinking! If you've got problems don't bring us all down with you! In less than a minute you might have just destroyed what we all have been working to build for the last twenty years!"

The senior pastor's chair slowly swiveled around until the two men's eyes met. In a voice that renounced former understanding, the conquered charismatic leader confessed, "It's going to fall sometime, Sean...we've built on the wrong foundation."

Pastor Hamilton rose from his chair and calmly walked past his co-conspirator. Without looking back he exited the rear door of the building, walked past his luxury automobile, and began his search for truth.

~

Jacob awoke to an empty house. The echoes of his footsteps on the hardwood floor of the Victorian mansion reverberated in the self-anointed ruler's soul. The subjects of his kingdom had fled.

Alicia, Jacob's daughter, escaped to college four years earlier, returning only for expected visits over holidays. College provided a living environment far removed from the innocence of her youth. Graduating with a degree in philosophy she discovered what could be gained from freedom of conscience. Alicia thanked her father for the education that opened her eyes to other possibilities in life and then deposed the ruler of her childhood.

Jennifer Hamilton began acting on her plan of escape shortly after Alicia left for college; secretly at first, then in full knowledge of her husband. She was willing to prolong the farce of marital bliss in exchange for benefits reaped from her husband's "Kingdom of God", but luster of wealth and position eventually diminished as emptiness crept deeper into her soul.

An affair hid itself within the walls of the stately structure the Hamiltons called home. Jennifer began content with conversations and friendship to help satisfy what she considered lacking in her relationship with Jacob, but as time went on intimate revelations of the heart gave way to passion.

Jacob hadn't noticed his heart's betrayal of the covenant made with the wife of his youth until it was too late. He was far too busy expanding his Kingdom. A drive to conquer and build, using the vast resources provided by parishioners who believed his gospel of prosperity, masqueraded as evangelism. Seeds sown had now born fruit, and Jacob stood alone amongst the harvest. *How did it all go so wrong?* "God, show me your truth."

~

Jacob spent most of Monday morning with his attorney and Pastor Sean signing legal documents to remove him from any relationship with The Victorious Church. The associate pastor's pleas to reconsider had no impact on the senior pastor's resolve.

During the afternoon Jacob worked at closing up the house that had never become a home. The purchase of this "fruit-of-faith" had come about well after the hearts of the family unit had begun to grow apart. The size of the mansion provided ample space for independent lives to blossom.

Jacob took one last walk through the house in an attempt to capture memories worth packing. He came up empty, grabbed a duffle bag from his walk-in closet, and walked past his designer suits to the drawers that held t-shirts and blue jeans. He packed only the bare necessities and then planned his own escape. *I'll head to Duluth... I can't stay here.*

~

The two-and-a-half hour drive north was made in Jacob's 1980 Chevrolet pick-up truck. The rusty relic was the only possession he retained from his pre mega-church pastoral days. The old workhorse was kept around to haul lumber, sod, plants, or whatever else was needed to fabricate the façade that concealed the deteriorating home-life of the Hamiltons.

Jacob had stripped himself of power, wealth, and the burden of pretense in a matter of just over twenty-four hours. The chains of deception began to fall to the ground once the decision was made to confess his life of lies. Remorse only reared its head when thoughts of deserting his flock rose to the surface. His family ties had been broken for years. There was no agony of abandonment when it came to Jennifer and Alicia, those feelings had been discarded long ago in order to maintain eminence in his all important work for the Kingdom.

Relief began to replace the fear of loss as Jacob saw how much a prisoner he had become to his own desire. Trying to sustain the stature of a "Man of God" became increasingly futile from his foundation of selfishness.

The sparkling beauty of the Twin Ports at sunset filled the windshield as Jacob descended Thompson Hill. Duluth, Minnesota and Superior, Wisconsin, cities sharing the same bay waters at the tip of Lake Superior, were a welcome sight. The soothing view offered his spirit the first impression of calm since his Sunday morning abdication process began.

Jacob, emotionally fatigued, exited at Twenty-seventh Avenue West and registered at the motel. The green light that appeared after pulling the keycard from the slot of his door lock flashed in his mind...pain gave way to darkness as he slumped forward against the door and fell to the ground...

...The pain was acute. Disoriented, Jacob instinctively reached to the back of his head with his right hand. The sticky wetness sent a surge of fear through his stomach; he realized he was bleeding profusely.

What happened? Why am I on the ground? It took a full minute for Jacob to clear the confusion in his mind. He struggled to his feet and began to comprehend that he had been attacked from behind. *How long have I been lying here?* He turned his wrist to check the time on his watch before remembering he had purposely left the two thousand dollar piece of jewelry on the dresser in his bedroom.

The door to the motel room was cracked open; he gave it a shove and attempted to look past the darkness. Jacob was unaware of the trail of blood he left behind as he slid his hand down the wall to find the light switch. He staggered forward and fell face down on the bed. The comfortable sensation of not having to force himself to stay on his feet lulled him to unconsciousness...

...A muddled mind worked at trying to understand the scream; somehow it just didn't fit into Jacob's dream. Voices began talking over each other, drowning out what he thought had been making sense. Two worlds overlapped until the confusing one overshadowed the pleasant walk on the river's edge.

"Mister...hey mister, can you hear me? We've called the police. They should be here any minute. We've got help coming."

Jacob knew something was very wrong, he just couldn't figure out what. His head felt like dead weight on a pillow he viewed through blurry eyes. A groan was all that came from his attempt to communicate. He soon became aware of being worked on by paramedics as he faded in and out of consciousness. His eyes were jarred open by the annoying sound of a siren. He was in full command of his faculties by the time the ambulance arrived at the hospital.

"How are you feeling, Mr. Hamilton?" The emergency room doctor went right to work as he waited for a reply.

"I hurt. My head is throbbing like crazy."

"Please look at my finger and follow it with your eyes without turning your head."

"That won't be a problem; I don't think I could turn my head if I wanted to. What happened to me anyway?"

"Well, I wasn't there. All I know is that you were hit in the back of the head with a blunt object, and I have to make sure you're OK. I've ordered x-rays and a CT scan."

"How much blood did I lose?"

"You can bleed a good amount from a gash on the scalp, but you didn't lose much. We always think we lost more than we did when it's coming from our own head. I don't think we have any major problems, but we're going to make sure before we release you. I'll check with you again after I read the films."

A nurse helped Jacob lean back on the stretcher that was propped up in a sitting position. "I'm just going to stay right here and make sure you don't go to sleep on us. We want you to stay awake until we're certain you're alright. A police officer would like to come in and talk to you if you feel up to it."

Jacob's mind searched for a reason to explain the attack. His last recollection before the pain was unlocking the motel room door. Then it struck him, "I got robbed. I bet I got robbed!" The nurse turned and stared at him to make sure he was OK as he reached into his right pants pocket to see if his check card and driver's license were still there. They were gone.

"Nurse, would they have emptied my pockets in the ambulance?"

A police officer slid the curtain aside before the nurse could answer. He looked at her patient and asked, "Mr. Hamilton, are you up to answering a few questions?"

"Yes. I even have a couple questions of my own; like did you empty my pockets?"

"No, I checked them, but they were already empty. Mr. Hamilton, I'm Officer Halden. I was the first officer to arrive on the scene at the motel."

"How do you know who I am if you didn't find my driver's license?"

"We took your name from the guest registry at the motel desk. Is there anyone you would like us to contact to come and help you out here...wife...next of kin?"

Jacob felt emptiness in his soul. "No...there's no one. I think I'll be OK. I should be able to handle things on my own."

"So, you say your driver's license is missing?"

"Yes, and my check card and some lose bills, about forty dollars in cash. I never carry a wallet; I just put what I need in my pocket. I didn't think to check my pocket until just a minute ago. I've been robbed, haven't I."

"It looks that way. Do you remember anyone approaching you?"

"No, all I remember is intense pain in my head and collapsing against the door."

"Do you remember how you got on the bed?"

"I...I think I got up and stumbled to the bed. I don't know. Everything is kind of fuzzy."

"Did you have any other possessions with you?"

"Possessions? I had a duffle bag. Is that gone too?"

"Well, we didn't find anything like that in the room. We also noticed on your registration card at the motel that you were driving a 1980 Chevrolet pick-up truck. Could you give me a description of that?"

"Don't tell me they stole my truck!"

"There's no truck in the parking lot at the motel, so unless you parked it somewhere else..."

"No, I parked it in the motel lot." Jacob smirked and painfully shook his head, *I didn't give up enough in the last couple of days, did I God. Well, I'm down to nothing now.*

"The truck was blue with a white roof. It's pretty rusty and has a lot of miles on it. I can't imagine why anyone would want that ol' beat up thing."

"Is there a number where you can be reached if we locate any of your things?"

"My cell phone! Unbelievable! That's gone too!... I guess I'll just have to check with you guys."

An orderly entered the curtained area with a wheelchair, "Mr. Hamilton, I'm your ride to x-ray."

Test results revealed no internal cranial damage. Jacob was given clearance to leave the hospital after signing release forms. *But to go where? I have no vehicle, no clothes other than what I'm wearing, no money, no check card, and I don't know anyone in the Twin Ports area.*

Jacob took a seat in the waiting room before heading out the door into a night of unknowns. *I have got to figure out what to do before I leave here, I need a plan. God, I can't believe how broken I've become in the last forty-eight hours. I've gone from having everything I needed right at my fingertips, to having nothing... I need Your help!* He lifted his head to see the nurse who had attended him walking in his direction. Stopping next to his chair she hesitantly handed him a piece of paper. "I could get in trouble for this...but you seem so lost. It's my pastor's name and phone number, I know he'll help you in any way he can." She looked around as if worried she was being watched, then turned and disappeared through double doors. Jacob opened the slip of paper and read the name: Pastor Herman Groves.

TRUTH

Chapter

13

"Hello"

"I'm calling for Pastor Groves. Is he available?"

"Sure, just a minute. DAD, TELEPHONE!"

Jacob pulled the phone from his ear to avoid the full effect of the blast coming from the young voice on the other end of the line. A nurse at the desk looked up at Jacob as if to say, "I heard that way over here."

"Seth, you know I've asked you not to yell like that near the phone. Hello."

"Pastor Groves?"

"Yes, I'm Herman Groves."

"Pastor, my name is Jacob...ah, Jacob Hamilton," he hesitated, deciding whether or not to give his full name to a pastor. "I got your name and number from a nurse at the emergency room. Um...to tell you the truth, I feel a little awkward even making this phone call."

"That's all right. It must have been Susie Johnson; she's a part of our church family. What can I help you with, Jacob?" Pastor Herman's voice was warm and welcoming.

"Well, I kind of have myself in a little spot here." Jacob couldn't remember the last time he found himself in a place where he was in need of asking for help. The awkwardness of the situation began to swell in his throat. "I...I don't even know what to ask... I don't know what I expect you to do for me."

"What kind of spot are you in?"

"I got robbed. They took everything I had and stole my truck."

"Are you still at the hospital?"

"Yes, I'm in the Emergency waiting room."

"Stay there, I'll be right down."

Jacob heard the phone disconnect. He was surprised at how quickly the conversation ended. *I would have asked twenty more questions before I'd leave my home to go pick up some stranger... I wonder if I WOULD have left my home to pick up some stranger?* He thanked the nurse for the use of the phone and reseated himself to wait for this willing heart that seemed eager to come to his rescue.

"Martha, make sure the guest room is in order. I think we're going to have company tonight." Herman grabbed his keys and jacket and hustled out the back door. His eighteen-year-old Dodge minivan was a little rusty and had over two hundred thousand miles on it, but it was fairly good on gas and served its purpose for this father of five. "Lord, thank you for giving me this mission tonight. Lead me to accomplish Your purpose."

Ten minutes after Jacob had hung up the phone he noticed a man in his late thirties enter through the Emergency Room door. *He can't be the pastor, the way he's dressed he looks in need himself.*

Herman walked directly over to Jacob, "You must be the man in a spot."

"Do I look that desperate?"

"No, but you are the only man sitting in this waiting room. I'm Herman Groves." Herman extended his hand and a warm smile.

"Hello, Pastor Groves, I'm Jacob."

"Please, Herman will do just fine. Looks like you got a nasty blow to the head."

"Yah, it was quite a welcome to Duluth."

"We'll try to change that first impression for you. Come on, let's take you home and get you settled in for the night."

Jacob was amazed at the earnest desire Herman seemed to have to help him. "Don't you want to know something about me before you take me into your home?"

"What's there to know? You need help, Susie gave you my number, and God spoke to my heart. That's enough for one night. We can talk in the morning."

Jacob followed Herman out the door and into the waiting van. The drive to the Groves home would take less than seven minutes. Passing the Fortieth Avenue West exit sign Jacob spoke up, "This is West Duluth, isn't it?"

"Well, the name's been changed to Spirit Valley, but I can't seem to get used to that. It'll probably always be West Duluth to me. I have to warn you, we have a houseful of kids. They'll be in bed when we get home, but the house might explode come morning."

"How many kids do you have?"

"Five, ages seven to fifteen."

"Wow, a busy household. What time do they leave for school?"

"School starts at eight, but they don't leave, they're home-schooled."

"Home-schooling five kids? You must be married to Wonder Woman."

"She is a wonder, that's for sure. The kids do very well; the older ones help the younger ones, and once school starts they stick to business. Here we are....home." Jacob noticed a joy in Herman's voice when he said the word, a joy unfamiliar to this man who had just left his house of deception.

The alley parking spot offered the backside view of a two story red brick house. The porch light revealed freshly painted cream color railings, steps, and door. What he could see of the back yard was well kept, and there appeared to be a harvested vegetable garden in the far west corner, bordering the back of the garage. *Reminds me of the façade I lived behind, but on a much smaller scale. I wonder what this pastor's home life is like.* Jacob's skepticism delivered a rush of guilt for questioning this man who was going out of his way to help a soul in distress.

Jacob soon found himself in a back hall that was smaller than the broom closet of his Victorian mansion. The wall on the left was loaded with hooks holding a multitude of different size jackets. Shoes and boots lined the left side of the basement stairs all the way to the bottom. Herman skillfully hung his jacket on a hook that already appeared overburdened.

Stepping into the kitchen from the back hall was a joy to Jacob's senses. The brightly lit room revealed a décor of reds and whites. The warmth of this home was a pleasant relief from the cool fall air following them in from the back porch, but what overwhelmed him was the aroma of the freshly baked apple pies cooling on the counter.

"Welcome, I'm Martha." Martha began her greeting in the hallway on her way to the kitchen. "Come in, sit down. I just got the guest room ready for you. I hope you're willing to test some apple pie for me."

Jacob took a seat on a ladder-back chair at the head of a long rectangular kitchen table. Homemade apple pie would have been the last thing on his mind an hour earlier, but the pain medication the doctor had given him helped to refocus his attention on his hunger. "Boy that would taste great."

Jacob's spirit was lifted by the cheerful attentiveness he received from this woman. He couldn't help but notice her beauty; it flowed from her, not from physical features, but from her eyes...her smile...her heart. *Wow, this woman has five kids?* It was almost apparent that children added to her beauty, as did her husband. Jacob had never been in the presence of a woman - a mother - a wife who seemed so at home with who she was.

The warm apple pie encouraged drowsiness. Herman was right on top of his guest's needs. "Jacob, let me show you to your room." Instructions were given on the way up the stairs, "There's a private bathroom for your use and a new toothbrush in the top right drawer under the sink. Get a good night's sleep and we'll talk in the morning."

"Herman, I can't thank you and your wife enough for your kindness."

"Don't mention it. See you in the morning."

Jacob sat down on the side of the bed totally exhausted, physically and emotionally. *Where do people like this come from,*

God? I can't say I'm crazy about how You got me here, but I think I'm where You want me to be. Thank you."

~

Jacob was awakened by children in the hallway trying desperately to maintain their understanding of quiet. The loud whispers from these youngsters who meant well flowed under the solid oak door, invading the half-conscious mind of their parents' house guest.

Squinting at the clock on the bedside table Jacob realized he had slept straight through the night, although six a.m. was not his idea of rise-and-shine time. Slowly he lifted his aching head from the pillow, maneuvered his body to the edge of the bed, and sat up. *This is not going to be a good day if I'm going to be hurting like this.* He remembered the pain medication the emergency room doctor sent home with him. He reached for his pants, searched the pockets, and found the promised relief.

The reflection in the bathroom mirror was a staggering sight; nothing seemed to remain of the man who, up to a few days ago, had reigned over the largest church in the state of Minnesota. The meticulously well-groomed man of God was gone. *I look like a homeless bum that got beat up in a back alley. Hmmmm...not far from the truth... God, I am so empty...so empty that I don't even know if I know You. Nothing I did was for You, was it. It was all about me...ME... I used Jennifer, I used Alicia, I used the people of my church...and I used You. I'm the farthest thing from the Godly shepherd I pretended to be.*

Jacob got dressed after a wonderfully warm, soothing shower. He noticed that the blood stained t-shirt he had taken off the night before was replaced by a clean, long sleeved flannel shirt. *These people are beyond belief.* Opening the guest room door he could hear sounds of conversation. He descended the staircase and determined the sounds were coming from the kitchen. His attention was drawn to pictures that covered the walls as he passed through the hallway, family pictures full of joyful interaction. Jacob, being an only child and having only one child himself, had never known the kind of family dynamics that surrounded him.

"Good Morning," Herman stood to welcome their guest to the table. "We have a seat for you right here next to Marni."

Marni, the youngest of the family, looked up at Jacob and exposed a gapped tooth smile. Jacob couldn't help but break out in a friendly laugh at the scrunched up nose and toothless grin that welcomed him to the side of this bubbly fountain of joy. As he bent down to slide onto the end of the bench his eyes fell on the pair of prosthetic legs that didn't quite reach the floor. A stutter in his movement was noticeable before he landed. "Good morning, Marni, thank you for letting me share this bench with you."

"You're welcome," bounced back the quick, cheerful reply. "Daddy said not to wake you this morning. Did we wake you up?"

"I think my headache woke me."

"I'm not even going to ask how you slept. I don't want to obligate you to the expected answer." Herman raised his eyebrows and gave a smirk as if to say he hated that question when he was a guest at someone's house. "Let me introduce you to the family. You've met Marni, she's seven. This is Pete, our oldest at fifteen. Of course you know Martha, I'm not telling her age, Mary -

thirteen, Seth who is eleven, and Sarah Beth at seven-and-a-half. Sarah Beth always wants to make sure people know she is not the baby of the family."

"Marni's the baby of the family and I'm her older sister!" Sarah Beth announced with great delight, as Marni giggled in agreement.

"French Toast this morning, Jacob," Martha passed a plate stacked high, "and here's some maple syrup; tapped, collected, and boiled down as a home-school project."

Breakfast was full of conversation amongst the family, goals for the day, questions about Mary and Seth's science project, and talk about Pete's tennis lessons. Jacob found himself looking for cracks in the façade. *A family can't have it this together.* Just then, Sarah Beth reached for another helping of French Toast, knocking over her almost full glass of orange juice in the process. Four napkins appeared out of nowhere dabbing up juice from the table while Martha jumped up to grab a towel.

"I'm sorry mommy. I didn't mean to spill it."

"I know honey, but it does show us why we need to ask for things to be passed. That was the last of the orange juice."

"You can have some of mine!" Marni seemed eager to share from her full glass.

"You don't like orange juice so much, huh Marni?" Jacob thought he was helping by making light of her obvious desire to lessen her liquid intake.

"I like orange juice. I just don't like seeing my big sister sad."

I don't believe this. I'm sitting next to a seven year old with two prosthetic legs and she's worried about her sister not having orange juice? What is this, a Norman Rockwell family?

When breakfast was over, Herman asked Jacob if he would come to the church so they could talk in his office. Jacob was glad for the invitation and began to sort out just how much he would tell this brother-of-the-cloth.

Herman tossed his guest a spare Jacket, "It's a bit chilly out there this morning," then exited the back door and bent down to grab the daily newspaper wedged between the railing posts. Sticking it under his arm exposed the lower portion of the front page to the man following close behind; "Mega Church Pastor Abandons Flock".

The drive to the church offered little time for anything more than small talk. Jacob now knew that he would have to be completely open with Herman about who he was and what he was doing. The problem with that was obvious; he didn't know what he was doing. *God, how do I explain to this pastor why I ran? How can I tell him what a complete failure I am? He's probably already been looking at me and wondering what happened to bring the senior pastor of the largest church in the state to his door step.*

Herman parked his minivan in front of what looked to be an old Ben Franklin Five-and-Dime. A sign above the plate glass windows read "Duluth Christian Fellowship" and listed the times of worship services and Bible studies. "Well, this be da place. We can settle down in my office with a cup of coffee and talk."

The sight of the converted five-and-dime building began to gnaw at Jacob's pride. *Here I am, WHO I am, and I'm going to sit down in a church office in an old dime-store with a pastor driving a rusty minivan and spill my guts. I bet he's the janitor in this place too*. Suddenly the reality of confession didn't seem so appealing.

Jacob was surprised at how packed with chairs the "sanctuary" was. "Do you fill all these chairs for your worship service?"

"Pretty much. The first service on Sunday morning doesn't always fill, but the rest do."

"How many services do you have?"

"We meet on Friday night, two services on Sunday morning, and one on Sunday evening."

Jacob was struck by the nonchalant manner in which Herman spoke of his success. *I'd brag it up a little more if I was doing that well with what he seems to have to work with here.* "With so many people I suppose you're ready to build a church and expand."

"No, actually we're talking about splitting and beginning another fellowship out in the east-end. We really don't want to spend money on buildings right now, there's too much need all around us."

"Are you against replacing this old storefront with a new church building?"

Herman successfully held in the smile that would have given away his insight into Jacob's question. He put his trust in the answer rising from his spirit rather than the one running through his mind, "I'm for the will of the Father, whatever that might be."

Jacob followed Pastor Herman into a ten-by-twelve foot room that was made to feel even smaller by the desk, bookshelf and three chairs it contained. He thought of his office at The Victorious Church where there was room for three black leather couches, his impressively large desk, and a fairly decent library. "You must have a conference room where you hold your staff meetings."

Herman answered with a chuckle, "Our staff meetings fit nicely into this room. When I meet with the elders we use the sanctuary."

Jacob looked back at the chair-filled area and thought of how long it had been since he considered a place like that a sanctuary. *God, please help me here, I know my pride is getting the best of me. I said I wanted You to show me Your truth. Give me strength not to fight this. Humble me so that my pride doesn't get in the way of what You want me to know.*

"Have a seat. I'll get us some coffee."

Jacob sat down and scanned the bookshelves in Herman's absence. *I wonder which of my books he's read...*

"I've brought some cream packets if you don't drink yours black." Herman set the coffee and cream on his desk and then turned the second chair so that he could sit facing Jacob. "Before we talk and see if I can be of any help to you, let's pray."

Herman bowed his head without waiting for a response. "Father, I am humbled every time You give me an opportunity to share with someone the truths You've taught me. As Jacob and I talk, I pray that You make it clear to both of us what Your will is in the situation Jacob finds himself. Father, give me wisdom about how to be Your servant to Jacob. Amen."

Jacob couldn't help but contrast this pastor's prayer with prayers he had offered at the start of counseling sessions. Never had he asked to be a servant to someone. He always prayed for victory over whatever the problem was; a positive attitude to strengthen faith. He felt it important to hype the emotions of the "counselee" a bit so that the "counselor" could shape and mold the solution to overcome whatever problem existed. He looked at counseling sessions as a mind game, one that demanded a positive attitude to prevail. This pastor's prayer seemed too simple. *To be humbled? To be a servant? He doesn't sound like someone who's got answers.*

"So, Jacob, tell me...what has happened to you?"

That's it? That's how you're starting? You want me to just blurt out the whole story? Jacob sat silent for a moment, wondering how much information he should divulge. He gave in to the thought of at least confessing his identity as he watched Herman reach for his coffee. *He must already know who I am anyway, and sooner or later he's going to read that newspaper article.* "I'm sure by now you know who I am."

Swallowing hard a sip of coffee that was hotter than expected, Herman answered, "Jacob Hamilton is all I know."

"I'm Pastor Jacob Hamilton."

"You're a pastor?"

"Yes...Senior Pastor of The Victorious Church...in Minneapolis." Jacob was mystified that the divulged information didn't seem to open Herman's eyes. "You are familiar with The Victorious Church, aren't you?"

"No, I'm sorry, but I can't say that I am."

What kind of hick pastor is this that he's never heard of the largest church in the state! "Maybe you've read one of my books?"

"Ahh...I don't think so. How many books have you written?"

"Eight. Do you really not know of any of them?"

"Eight! Maybe you should be counseling me."

Is he serious? Does he really not know about The Victorious Church or my books? Is he pulling my leg?

"I'm sorry, Jacob. I don't get out much. A hundred percent of my time is spent with my family and our church. There are a few outside ministries that I know well and trust, and those ministries are a great help to me. But I guess I'm so focused on what God has put before us that I don't pay a whole lot of attention to what's going on in other ministries unless God draws me to them. We're so busy right here in this city that I don't have time to check out what others are doing. So tell me, is there someone from your church we should contact?"

"No...actually, I resigned as pastor on Sunday." Up to now Jacob had been feeling sacrificial, like he had been giving everything up for God. *I'm still running things, aren't I God. I'm still making the plans. I'm giving everything up thinking You'll be impressed with me. You brought me here to humble me. You brought me to this man, who doesn't know anything about me, to show me that I'm not as important as I think I am. What a fool...what an arrogant fool I am.*

Reaching over to pick up the newspaper Herman had lain on his desk Jacob spoke with the first smattering of shame to seep from his prideful heart, "Please, read this. Read it out loud... I need to hear it too."

TRUTH

Chapter

14

"...Many members question whether the church can survive the loss of its senior pastor. 'Pastor Jacob was the main reason I came here,' said Jack Hankle, a Sunday morning regular. 'Without him, it just won't be the same.'"

Herman slid the paper back down on his desk, "They weren't very kind, were they."

Jacob stared at the floor and confessed, "I can't sue them for slander...everything they said is true. I did abandon my flock. I walked out and left them sitting there with their jaws in their laps. One Sunday I'm preaching about claiming victory over any problem Satan throws at them and the next Sunday...the next Sunday I'm telling them I've had so many problems thrown at me that I have to run away."

"Did Satan throw all those problems at you?"

Jacob lifted his head, questioning Herman with his eyes, "You think God threw them at me?"

"Usually our problems grow out of seeds we've sown; and most of the time those seeds are temptations we've fallen to. Is it possible that you are responsible for most of your problems, and their size has come from what you've fed them?"

The question penetrated every line of defense in advance of Jacob's response. "Wow, you don't pull any punches, do you. Do you think you could maybe stroke my ego a bit before you finish what God started?"

Herman spoke with compassion as he recognized the empty cavern Jacob was peering into, "I was there once... The circumstances weren't the same, but I'm well acquainted with the hole of the unknown you're afraid to jump into. Dying to self is painful; but the joy of new life, received from the Giver of Life, is worth the plunge."

Tears began to well up in Jacob's eyes. "How did you do that?.... How did you bring me to the root of the problem in less than a minute's time?"

"You've always known the root of the problem; you're just finally willing to admit it."

Jacob leaned forward in his chair, buried his face in his hands, and fell head first into the waiting arms of Jesus. Tears became rivers, flooding his soul with remorse. Gasping for air, Jacob realized he was breathing in new life in Christ for the first time. "What games I've played...what religious, stupid, self-serving games I've played."

Herman knelt beside Jacob, placing his arm around shoulders weary of the burden of pride. He gave way to the Holy Spirit who was speaking volumes to this repentant sinner...

Jacob and Herman remained yielded before their God until He transformed a heart once governed by selfishness into a heart yearning to surrender.

"I don't understand. How could I not have known Him?... All these years...how could I not have known Him?"

"You don't become a new creation by playing a role on a stage; you become a new creation when you succumb to the Truth." Herman maneuvered his way back into his chair. "Jesus told Nicodemus, '...unless one is born again, he cannot see the kingdom of God.' He's waiting...to welcome you into HIS kingdom."

"That's the emptiness I've known all these years, ruling over MY kingdom. I've never stepped aside. I've never said, 'Your will be done.' I've shaped God into what I wanted Him to be, how I wanted Him to fit into my life... No...I really wasn't shaping God at all. I was shaping...me. I became my own god. I wasn't building a kingdom for God. I was building one for me, and I expected His help... That's what I taught others... Oh, Father, forgive me. How many lies have I convinced people to believe?"

The weight of guilt forced Jacob to his knees. Then, as though a millstone had been hung from his neck, he fell forward, drowning in a sea of faces that had been led astray.

Now prostrate before his God, Jacob Hamilton, senior pastor of the largest church in Minnesota, author of eight best-selling books, self-appointed ruler of his contrived kingdom...was no more.

Herman quietly slipped from the room, leaving this new babe in Christ to the loving care of the Holy Spirit.

Over two hours passed before the office door opened. The man God had led Jacob to was on his knees in the sanctuary. Jacob's approach fostered a prayer of his own, *Thank you, Father, for this man who prayed to be your servant.* His heart was grateful for the spiritual sensitivity Herman possessed: knowing when to speak God's truth, knowing when to yield in silence. *How many counseling sessions have I dominated, spewing the wisdom of a fool?*

"Jacob! How are you doing?" Herman pushed himself up from the floor.

"I'm exhausted, humbled...and in love with my Savior." Jacob's proclamation was drenched in emotion.

"I've been praying for you. I want you to know that I will help in any way I can."

"Somehow, I already know that. I know we need to sit down together again and talk...but I think I need some time to let all this sink in." Jacob once again began to break down, "I didn't even know Jesus as my Savior. Can you believe that? I claimed to be doing His work, and I didn't even know Him." Tears reappeared as he dropped onto the padded chair behind him. "I would really like to just sit here for a while and spend some time praying."

"I can understand that. I've got some things I need to run and do. You're welcome to stay here as long as you need. My cell phone number is on my desk next to the phone. Call if you need me for anything before I get back."

The remaining morning hours passed quickly into the afternoon as Herman endeavored to get his Tuesday schedule back on track. By two-thirty he was caught up, making a hospital visit to see Fred Carlson; a man who, eight months earlier, had visited Duluth Christian Fellowship for the first time. Fred was invited by his best friend, Jess Rivers, and before he left that Friday night meeting he had surrendered his life to Christ.

"How are you doing, Fred?"

"I'm doing great. The doctor says one more day and he's kicking me out of here."

"Are the lungs cleared up?"

"Pretty much. I'll tell you, this was the worst case of pneumonia I've ever had."

"It'll be good to see you back on your feet. We've missed you at the men's Bible Study."

"Not as much as I've missed being there." Fred dropped his head just a bit and gave it a slight shake. "I never would have said something like that a year ago. Isn't it amazing what God can do to a heart in such a short time; I'll be grateful to Jess for as long as I live," then added with joy overtaking his face, "and beyond! His gentle, straightforward honesty is what convinced me to open my mind...and then my heart to Jesus..."

Herman gave time for Fred to reflect before changing the subject. "Fred, I know a while back you mentioned you and Julie had a bedroom set you would offer to anyone who had a need. Do you still have it?"

"Yes we do. Have you found someone who can use it?"

"I think we need it at the church."

"What, you got more kids coming and you're running out of room at home?"

"No, nothing like that. I'm seeing a need to have a place to offer people as a refuge while God is dealing with their lives. Kind of like a halfway house. Some people find themselves with nowhere to turn. We have the old store office in the back of the church that would be perfect for something like that. Let me run this by the elders tonight at our meeting, I'll let you know tomorrow if we can take that set off your hands."

"Don't check with me here. By tomorrow afternoon I'm going to be finishing my recovery snuggled between the arms of my recliner at home!"

Herman prayed with Fred and made tracks back to the church. He had thought about dropping off lunch for Jacob earlier, but decided God was surely providing spiritual food that would silence any hunger pangs. He found Jacob kneeling in front of the chair he had left him on hours before. He slipped into his office to begin working on his sermon for the weekend's services so that he would not disturb the precious quiet time this man was savoring before his heavenly Father.

At four-thirty Herman's office door finally opened, revealing a man who appeared to have been taken to the woodshed and then set upon his daddy's knee to be lavishly smothered in love.

"Are you all right, Jacob?"

Jacob turned a chair to face Herman's desk and buckled under fatigue. "I thought I was broken Saturday night when Jennifer left me, then I thought I was broken when I stood before my congregation on Sunday morning resigning as their pastor, and again when I was mugged and left with nothing. For three days I believed I was enduring the final blow, only to discover another pile of pride rotting under the last one exposed. Now I'm afraid I haven't come close to the bottom of what He wants to dredge from my soul.

"I've had things so backwards. I shoved my plans in God's face demanding He bless them instead of sitting before His throne and digging into His word to understand His will."

A knowing look of delight gradually spread across Herman's face as he remembered the sweet aroma of truth's first breeze, "Oh, Jacob, you are going to love this God you now serve."

The two men began to pray, praising God and thanking Him for His gift of salvation.

Herman raised his head after the Amen, "Jacob, we should be home for supper by five-thirty. On the way I want to stop at K-Mart across the street so you can get some things I know you need. Let's head out so we have time to do that."

"I don't have any money on me. If you can take me to the bank, I can get some cash."

"How are you going to do that with no I.D.? We'll deal with that later. For now I know you at least want a change of underwear and socks." Herman opened the bottom left drawer of his desk and grabbed eighty dollars from a box. "Here, we keep some cash around for things just like this. You can pay it back when you're able."

"Thank you, Herman. I have never known a servant's heart like yours...and I now know...I have never possessed one."

Shopping was not one of Jacob's favorite things to do. His dislike of the pastime goaded him to make good time in securing a couple changes of clothes and some needed personal items. Herman waited patiently in the car, but was pleased to have his new friend return quickly.

"Find what you need?"

"Yup."

"I have an elder's meeting tonight at seven; do you want to tag along?"

"If you don't mind, I would really like to borrow a Bible and sneak off to the guest room tonight. I have never, never in my life, had such a craving to read the Bible."

"I'll make sure the kids know you're not to be disturbed."

Jacob's mind returned to that morning's breakfast. "Herman, how did Marni lose her legs?"

"She didn't lose them; she never had them. Marni was the daughter of a teenage girl who decided not to have an abortion. We lived in Denver at the time and were part of a ministry there that prayed in front of the abortion clinic near our church. Marni's mom decided not to go through with her abortion after talking and praying with Martha. Her parents were not very supportive, but willing to allow us to help their daughter through her pregnancy if we were also willing to help her find a home for the baby. After working with Marni's mom for several months, we knew God was speaking to our hearts to adopt the baby ourselves.

"Marni was perfectly healthy when she was born, except she had no legs below her knees. Marni's mom was devastated and afraid we weren't going to go through with the adoption, but we loved that little girl from the moment we laid eyes on her."

"She seems to be a sweetheart."

"Oh, she has a sweet heart for sure, one that is very sensitive to others around her. She's also very honest." Herman turned to Jacob offering a playful warning, "Sometimes, maybe too honest... Well, we're home."

There was that word again, home. As they entered through the back hall they were greeted by the loving aroma of homemade bread. The house itself seemed to welcome this husband and father who was eager to leave behind the cold crisp air of the autumn evening. Jacob was grateful to be in this place, even if just for a moment in time, to savor the love radiating from this amazing family.

A chorus of "Hi dad" rang out from the oldest Groves children as they finished setting the table for supper. Martha zigzagged her way around the busy helpers to give her husband a hug, "Hi hon, we're just about ready to eat. Hello Jacob, I hope your day went well."

"It was quite a day, one I didn't see coming. Your husband has been a real blessing to me."

"I've been praying for both of you most of the day. The kids have too." Martha turned her attention back to Herman, "As a matter of fact, they've been prayer warriors today."

"Oh? Something happening I should know about?"

"Natasha stopped by, but let's get supper on the table and I'll fill you in later."

All during this welcoming conversation Jacob's attention had been divided. The sounds coming from down the hall and up the stairs painted a picture in his mind of Sarah Beth helping Marni descend to supper.

"Daddy, daddy," Sarah Beth rushed into the kitchen first, throwing her arms around Herman's waist and giving him a hug. Her little sister was close behind. Marni reached up, signaling

Herman to bend over so she could squeeze her daddy's neck. Then she turned to Jacob, took two steps, and did the same to him.

Jacob wasn't prepared for such a welcome. He fought to hold back the tears, but all for naught. After Marni's skinny little arms pulled Jacob close, she whispered in his ear, "I asked Jesus to give you a hug today."

With tears now flowing, Jacob struggled to whisper back, "He did, honey, He did."

Chapter

15

Herman, Martha and Jacob each lingered over a cup of hot coffee as they enjoyed the peacefulness of the now vacated supper table. Jacob sensed he was witnessing a nightly ritual when Martha began to brief her husband on the days' events. Herman injected a number of questions, ending with, "So, how is Natasha doing? Did you get an opportunity to really talk with her?"

"Yes, and I think she's doing great. She's grown so much and the relationships she's developed over the last few months with women from our Bible study have provided a tremendous support group for her... But from her side of things, she's struggling. God is doing the very thing she feared the most, speaking to her heart about joining our prayer ministry in front of The Women's Center. She stopped by to ask for prayer. The kids prayed for her right then and there; and you know Marni, she stood in front of her, took her hand and said, 'You know you have to do it, who can pray for them better than you?'... Well, Natasha lost it, and it took her a good twenty minutes to pull herself together enough to head for home. There's no doubt in my mind she'll be joining us, but God still has some work to do before that will happen."

Herman turned his attention to Jacob, "This lady has been through a lot, a story I'll share with you when we have a little more time. For now I'll just share that she worked at The Women's Center for years and before that was very active in any way she could find to help secure a woman's right to an abortion. She turned her life over to Jesus six months ago."

Martha picked up the story. "The women at the Center were her friends. Besides friendship, they were united by another common denominator; hatred for the people who prayed in front of their place of work. Natasha has been continuously praying for those still working at the Center. Of course, they don't understand what has gotten into her. She left her job after her husband was in a terrible car accident, and..."

"I'm sorry to interrupt you honey, but I didn't realize it was so late. I have to get to the elder's meeting."

"That's OK. I need to sit down with Sarah Beth and Marni tonight, a little trouble with math. We'll talk when you get home."

"Jacob, I'm sorry to leave you hanging like this."

"I understand. I have a lot to do myself. Is there a phonebook around? I'd like to give the police a call to see if they found my truck."

Martha headed upstairs, Herman out the back door, and Jacob, after receiving good news about his truck, retired to the guest room with a Bible in hand for another open-ended meeting with the God of all creation.

~

Wednesday morning's routine at the Groves' was hampered only by the excitement over Marni's loss of another baby tooth. By 8 a.m. Herman, Jacob, and Pete were in the car heading to the indoor tennis club for Pete's lesson. Herman looked forward to Wednesday mornings with his eldest son, normally being their time to hang out together. Pete would go to the church with his dad after his tennis lesson to do some schoolwork and then help set up for the evening's children's programs. Lunch at Big Daddy's Burgers provided time for father-son conversations while devouring a "man's meal".

This Wednesday morning, however, would be different. After dropping Pete off for his tennis lesson, Herman and Jacob would drive to the police station to complete the paperwork necessary to recover the stolen pick-up truck and to retrieve Jacob's driver's license which had been found on the seat. Jacob had already called the bank to cancel his check card, so not finding that wasn't a problem. Later in the morning Pete would be on his own setting up for Wednesday night, allowing Herman and Jacob the opportunity to once again sit down behind a closed office door.

~

"Herman, if it's all right with you, I would like to open in prayer this morning."

"That would be wonderful."

Jacob, leaning forward with elbows on knees, hands folded, and head bowed, came before his Savior as a man deposed from a throne he now understood had no eternal value. "Jesus, over the last twenty-four hours You have revealed to me how empty and useless my efforts to build a 'Heavenly Kingdom' here on earth have been. Your Kingdom isn't made up of physical buildings or earthly riches that You want to pile on us to prove to the world who You are...Your Kingdom is evidenced in the heart of a man who puts others before himself... Thank you for this man You have led me to. Keep my heart open to being humbled so I can learn what You want to teach me through this brother. Amen."

Herman silently breathed a prayer of his own; knowing that what had taken place in Jacob's life was by the work of the Holy Spirit. "Jacob, you've spent a lot of time alone with the Lord since yesterday. Tell me where you're at."

"I'm not sure... I see how wrong I've been on so many things...but there's still something missing. I know now that I belong to Jesus. I am so very, very grateful for my salvation. I spent more time in the Bible last night than I have in...in years. The Bible to me has always been like a reference book, someplace to get quotes from to support a teaching. Now, somehow, it's come to life...

"Anyway, there are so many things I need to deal with. Maybe we should start with my marriage. I don't even know where Jennifer is right now... Years ago our marriage turned into...some kind of 'agreement'... When she left she broke that agreement, and my world crashed..."

"Did you ever love her?"

Jacob's first thought was to say, *Oh, sure I did, when we first met,* but the answer seemed too glib. Instead, he fell into thought. *What was it like to love her? Do I even remember?...* "I'm ashamed to say, I've forgotten that I loved her."

Memories trickled from the recesses of Jacob's mind. His heart began to ache as he shared with Herman something that happened in their first year of marriage. "I remember the night we had my parents over to our first apartment. Jenny had worked so hard at making the place look nice; she wanted the evening to be perfect. She wasn't a great cook so she asked her best friend to come over in the afternoon and help her make the meal." Jacob paused as the memory became more and more vivid. "It's not that she wanted to deceive my parents into thinking she was a tremendous cook, she just didn't want them to know she was a terrible cook. After my mother complimented her on the meal, my big mouth spewed out the truth... I remember the look on Jenny's face...and how my heart sank... I felt her pain like it was my own... Yes...I loved her..." Jacob's thoughts drifted in and out of the two worlds he had shared with Jennifer. "How did we let that love slip away?"

"Love of self kills love for others... The flower that blooms is the one that's tended."

"I didn't tend my love for Jenny." The admission uncovered another pile of rotting pride that once again brought Jacob to tears.

"Do you know what God's Word says about marriage?"

Jacob managed a sarcastic smile after wiping wet cheeks, "You want to hear something funny? I wrote a book on it."

"On what God says about marriage?"

"Well, how to be happy in your marriage, whether it's your first or fourth. Maybe I should go back and read it."

"Do you think you'll find answers there?"

"No... When I wrote that book I didn't read the Bible to prepare, I read all kinds of books written by other people. It sold like hotcakes...but it didn't have any answers...not really. I quoted some verses here and there, but only to justify a point I was trying to make. When I look back now, I see it was just another exercise in explaining how you can get what you want..."

"That's something man's been doing ever since Adam and Eve ate the fruit from the tree in the middle of the garden. We have only a very small glimpse of what marriage was like before sin, but that glimpse can tell us a bunch about how far off the mark we are today."

"You think Adam and Eve really had it figured out? I've got to tell you, I'm not sure there really was an Adam and Eve in the first place."

"I'm not surprised. By your own admission you've been willing in the past to twist scripture for your purposes. Reverence for the word of God is the first sacrifice offered on the altar of personal gain."

Jacob felt as though a sword had pierced his heart. Bearing a look of anguish, he threw his hands up against his face and dropped his head in an attempt to hide from the truth. Sobs laid bare the rawness of a soul completely exposed by the Holy Spirit. "I'm responsible...I AM RESPONSIBLE...for leading so many people away from God's word!"

Herman began to pray for wisdom - words of knowledge - anything to help this man seated in front of him. Nothing came.

Jacob finally lifted his head and, through deep breaths, yielded to the Spirit of truth. "I spent years listening to garbage...allowing myself to be deceived by men who claimed to know truth...but the worst thing...the worst thing of all is that I BECAME one of those men and turned right around and fed those same lies to others...thousands of others. I don't even know how many.

"I read a verse in Luke last night that scared me to death. Luke 17:1, '...It is inevitable that stumbling blocks should come, but woe to him through whom they come!'... You know, I've never believed the Bible was really the word of God. I've always believed it was just writings of 'Godly' men. I've believed it had mistakes and was open to interpretation... But if it is the word of God...and everything in it is true...oh, Jesus, what have I done?... And what do I deserve?"

"Jacob, I have to tell you that your brokenness is ministering to me. In your pain I'm beginning to see, like I have never seen before, the responsibility we have concerning God's word toward others. I've always known that truth, but never to this depth."

"That's what scares me. If you only knew the things I've told people in the name of God's word. Even now I'm questioning...is it true? Is all of it true? Was there really an actual Adam and Eve? My mind is telling me not to go there because I'll become vulnerable to what scripture says. My heart is telling me that the Holy Spirit has already revealed the truth, and I have no excuse for rejecting the authority of God's written word."

"Oh, Jacob, I can tell you this. There is forgiveness for our sins. As abominable as they are to the God who created us, there is forgiveness for those who repent through the shed blood of Jesus Christ. Can I pray for you right now?"

"Yes, please, yes."

"Jesus, through your Holy Spirit, make known to Jacob the reality of his new birth; that he is a brand new creation and that old things have passed away. Impress upon his heart that he is no longer the man through whom stumbling blocks have come. THAT Jacob Hamilton is dead! Open his heart and his mind to the truth of Your word. Amen.

"Jacob, there are all kinds of studies you can do to confirm the truth of scripture, and I encourage you to check them out. But for now, I'm going to ask that we deal with what's before us using scripture as our standard." Herman lifted his Bible from his desk, "I have no doubt God will establish the foundation of His word under your feet as you see the truth contained in this book take root in your life.

"Let's take a break for lunch. Pete and I will introduce you to the best burger joint in town, and then we'll come back here and get into marriage. This would be a good time to tell you about Natasha's husband; an amazing man. I think his story is going to minister to your heart."

Chapter

16

Lunch at Big Daddy's Burgers lived up to its billing. The old fashioned burgers and homemade fries were some of the best Jacob had tasted. Herman took advantage of the satisfying moment after the last bites of burgers were swallowed to offer Jacob a room at the church.

The offer was received as another ingredient of God's intervention in Jacob's life. "God spoke to my heart about something last night. He said the money in my bank account isn't mine. Every penny I have was received through spiritual deception. I'm to walk away from it all. The only thing He hasn't spoken to me about is my truck. It may be He's allowing me to keep that because I bought it with money earned before I was in ministry." Jacob looked Herman straight in the eyes, "God has shown me that I was already spiritually bankrupt, now He's making sure I'm financially bankrupt so that I depend completely on Him. Offering me a room at the church is a gift straight from His hand, and I accept it. But I would like to contribute somehow. What can I do around the church to help out? Are there any jobs to be done? Anything to fix?"

Herman appeared hesitant. "Well...as long as you asked. The couple who normally do the custodial work at church are in the middle of a two month mission trip to Africa. They won't return for another month, and I've been picking up the slack while they're gone. If you would be willing to take that over until they return it would be a tremendous help."

The irony hit its mark. *He IS the janitor...and now I'M going to be!* "Yes, I'll do it."

"Great. When we leave here we'll drop Pete off at home, pick up your truck at the impound lot, and stop by Fred Carlson's house to load up the bedroom set. We can put the room together tomorrow morning. This afternoon we've got some work to do on a marriage!"

Herman's enthusiasm caught Jacob by surprise. In his mind there was no marriage to work on, just what remained of a deceptive agreement. As he had told Herman earlier, the marriage ended years ago. Now the legal loose ends had to be tied.

~

"Father, we place before you the marriage of Jacob and Jennifer. I pray that You reveal to Jacob's heart Your will so he knows how to minister to his wife. Instill in him Your strength, enabling him to shun the desire for the wisdom of man. Render a hunger in his gut and a thirst on his lips that will be quenched only by the digestion of Your truth. Amen."

Man, this guy gets right to the point even in his prayers. "Herman, I'm a little afraid of the direction you might want to take this counseling session."

"Afraid?"

"Well, nervous maybe. I get the feeling you think there's a marriage here that can be salvaged. I can't see that. Jennifer and I have not really been married for so long, and besides, she's been with another man."

"Is it your desire to get divorced and move on so you can be happy?"

"I don't think I would put it that way, but...but I'm sure that's how it will end up..." Jacob's posture was now defensive, "Look, we are divorced and have been for some time. We just lived in the same house. We even slept in separate bedrooms. I need to make it legal. She's going to want to sell the house and...and I want to get all that stuff out of the way."

"By worldly standards you have the right to do that, but as a brother in Christ I am going to tell you that God's word speaks against it."

"Jennifer is living in adultery. I have scriptural grounds for divorce."

"That was one of the verses you used in your book to support a teaching, wasn't it."

"Yes, Matthew 19:9, 'And I say to you, whoever divorces his wife, except for immorality, and marries another commits adultery,' Jennifer has committed immorality, which gives me scriptural ground to divorce her and move on to what God has for me."

"This morning you were telling me you weren't sure if everything in scripture is true...but you're pretty sure about that one?"

For the first time Jacob was feeling anger toward this man he believed God led him to. "I'm sorry. I know I'm getting defensive. Maybe this isn't an area you can help me with."

"You're not closing the door on me, Jacob; you're closing it on God. Would you be willing to at least listen to what I believe God has to say about this and consider praying about it? You don't have to believe a word I say, as a matter of fact you shouldn't. But would you be willing to listen and then take it before God, with scripture in hand, and ask Him to show you His truth?"

Jacob's spirit began to settle. "Yes...yes, I can do that. Again, I'm sorry for my attitude. Maybe there's more here than I think there is. I don't know why I'm having such a hard time with this... Maybe I care for Jennifer more than I think I do, and I want her to be happy."

"I don't think it's Jennifer you're caring about. I think it's you you're caring about. You have been so willing to relinquish other things that God has asked you to trust Him in, let go of this too. Allow Him to transform your heart so you can walk in His will."

..."You're right. I'm clinging to the thought that after all this passes...someone might love me again."

"You may find some earthly pleasure in that, but the joy of walking in the will of God is where you'll find fulfillment." Herman reached over and placed his hand on Jacob's knee, "Brother, I'm going to say some things that you're probably not going to accept right away, but understand that I believe God has proven these things in His word. Take them to His word yourself and ask the Holy Spirit to bear witness to the truth before you accept or reject what I have to say."

Jacob settled back in the chair as his tense muscles relaxed. "I'll listen with an open mind, and I promise...I'll take it to scripture."

"Thank you. I want to start by giving you something to think about concerning Matthew 19:9. Scripture confirms scripture.

Consider some early manuscripts of this verse that read, 'And I say to you, whoever divorces his wife, except for immorality, and marries another **makes her** commit adultery, **and he who marries a divorced woman commits adultery.**' In light of these manuscripts we see how this verse is completely consistent with what Jesus taught in the Sermon on the Mount. Matthew 5:32 says, '...but I say to you that everyone who divorces his wife, except for the cause of unchastity, makes her commit adultery; and whoever marries a divorced woman commits adultery.'

"Jesus was not giving justification for marriage after divorce, as so many Christians want to believe. He was telling them that marriage after divorce is adultery and then explained who would bear responsibility for the adultery when it occurred. If a wife is divorced because she is unfaithful, and the husband has been faithful, then he does not bear responsibility for her adultery when she is with another man, because she has already committed adultery through her unfaithfulness. But if she has been faithful and he puts her out, then he does bear responsibility for her adultery when she ends up in the arms of another man. In this instance, it is his lack of faithfulness to the covenant of marriage that has placed his wife in harm's way to the sin of adultery.

"Look at how Jesus puts it in Mark 10:11-12; And He said to them, 'Whoever divorces his wife and marries another woman commits adultery against her; and if she herself divorces her husband and marries another man, she is committing adultery'. And again in Luke 16:18; 'Everyone who divorces his wife and marries another commits adultery; and he who marries one who is divorced from a husband commits adultery.' Jesus makes it very clear that whenever there is marriage after divorce there is adultery."

"Are you saying there is no scriptural justification for marriage after divorce?"

"I'm saying that we shouldn't be looking between the lines for scriptural justification for our sin... We know, within the conscience of our soul, the righteousness of God's design. The unrighteousness of ripping and tearing apart what God has made one flesh is painfully evident to the husband and wife involved. This is why God states in Malachi 2:16 that He hates divorce. He describes that ripping and tearing apart of the covenant as a 'treacherous deed'."

Jacob's disagreement was obvious and threatened to put an end to the counseling session.

"Jacob, I told you I was going to say some things that you won't agree with right away, and you promised me you would listen and bring them to scripture. I only know one way to give counsel and that is to speak the truth God has so graciously planted in my heart. If you do a scriptural study, not listen to man, but listen to the Holy Spirit, He will show you the same truth, because it's His truth.

"We, in the church, have made a terrible mess of the covenant of marriage by following the heart of man rather than the word of God. As a result, Christians are forced to deal with the consequences of broken families, blended families, and in many cases children growing up without a father or mother in the home; hearts are shattered by broken trust.

"I fully understand it's not possible to go back in time and undo our sin, but true repentance demands that we admit our sin and turn from the lie that we believed justified our fall. God calls us to stand on the truth, walk in the truth, and teach the truth.

"The important thing to remember is that we serve a forgiving God who, upon seeing our repentant hearts, will wash us clean by His blood shed on the cross and take our broken lives and make them whole. Any attempt at justification for our sin outside of the blood of Christ will only leave us in bondage."

Herman waited until he saw in Jacob's eyes that he was willing to continue. "I want to get past divorce and talk about what I believe God wants you to know about marriage.

"This morning I mentioned Natasha's husband, Jess Rivers. Jess came to see me a year ago. He had to remind me that we had actually met when I was a kid. He worked for my Grandpa selling used cars. When he walked into the office he was recovering from a car accident that nearly took his life. That afternoon he shared with me a story that tied my emotions in knots. A story that I want to share with you..."

For the next hour and a half, Herman ministered to Jacob by recounting truths learned by a man in a coma. When he finished, two men wiped tears from their eyes.

"Jess came to me because he didn't want to fall prey to the same mistakes he made in his dream. He wanted counsel on how to share the love of Christ with the woman he loved. Natasha hated the idea of even driving him here to meet with me. She was fearful of losing, not only the man she loved, but also the life she loved. A different man lived behind the eyes she knew so well.

"I met with Jess twice a week. He became a part of our men's Bible study and regularly worshiped with us on Friday nights. That is until he led his best friend, Fred Carlson, to the Lord. After that they both came Sunday mornings, and soon Fred's wife, Julie, started coming. Natasha didn't know about Julie coming to church until a women's Bible study conflicted with something Natasha had invited Julie to do with her. By this time Julie was so in love with Jesus that she couldn't keep her joy a secret from her best friend any longer. Needless to say, Natasha felt pretty ganged up on."

"How did Jess end up sharing with Natasha?"

"That's what makes this man so amazing... I have to tell you that Natasha manifested more hate towards Christians than anyone I had ever met. I'm sure she was influenced by her parents as a child, and she's admitted to having some bad experiences with Christians through the years, but I believe most of her hate was spiritually introduced by Satan, and a lot of the fuel he used to stoke the flames was gleaned from her defense of abortion.

"In one of our regular counseling sessions, Jess shared with me that Natasha came to him and blew up. She told him, 'I hate who you've become. I want my husband back!'

"Jess sat with her and explained that he asked God to give him strength to lay his life down for her, which she didn't understand at all. He told her he couldn't go back to being the man he was, a man so wrapped up in himself that he was willing to trade an opportunity for her salvation for his own happiness. 'If I deny what Jesus has done for me, shedding His blood on the cross and rising from the dead, in order to retain your love,' he told her, 'I will never again be able to tell you that I love you with all my heart. Natasha,' he said, 'Jesus loves you more than I do, I long for you to know that. Where you'll spend eternity means more to me than any happiness I could ever gain from a return to our old life.'

"He said Natasha had calmed down enough to listen, but then got up and walked away in anger. Two very silent days later, she told Jess she would divorce him if he didn't come to his senses.

"Jess believed she only made an appointment with the divorce attorney to force him to change his mind, so he decided to go downtown with her, thinking his presence would make it harder for her to go through with the meeting. After they parked the car on Superior Street, they hesitantly walked side by side in a direction neither one ever expected to be heading.

"At the stop light on the avenue, Jess turned to Natasha and, with tears in his eyes, said, 'Tash, I can't go any farther. I love you more today than I have ever loved you in my life. Please know that I don't want this. Please know that I would do anything for you...except deny my Savior. I would do more than give up our marriage, I would give up my life if that's what it would take for you to come to know the love of Jesus.'

"When the light turned green Natasha turned away from Jess and stepped into the street... Everything happened so fast, but eyewitness accounts said they didn't believe Natasha ever saw the car coming... They said Jess lunged forward and threw himself against his wife to knock her out of the way... The driver of the car was a teenage girl texting on her cell phone..."

"Are...are you saying Jess was killed!"

..."Natasha said she hit her forehead on the pavement, blood was running down her face. When she lifted her head and looked back...in a blur she saw Jess lying in the street. She crawled over to him, begging, she said she didn't know who, to let him be alive. When she reached him she said she stared into eyes that were full of love. Leaning down, she laid her head on Jess' shoulder, pressing her cheek against his...hugging him...clinging to him in an effort to hold captive the warmth of life...

"Jacob...Jess knew that if Natasha had died at that moment instead of him, she would have entered eternity without her Savior. He was not only willing to lay down his life for her...he did lay down his life for her. This is what God wants you to know about marriage. Ephesians 5:25, 'Husbands, love your wives, just as Christ also loved the church and gave Himself up for her...'

"Put Jennifer before yourself, Jacob. Love her unconditionally. Lay your life down for her. Don't look for loopholes to provide you with justification for worldly love. Don't look for excuses to justify your fleshly desires. Don't be shortsighted; consider the infinite value of Godly faithfulness over the finite value of worldly happiness. You still have the opportunity to be true to the covenant you made with the wife of your youth. She needs your steadfastness now more than ever.

"Yes, Moses allowed a certificate of divorce to be written, but Jesus made clear it was because of the hardness of their hearts. And what were their hearts hardened against? Their wives?... No... It was against the word of God.

"Jesus said in Matthew 19:8, '...from the beginning it has not been this way.' He quotes to them Genesis 2:24, 'For this reason a man shall leave his father and his mother, and shall cleave to his wife; and they shall become one flesh.' He adds in Matthew 19:6, 'Consequently, they are no more two, but one flesh. What therefore God has joined together, let no man separate.'

"I want to go back to what I said this morning about only having a glimpse of what marriage was like before sin. We don't really know how long a period of time there was between the creation of Eve and the eating of the fruit, but can you imagine the love in that union of two hearts before there was sin? Whether it was one minute or one year, there was a purity of love between two people which the world has never again known. No demands of self, none, only love between a man and a woman the way God intended it to be.

"Think back to the moment your eyes were first opened to the revelation of your love for Jennifer. What that moment must have been like for Adam when he awoke; there before him stood in the fullness of unblemished beauty...woman...created for him by the hand of God.

"We need to understand marriage for what God created it to be, not for what man has made it. Marriage requires leaving, cleaving, becoming one flesh. Marriage requires you and me, as husbands, to love our wives as Christ loved the church and died for her. This is the foundation that God has placed marriage upon. And when things go bad, no matter how bad, this is the foundation to which we must return.

"Will you view marriage through the precepts of scripture, or the precepts of man? And if through scripture, Jacob...will you be willing to lay your life down for Jennifer?"

Jacob sat motionless, peering deep into his own soul. Then, in a voice broken by inner disgust, he spoke, "I've never come close to knowing the kind of love Jess had for Natasha, not even in my best days with Jenny... I don't think I know how to love..."

"Father, You have brought Jacob to the bottom. You have completely torn down his dwelling place of the past and discarded the rubble. You have made ready the ground to lay a new foundation for his life in You, Your Son being the cornerstone. Father, as the house goes up, fill the room known as Jenny with an ache for her salvation. Minister peace to Jacob through Your Holy Spirit, and give him rest for his soul as You prepare him for what lies ahead. Amen."

Chapter

17

Jacob looked longingly at the back door of the red brick house as Herman's minivan backed out of the driveway Thursday morning. He was leaving a family unit where, just three nights earlier, he had been received with love and homemade apple pie; no questions asked and no conditions placed upon his lodging.

"Herman, I feel as though I'm leaving home to check into my dorm room. I'm going to miss your family more than I could've imagined I would miss anyone."

"What? You mean you're not going to come and have dinner with us in the evenings?"

"Oh man, I've imposed on you and your family long enough."

"You have not imposed once, and you are welcome anytime. Personally, I think it would be a good idea if you ate supper with us until your life gets a little more settled. You're going to need that daily Marni-hug to help build your strength."

"What a sweetheart. I would love to have one of those skinny armed hugs every day for the rest of my life... I...I can't imagine that Marni's mom ever would have even thought about an abortion if she would have known who that little girl was."

"Makes you think, doesn't it; about all those kids who were aborted. Who were they? And what is this world missing out on?"

Jacob pondered the thought in relationship to his own daughter. "I wonder how different I am from the parents that abort their kids before they're born? I aborted Alicia from my life early on. I was never a father to her. I never allowed her to be a daughter to me... I used her for a prop."

Herman turned to Jacob after parking the van, letting him know he was there to listen.

"By the time we had Alicia I was already into my 'Plan for the Kingdom'. Never once did I stop to find out who was living inside that little body... I told her who to be...who I needed her to be."

"Where is she now?"

Jacob paled and turned to Herman, "I don't know... Can you believe that?... I don't know. The last time she was home she made it very clear she was severing any cord of control I might've believed I had over her. She's living with a guy she met at college. Jennifer knows where she is, but...I never asked her to tell me, and now I don't know where Jennifer is." Jacob's heart filled with regret.

The first two hours of the morning were spent setting up the church's new halfway house. The room had previously been cleaned and painted in anticipation of expanding office space. The bed coverings didn't quite match the color of the room or the window curtains, but to two guys who only had privacy on their minds the place was deemed sufficient. Jacob needed no more than a minute to move in all his earthly possessions.

"This should work out fine. You can use the church kitchen as you need and there's a shower in the men's restroom. Jacob, I have a hospital visit to make. I want to pray with someone who is having surgery tomorrow morning."

"Sure, I'll be ok. If you'll tell me what needs cleaning I can get some of that done."

"Well, both restrooms need to be cleaned and the sanctuary needs to be vacuumed. I'll be back in a couple of hours, but then I'm going to have to finish my sermon. If you need to talk more today we will, otherwise let's plan on sitting down first thing tomorrow morning. Come on, I'll show you where all the cleaning supplies are."

Jacob decided to vacuum first to ease into this new life as a custodian. By the time he was on his knees scrubbing the last toilet in the men's room he realized how at peace he was with the situation he found himself in. *Jesus, thank you for giving me what I need. I have a place to sleep, a place to eat, and a place to learn what You want to teach me. And Lord, I want to learn... Whatever You want to teach me, I want to learn.* He worked his way to his feet and backed out of the stall. The former self made Man-of-God turned and came face-to-face with the man he had now become. The mirror above the sink reflected the transformation. Where once towered an egotistical fool who believed God must honor every request his heart desired, stood a servant, toilet brush in hand, overwhelmingly grateful just to be allowed in his Master's presence.

"Jacob! Hey, Jacob!"

"I'm in the men's room!"

Herman poked his head past the half-open door. "Will you come to lunch with me? Natasha called and would like to meet me at Perkins. I never go to lunch with a female alone unless it's my wife, so it would be a great help if you would come."

"Can't pass up an offer for lunch."

"By the way, you look pretty good wielding that brush."

Jacob raised the implement as if a sword and in a voice rendering knightly homage declared, "I have come to respect this mighty weapon, for it has pierced the prideful heart of a lofty king."

Herman laughed out loud. "Come along, Sir Jacob, our chariot awaits."

Jacob washed up and rushed out to join his new friend.

~

"Natasha, this is a friend of mine, Jacob Hamilton. Jacob, Natasha Rivers." Greetings were exchanged while the threesome settled into a corner booth.

"You know, whenever I come in here," Natasha paused, considering whether or not to finish her statement, "I look around and wonder if...if Luke might show up."

"I would like to meet him myself one day," Herman admitted.

"I thought Jess was nuts when he told me about his dream... I wish I would have known the author of that dream then as I do now... I've always felt Jess didn't share everything with me. There always seemed to be something he wanted to ask, but was afraid to... I'm sorry, that's not why I asked to meet with you, to talk about Jess' dream. There's something else I want to talk to you about."

"Hi, can I get you something to drink?' The cheery waitress placed menus in front of her guests.

"Coke for me," Natasha responded. Coffee and water were requested by her companions.

"So, what's on your mind Natasha, anything I can help you with?"

Jacob sat silent, hoping his presence wasn't an intrusion into Natasha's business.

"I think you can help me. I'm going to move off the farm... I'm finding it too lonely, with too many reminders to stay there. I've purchased a small house close to Julie and Fred, and being in town will allow me more time to check on Jess' mom... I don't think it will be long before she goes home, she has really gone down hill the past couple of weeks."

"Yes, I know. I stopped to visit her last Thursday. She talks of nothing else but being with Jesus...and seeing Jess again."

"I have so many regrets from my past life," Natasha spoke with determination, "I'm not going to let that wonderful woman die alone; she's going to have family around her."

"If there is anything Martha and I can do, you know you only need to ask."

"Yes, I do know that."

Drinks were set on the table. "Are you ready to order?"

Jacob couldn't help but notice the servant's heart in this young girl. "Do you know Jesus?" The words just popped out of his mouth as though they had been served up by the Spirit of God Himself.

"Yes, He's my Savior."

"I have a daughter about your age. I would give anything to see her know the joy that is shining through you."

"What's her name? I'll pray for her."

"Alicia. And thank you, I appreciate that."

After orders were taken, Natasha returned her attention to Herman. "I don't want to sell the farm; I want it to be used for ministry."

"Wow! That would be a blessing. Do you have something in mind?"

"I do. Having worked at the clinic as long as I did, I know there are girls that have nowhere to turn. They would allow their babies to live if they could get help... I want to donate the farm to the church if you're willing to put a ministry together that would offer girls a home. I know it would cost money to make something like this happen. Jess was a very good business man. I'm almost ashamed to tell you how much money we have amassed over the years, money that we believed would allow us to live the American Dream in retirement... I know that Jess would have gone along with this if he was still here...if he had known what I had done..."

Herman spoke directly to Natasha's heart, "You know, when Jess came to me he had already given his life to Jesus. I have never known anyone to have more Christ-like love for his wife than Jess had for you. There is nothing in your past he would not have forgiven."

The air of ministry caused the waitress to pause before placing orders in front of three people who seemed more interested in spiritual food than what she was serving. When the moment passed, and the food was on the table, Jacob cautiously entered the conversation. "Natasha, Herman has shared Jess' story with me. Your husband's love for you has helped me see how selfish I've been in my relationship with my wife. He stopped short of telling me how you accepted Jesus. Would you be willing to share that with me?"

Instantly, Jacob could see tears flooding Natasha's eyes. "I'm sorry, I didn't mean to cause you pain. I understand if it's too hard to share."

"No...I want to share. I haven't yet put this whole thing into words. It will do me good to say some things out loud."

Natasha took a deep breath and then released it, giving her emotions time to catch up to her desire. "I began to die the day Jess died, I just wasn't aware of it at the time. We loved each other...but his love was so different after he crashed the Vette. Before the accident we were on a level playing field. I know it sounds crazy to describe love in that way, but there really was some sort of game to it all. Deep inside, both of us knew we thought about ourselves as much as we thought about each other...maybe more. I wanted him, and he wanted me... It was more about getting than giving. I'm beginning to think most marriages are like that.

"I know now that when Jess woke up from his accident, he was a brand new creation. The old had passed away, and a new life had begun. That new life ushered in a love unfamiliar to me; a selfless love, a love that was in total contrast to what we had shared for thirty-nine years...and it scared me to death. Without meaning to, Jess loved me into a corner.

"You would think a woman would melt when loved unconditionally...but my heart had become so hard. This love was from a source that I had grown to hate; hate so much that I tried to deny its very existence. In my mind, Jess had gone over to the enemy, and that enemy was stealing everything I treasured...

"Jess' mom and Fred and Julie handled the funeral arrangements. I couldn't do it... I wouldn't do it. I knew Jess would want a Christian funeral, and I wanted no part of it. Pastor Herman came to see me, and I begged him to get out of my sight. I screamed at him as if he was the devil himself.

"...I didn't go to the funeral... I didn't go anywhere for two weeks. I stayed cooped up in the house, blaming a God I refused to believe existed for the death of my husband. This is how demented I became: I began to believe Jess had died in the Vette. I convinced myself that the man I lived with since the accident wasn't my husband... It wasn't my fault that Jess was dead, it was God's fault, and I was now willing to acknowledge Him to have someone to blame." Natasha allowed time for her own words to penetrate her mind.

"Julie, Fred, Pastor Herman, and even Jess' mom came to the house after the funeral to try and help me. I turned them all away. I let Julie in on her first visit, but she brought with her a CD of the funeral message Pastor Herman had preached. When she handed it to me I threw it on the floor and told her to leave. I didn't let anyone in after that. The CD lay on the floor for a week and a half. I didn't have the courage to listen to it, and I didn't have the courage to throw it in the garbage.

"I drank every night until I passed out. I wanted to kill my mind...make sure it didn't remember. Then one morning I woke up to the sound of someone talking. My head was such a mess that I couldn't understand what was being said or where it was coming from. When I gathered my wits, I realized I had passed out on the leather couch in Jess' den. The CD of Pastor Herman's sermon was in the CD player, and the player was set on repeat. His message had been playing over and over all night long. I must have put the CD on while I was in a drunken stupor, unaware of what I was doing. Or...maybe an angel...

"I tried to block out the sound of Pastor's voice, but his words couldn't be stopped from entering my defenseless mind. God came to me when I was too weak to fight...when I was vulnerable to hearing His truth.

"The first words that made sense to me were from scripture. Pastor was quoting John 15:12-13, 'This is My commandment, that you love one another, just as I have loved you. Greater love has no one than this, that one lay down his life for his friends.' At that moment I understood the love in Jess' eyes as he slipped away... It was the love of Christ...

"I broke down in utter despair. It was like my heart was fully exposed by the light of a love I couldn't comprehend. The ugly, ugly truth in my heart had nowhere to hide... I would not have done for Jess what he did for me... I would have recoiled to save my own life instead of lunging forward to save his. This I knew...because I had already done it...to my baby."

Natasha looked straight into the eyes of the two brothers in the Lord who sat across the table from her. "When Jess and I were first married, I had an abortion. From the moment I walked out of that clinic I worked as hard as I could to convince myself I hadn't killed my baby...to keep it from ruining the life I wanted. I spent a lifetime trying to justify what I had done...but justification only turned my heart cold. That's why I hated the people praying in front of the Women's Center; they didn't know it, but they were praying for me to admit my guilt.

"And now...Jess was dead...because of me. I rolled off the couch onto the floor and, in agony, begged God, a God I didn't want to believe in...to let me die... Instead, He spoke words of life to me through Pastor's sermon. 'Come to Me, all who are weary and heavy laden, and I will give you rest. Take My yoke upon you, and learn from Me, for I am gentle and humble in heart; and you shall find rest for your souls.'

"I fought against God all my life. I hated Him. And what did He do when I wanted to die?... He said, 'Come to Me.' He knew I was weary from battle, and even though the battle was against Him...He offered me rest.

"I rejected God at an early age, and He loved me. I considered Him my enemy, and He loved me. I denied His very existence...and yet, He loved me... Here I was, too weak from a drinking binge to pull myself up off the floor; too filthy from a lifetime of sin to turn my face toward Him...and He loved me... Every word that Jess had shared with me about his Savior passed through my heart as I lay there, and every ounce of Christ's love he had shown me ministered to my soul.

"The next thing I knew, my head was resting in Julie's lap. She and Fred had come to check on me. When they got no response they started to look through windows. After they saw me on the floor, Fred kicked in the front door. I could hear them praying for me, and all I could say was, 'Thank you, Jesus...thank you, Jesus...'

"In the weeks to come Fred, Julie, Pastor Herman, and Martha showered me with love, nursed me in the faith, and introduced me into fellowship with sisters in the Lord that I don't know what I would do without."

Jacob spoke tenderly through his tears, "Thank you. Jess' testimony has born witness of how to love my wife, Jenny. Your testimony has given me hope for her salvation."

Three spiritually fed hearts turned their attention back to their food and their conversation back to the possible birth of a new ministry; one that would shower the love of Jesus on pregnant moms willing to nurture new life.

Chapter

18

Jacob leaned on the cold steel railing atop Enger Tower, a five story bluestone monument built on a hill rising 530 feet above Lake Superior. He surveyed the dying beauty of the city below. Fall was struggling to draw its final breath; once vibrant colors were dulled by frigid air, leaves clung to a finite hope of life, and gardens fought against hibernation.

Looking southwest he could see the winding path of the St Louis River; while northeast offered a view of the rocky shores of the lake the Ojibwe called Gichigami. Jacob was glad to have been introduced to this favorite local tourist spot, even though he was sure his friend's real objective was to secure an afternoon to work on his sermon.

Lord, so much has happened in such a short time. You've reached in deep and turned me inside-out. I know you have a lot to teach me, and I need to be patient...but I'm worried about Jenny and Alicia. I feel like I should be looking for them. I failed them in so many ways... I failed them most by not walking in Your truth.

Jacob stared past tops of trees and the houses they sheltered, past the harbor and the uniqueness of the Aerial Lift Bridge that connected the mainland to a long narrow sandbar known as Park Point. His eyes drifted outward until they refused to take notice of the vast body of water his mind had traversed.

...Jenny's face was soft and inviting. Her smile warmed the air around him. She stretched out her arms as if to say, come to me...and Alicia did. At ten months, she let go of the couch and wobbled her way through her first steps to the open arms of mama...

The vivid memory cut deep into Jacob's heart. Its existence owed nothing to his fatherly involvement. He just happened to be in the right place at the right time, passing through the living room of their cramped apartment on his way out the door. There was no time for a daddy-hug, or to celebrate this first in his little girl's life; people were waiting, important people, people who devoured his vision of the kingdom that could be.

A wave washed the image from Jacob's mind, leaving remorse in its wake. *Oh, Jesus, if I just had it to do over again...but I don't.* The wetness of Jacob's cheeks disclosed the futility of over twenty years of selfish manipulation. *I had everything I wanted, Lord, and nothing I needed. What did the accumulation of wealth and stature have to do with the salvation of my wife and daughter, or of anyone else for that matter? Nothing! I see that now. How could I have been so stupid as to think that You would put my worldly desires above someone else's eternal needs?*

Descending the tower reminded Jacob of his "fall from power". The people in the parking lot no longer looked smaller than him. He could hear their conversations. He could see the young girl slip her hand into the waiting grasp of her boyfriend and the middle-aged wife refusing her husband's touch as she picked up her pace to put space between them. *This is where you want me, Lord; in the trenches, down here where there's work to be done.* Jacob turned and lifted his eyes to the top of the monument, *not up there in my lofty tower.*

~

Jacob parked his truck on the street in front of the Groves' home. He walked to the back of the house basking in the knowledge that he was not front door company; family status had been offered him, and he eagerly embraced it. Homemade meatloaf, creamy mashed potatoes, and garden grown acorn squash, enhanced by the skinny-armed hug from a seven-year-old angel, welcomed him as he entered the kitchen through the back hall.

"Did you have a good afternoon, Jacob?" Herman took his turn at putting his arm around the shoulder of his new brother in Christ.

"I did. Enger Tower offers a beautiful view of the city. Thank you for suggesting the visit."

"I thought you might like that. I do a lot of thinking up there during the summer months. I imagine it was a little chilly today, though. Well, let's sit down and enjoy this feast. Peter, please go ask Seth and Sarah Beth to come for supper."

Jacob took a seat on the bench next to Marni as though it belonged to him. After Peter offered grace, Martha probed deeper into Jacob's day. "I understand you met Natasha."

"Yes, and she blessed my heart with her testimony." Jacob plopped a spoonful of fluffy white mashed potatoes on his plate.

"She's a wonderful person. Herman shared her plan for the farm with me. I think it's a fantastic idea, and I know the church will embrace the plan with a heart ready to minister to moms and babies."

"Speaking of Natasha," Herman passed the meatloaf on to Peter, "she called me later this afternoon to say she completely forgot to ask me something. She wants to move into the house she bought in town on Monday and thought I might know of some men who need work to help her move her things. Are you interested in making a few bucks next week, Jacob?"

"Absolutely."

"Great. I know of a few more men who would jump at the opportunity as well. They'll be hard workers, but a couple of them may need some direction. Would you be willing to be the foreman of this makeshift crew I put together?"

"Sure, it'll feel good to be useful."

"I'll talk to them on Saturday; they should be at the church bright and early."

"Oh? Do you have a Bible Study on Saturday mornings?"

"We have a party!" Marni's words barely made it past a mouthful of squash.

"Honey..." Herman's look told Marni all she needed to know about speaking with her mouth full. "Breakfast begins at seven Saturday morning, but a number of us will be there by six to set up. You're welcome to join us. There's no way you'll be able to sleep through all the noise."

Jacob's curiosity was heightened, but he questioned no further; deciding to enjoy the anticipation of the unknown.

~

Wind whistled through a torn weather strip on the back door outside Jacob's room, waking him from a restless night's sleep in his new quarters. He was thankful to have a room for shelter and a bed to sleep on, but the mattress was anything but comfortable. The morning counseling session with Herman served as motivation to place his feet on the ice cold floor and head to the shower.

~

"Good Morning." Herman sat down on a kitchen stool across the counter from the sweatshirt clad man who huddled over a hot cup of coffee. "A little cold in here this morning," He tried to restrain himself as long as he could, but finally let loose with a hardy laugh. "I am so sorry, Jacob. I never even thought about turning up the heat. I didn't know how cold it was supposed to get last night until I heard the weather report on my way here. It was close to freezing. It's too early for that to happen. I bet it got pretty cold in that back room."

"Well, thank you, for at least not asking how I slept."

"Have you eaten breakfast?"

"Yup, a nice big bowl of COLD cereal."

With a smirk still on his face, Herman grabbed a cup of hot coffee for himself and invited Jacob to follow him to where the thermostat lay hidden behind an open classroom door. "We'll get the heat cooking so we can have a hot counseling session this morning."

Jacob's warmhearted "chilly" reaction to Herman's attempt at humor bore witness to the roots beginning to anchor the fast growing bond between these two brothers in Christ.

Herman's office enjoyed the benefits of a window facing the morning sun; a welcome change for the man who spent the night shivering under blankets. Both men settled in their chairs, eager to venture into God's presence. After setting coffee cups on the desk, folding hands and bowing heads, they entered prayer.

"Father, we sit before You this morning in anticipation of hearing from Your word. You have taken Jacob out of the kingdom he had built for himself and placed his feet on holy ground before You. I know You only empty us of our will in order to fill us with Your will. Speak loudly and clearly this morning so that Jacob knows how to follow Your lead. Set Your path before him so he knows in what direction to begin walking."

Only seconds passed before Jacob seized the opportunity to pray for Herman. "Thank You, Father, for my brother. You have spoken volumes to me through him in just a few short days. You have allowed me insight into a shepherd's heart while at the same time receiving ministry. I willingly place myself under the accountability of this minister of the Gospel. Open my eyes to what You are going to show me through Herman this morning, and give me a receptive heart and a willing spirit to apply Your truth to my life."

Herman picked up his Bible, turned a few pages, and began to read John 15:4-5, "'Abide in Me, and I in you. As the branch cannot bear fruit of itself, unless it abides in the vine, so neither can you, unless you abide in Me. I am the vine, you are the branches; he who abides in Me, and I in him, he bears much fruit; for apart from Me you can do nothing.' John 8:31-32 says, '...If you abide in My word, then you are truly disciples of Mine; and you shall know the truth, and the truth shall make you free.'

"Abide means to stand fast, to remain and reside in. Wednesday morning you confessed your unfaithfulness to God's word. This morning, God wants you to understand the necessity of spending the rest of your life absorbed in it."

Jacob listened intently, now grateful for the no nonsense approach of his counselor.

"God's truth will set us free from every lie of Satan that we have been enslaved to, but we will not know God's truth unless we seek it out. We may hear God's truth spoken from the lips of man, but it will not flow through us and become our sustenance until we receive it through the Vine. Living outside of God's word, we wither and die. Abiding in God's word, we bear much fruit. This is a simple truth that will change the life of anyone who desires to know God. It is essential, Jacob, that you understand and apply this truth to your life in order to know the will of God.

"John 15:7-8 says, 'If you abide in me, and My words abide in you, ask whatever you wish, and it shall be done for you. By this is My Father glorified, that you bear much fruit, and so prove to be My disciples.' I bet you've used that verse quite a bit in the past, along with other verses, focusing on what's promised to you."

Jacob lowered his head, nodding in the affirmative. Before the words came out of Herman's mouth, Jacob knew he had subscribed to the interpretation of man.

Herman continued, "Our selfish nature draws our attention to what we think we can get from God. God's nature is to give us what's best for us. Look at what 2 Peter 1:3-4 says. '...seeing that

His divine power has granted to us everything pertaining to life and godliness, through the true knowledge of Him who called us by His own glory and excellence. For by these He has granted to us His precious and magnificent promises, in order that by them you might become partakers of the divine nature, having escaped the corruption that is in the world by lust.'

"How can we who live in the presence of the glory and excellence of God, having been granted everything that pertains to life and godliness, become partakers of His divine nature through His precious and magnificent promises...turn around and say...I want? When we come to the true knowledge of Him who called us...we bow and say...I am content in Christ."

"I understand where you're leading me. I see the difference now, but I didn't then. What I proclaimed as God's will was determined by my own lustful and corrupted heart. I was the center of the universe. I preached a prosperity gospel...because I perceived it as being beneficial to me."

"God WILL provide us with everything we need, Jacob, but those needs are in line with HIS will. Jesus specifically tells us in Matthew 6:19-21, 'Do not lay up for yourselves treasures upon earth, where moth and rust destroy, and where thieves break in and steal. But lay up for yourselves treasures in heaven, where neither moth nor rust destroys, and where thieves do not break in or steal; for where your treasure is, there will your heart be also.'

"What good is anything on this earth if it does not serve to bring glory to God? God wants us to walk in His will for our lives. For some that might mean attaining wealth by earthly standards because that wealth is in God's plan for spreading the gospel, feeding the poor, bringing rest to those who are weary. For others, worldly wealth would be a hindrance to God's plan for them to walk in the shoes of the impoverished and the downtrodden. The question isn't what assets we have at our disposal, the question is: who do these assets belong to, and what is their purpose? If we allow any possession to stand in the way of God's will, then we are worshiping idols and not the God of our salvation. He promises to fulfill our every need...every need necessary to walk in His will, and only He knows what those needs are.

"Jacob, when we come to the place that we are partakers of His divine nature, we simply will not pray for selfish desires. We will not pray to move mountains that God does not want moved. We will fall in love with His desire and pray only for His will to be accomplished, no matter what that means for our own lives. The more we abide in Him and His word, the more we will become partakers of His divine nature. It is exactly where He wants us to live."

"And exactly where I have not been living... How did I get it so wrong?"

"You didn't look at the whole picture. There are a number of verses in scripture that we can use to justify a teaching that says, 'If you only believe, God will give you whatever you ask for.' But scripture as a whole bears out the truth that what we ask for should be in accordance with His will.

"We have a number of people in our fellowship that have come from places of broken promises. They've followed the 'formulas' only to walk away disappointed, and sometimes even devastated. Their focus had been turned inward by motivational ministers -

charismatic speakers preying on victims fallen to the lie of lust. In the end, they were not able to speak healing into existence or wealth into their desperate lives.

"God's word is true; He will supply all our needs. In Matthew, at the end of chapter 6, Jesus tells us not to be anxious for food or clothing. In verse 25 He asks, '...Is not life more than food, and the body than clothing?' Verse 33 tells us to '...seek first His kingdom and His righteousness; and all these things shall be added to you.' Again, how can we seek the righteousness and the kingdom of God while turning around and asking God to satisfy our selfish desires? We're to think beyond food and clothing, toys and treasures - anything this world has to offer.

"Matthew 5:6 says, 'Blessed are those who hunger and thirst for righteousness, for they shall be satisfied.' A new car, a new house, a million bucks doesn't come close to satisfying a true hunger for the righteousness of God. A hunger and thirst for God's righteousness is only satisfied by walking in His eternal truth. People who declare that God's word promises unlimited earthly treasures in exchange for faithfulness are small-minded and shortsighted. They have no understanding of the value of forsaking all for the cause of Christ.

"Jacob...what would you give right now to see your wife and daughter come to salvation?"

..."Everything...even my life."

"Welcome to the Kingdom of God."

Chapter

19

The Friday night worship service would begin in less than half an hour. Jacob had spent the afternoon and early evening reading scripture; just now realizing he had missed supper. He dropped to his knees next to his bed, "Jesus, I'm hungry for so much more than food. I'm hungry to serve you, to do your work... But I've messed things up... Who could ever trust...oh, Jesus, the books I have out there...so full of garbage...how can You use me now?" Words, heavy with regret, slowly worked their way to the surface from an aching heart, "Speak to Jenny and Alicia, Lord. Minister Your truth to them through Your Holy Spirit... Bring them to salvation"

"Jacob, are you home?" The loud knock on the halfway house door startled the man on his knees.

"I'm here. Come on in."

The smell of pot roast filled Jacob's nostrils, "Martha thought since you didn't show up for supper that I should bring supper to you."

"Oh man, that does smell good, and I really should eat."

"The service starts in twenty minutes. I hope you'll join us."

"I wouldn't miss it for the world." Jacob shoveled in Martha's gift so that he would not miss a moment of savoring fellowship with the body of believers.

Jacob was surprised by the stillness as he entered the sanctuary. A sense of reverence, as people sat with their heads bowed, replaced the sounds of excited commotion he had heard from his room. The place was packed. Two men were quietly bringing in more chairs to form another row against the back wall. Before he could move in that direction he noticed Herman motioning for him to come his way. Jacob maneuvered to the front row and settled into the seat saved just for him between Herman and Marni. His heart took flight when the hand of the child of God sitting next to him landed on his knee. A look sideways momentarily transported him to another time and place; to a different church, with a different little girl's face looking into his. That day, he let the moment pass unanswered. This day, with all the love he could muster, he placed his hand on top of Marni's.

A tender female voice rose in melodic worship from the midst of still hearts gathered before the throne of God. Jacob was familiar with the song, but had never heard it sung quite like this; with the passionate sincerity of a prayerful heart. Others joined in on the second verse, as the swell of one spirit sharing one purpose overtook the sanctuary.

When the singing stopped Herman stood, turned to face his flock, and began to pray, "Jesus, You died on the cross to pay the debt of our sin so that we would be able to stand in the presence of the Father. We confess our need for Your sacrifice and give thanks for what we do not deserve. You arose from the grave and now sit at the right hand of the Father. You are worthy of our worship and praise. We turn our hearts to You to be shaped and molded by Your Holy Spirit in order to be witnesses to a lost world. Amen"

A time of worship through music and open prayer amongst the congregation followed. Then Herman, with Bible in hand, stepped behind a simply constructed wooden pulpit. "When church gets comfortable, we're not learning. I want us to learn today. That's why my sermon is entitled," he paused to allow a mischievous smile to cross his face, "Washing Feet." The tactic worked. People, including Jacob, began to shift in their seats; attempting to inconspicuously scan the premises for buckets of water and towels. "Don't worry; we're not taking our shoes off." A collective sigh could be heard over an uneasy chuckle.

"Before sharing this message, though, I would like to take a moment to explain who we are as a body of believers to the new faces I see in the crowd tonight."

Jacob wondered how many new people there were for Herman to feel it necessary to interrupt the flow that had been established. *Let the "experience" reel them in. You must have ushers ready to give out welcoming packets. Just have the new people raise their hands and give them the pitch through the material in the packet.*

"We are sinners saved by grace who desire to follow a narrow path according to Matthew 7:14, a verse that tells us the way is narrow and the gate small that leads to life. We believe the Bible is the inspired and infallible word of God and that Jesus Christ is the one and only way of salvation. We gather together to worship the God who by His spoken word created us and through His overwhelming love offered up His only Son to pay the debt of our sin. We study the word of God to equip us to share the gospel of Jesus Christ to a lost world.

"We don't go out of our way to advertise our existence in an effort to draw people to us, but rather we are drawn to a world in need, a world we were once part of. We were liars, adulterers, thieves, gossips, homosexuals. We've been drunks, drug addicts, prostitutes, and murderers. We have been entangled in deceit and enslaved to lustful and prideful hearts... Those are the things we have been. What we are today...is forgiven.

"We are by no means perfect; we struggle in our pursuit of His righteousness. But we are not what we once were. We are new creations in Christ. We have come to know the Truth and that Truth has set us free.

"Whoever you are, you have come to the right place. Not that you have come to us, but that you have joined with us as we come before Christ. If you are a redeemed sinner, a disciple of Jesus Christ, welcome. My hope and prayer is that you will be strengthened in your walk and encouraged to go from this place and minister to those around you. If you are an unredeemed sinner, one who does not know Jesus as your Savior, welcome. My hope and prayer for you is that you will come to know your Redeemer before you leave this place tonight."

Jacob was inwardly ashamed of his mind's regression to tactics employed in his former life. How easy it was to fall back into the "market oriented plan" way of thinking at The Victorious Church. He also now realized he had unknowingly entered this body of saints with an air of pretense, believing he had to hide what he once was, believing he had to pretend he was something he was not; a practice that in the past had become a weekly ritual for Pastor Jacob Hamilton.

"Please turn in your Bibles to the gospel of John, chapter 13. I'm going to begin reading at verse 2. 'And during supper, the devil already having put into the heart of Judas Iscariot, the son of Simon, to betray Him, Jesus, knowing that the Father had given all things into His hands, and that He had come forth from God, and was going back to God, rose from supper, and laid aside His garments; and taking a towel, girded himself about. Then He poured water into a basin, and began to wash the disciples' feet. And to wipe them with the towel with which He was girded.'

"I'm going to share some thoughts with you about these verses, and others that follow. I hope that you will take these thoughts home and chew on them for a while. Sit down with scripture and ask the Holy Spirit to speak to you about what to swallow.

"John begins his narration of this act by filling us in on what Jesus obviously knew. Jesus knew who was sitting at the table with Him - his betrayer. He also knew that the Father had given all things into His hands; that He had come forth from God and was going back to God. He was in the beginning with God; all things came into being through Him and very soon He would be sitting at the right hand of the Father to judge the living and the dead... Of the thirteen men sitting at the table...this is the One who removed his garments, girded Himself with a towel, and knelt before the others as a servant.

"To comprehend the significance of this, we need to understand the background of the act of washing feet. This custom is believed to have come into existence in a sandal clad culture that traveled by foot along dusty roads. A head of a household would offer water to his guests to clean their hot and dirty feet as a gesture of hospitality. If the household retained servants, the lowliest of the servants would wash the feet of the guests.

"It is important to understand that washing someone's feet has never been a job of distinction. Even in the days when the custom was in common use it was considered a task for servants or slaves, never something masters did. And yet here was Jesus; Master of all masters, King of all kings, stripped of His garments, girded with a towel...on His knees washing the feet of men who knew Him to be the Son of God...

"The next section of this narrative deals with Simon Peter and his forceful rejection, followed by his self-indulgent acceptance of the service Jesus rendered. Peter didn't have a clue what Jesus was doing. Jesus Himself told Peter that he would understand later. I believe this section speaks of Christ's service on the cross and is a sermon in itself that we will deal with another time. For now, I want to skip down to verses 12-17.

"And so when He had washed their feet, and taken His garments, and reclined at table again, He said to them, 'Do you know what I have done to you? You call me Teacher and Lord; and you are right; for so I am. If I then, the Lord and Teacher, washed your feet, you also ought to wash one another's feet. For I gave you an example that you also should do as I did to you. Truly, truly, I say to you, a slave is not greater than his master; neither one who is sent greater than the one who sent him. If you know these things, you are blessed to do them.'

"This is where some would bring out the towels and pans of water they had hidden around some corner. But I ask you, how many people here, right now, need to have their feet washed?...

The reality is - washing feet is a lost form of showing hospitality because the need is no longer there. A good host or hostess will always assess the needs of their guests and make every effort to meet them, but the custom of washing feet went by the wayside with the advent of paved roads, and shoes and socks.

"If I pulled out a pan of water and a towel from behind this pulpit and stepped down to wash George's feet there, what would you think?... Would you think, 'What a humble man to kneel down in front of all of us and perform an act like this?'... If I am doing something to demonstrate my humility, you can be assured that my heart is full of pride. And if the one receiving the washing is doing it, not out of need, but out of a show of humbleness...then he is in the same prideful state.

"This action by Jesus had nothing to do with SHOWING humility, even though it takes a humble heart to wait on others and a humble heart to receive from others. It had everything to do with having the heart of a servant. Using His disciples, Jesus was teaching us a spiritual lesson; a servant's heart commands action. He was not establishing a ritual to give us occasion to flaunt our piety.

"What if we renamed this narrative from John? Instead of calling it, 'Jesus Washes the Disciples Feet', we entitle it, 'Jesus Girds Himself as a Servant'. We would no longer be focused on ritualistically performing a custom from another time and another culture. We would become instructed to attend to the needs of those God has set before us in this moment in which we live.

"Jesus expected His disciples to 'get it'. He expected them to serve one another and to teach this principle to the church He was establishing. He expects the same from us. There may be a time when you run across someone who really does need their feet washed, but more likely you will hear that a friend needs a meal cooked, a leaky roof fixed, or a prayer warrior to help them through a difficult time. Jesus wasn't telling us to have water and towel ready by the door, He was telling us to have a heart ready to serve."

Herman looked straight at Jacob and, allowing the gentleness of the Father to speak, continued, "It doesn't matter where you have come from. It doesn't matter how messed up your heart has been. What matters is that you have turned your sin-filled human heart over to the Master and are allowing Him to transform it into a heart ready to serve according to His will."

Herman returned his attention to his flock, "God will not let us sit on the shelf for long. He will move us into areas we can serve Him while He continues to teach us. He will always have work for us to do no matter what stage of the learning process we are in. Don't think you need to graduate from Bible School in order to speak the truth of the gospel. Don't think you have to be a 'mature Christian' before you can minister to your neighbor. All you need is the transformed heart of a servant, derived from being daily bathed in the word of God, and you can gird yourself - kneel down - and serve the mission field God has set before you."

Jacob was seeing deeper into the depth of His Savior's love. *"Thank you, Jesus. Thank you for forgiving me, even though I have worked against Your word. Thank you for calling me to be a servant in Your kingdom."*

A small finger touched Jacob's cheek, catching a tear before it fell. Marni gently ministered child-like-love to a man who had never taken time to receive it in the past. He wondered what his rejection had done to his own little girl. With a smile he thanked Marni for her loving care, then breathed a one word prayer that added a new room in his heart next to the one named Jenny... *"Alicia."*

TRUTH

Chapter

20

Jacob awoke to the sounds of banging chairs. One glance at the clock on his end table told him he had overslept. *How could I not have heard the alarm?* This morning's air was not frigid. The warmth of the room induced a body to sleep. He jumped from bed, quickly dressed, and headed to the restroom; making his way through people who were scurrying around outside his door like ants. Once he was presentable, he set out to find the man in charge.

Herman was in the kitchen. The apron and clear plastic hair covering caused Jacob to question the authority of this man he had come to respect.

"Excuse me, are you the boss?"

"The boss? No. If you want to talk to the boss she's over there giving orders to the other grunts." Herman pointed to the love of his life and the mother of his children.

"I'm sorry I wasn't up when you got here this morning, I was sleeping so soundly I didn't even hear the alarm. What can I do to help?"

"Come on, I'll take you to Fred, he'll put you to work."

Jacob followed the "kitchen grunt" to the sanctuary where eight foot tables had been set up to accommodate over a hundred people, at least that was the calculation that quickly passed through his mind.

"Fred, Jacob here would like to be useful, got anything for him to do?"

"I sure do. Mark is looking for some help to finish his set up. Right this way, Jacob. I'll introduce you to the good doctor."

Doctor Mark Finly stood tall. His muscular arms and fine-tuned physique were obviously a result of many hours in the gym. Once you were on the receiving end of the gentle but firm handshake, though, a warm countenance overshadowed any first impressions of a compulsive body builder.

"Doc, I'd like you to meet Jacob Hamilton. He's just itching to dive in and help."

"I can use it. I'm a little late in getting here this morning, and I know there'll be a line at my table in twenty minutes. Could you come and help me carry some boxes in?"

Jacob followed the powerfully built medical man as he headed out the back door towards a Suburban in the alley, all the while continuing to size up this new boss. *He must be in his seventies, but he's very well preserved. I might not be able to keep up with this guy.* Jacob had already broken into a trot just to stay close to the long fast strides of the good doctor.

"If you'll take those two boxes, I'll take the rest." Jacob struggled to lift the two boxes at the same time, while Doc rose from a squat with four in his arms as though they were empty. *They must be filled with cotton balls.* Jacob tried hard not to pant after he set his boxes in front of Doctor Mark's table.

"There's a white tablecloth in your top box there, Jacob. Would you please take that out and put it on the table."

Jacob noticed that the rest of the box contained fruit. When all six boxes were unpacked the table was heavy-laden with health bars, apples, oranges, grapefruits, and small bags of mini carrots. A box and a half of a variety of medications sat next to the metal folding chair Doc planted himself on.

"My patients don't eat well so I try to encourage them a little by giving them 'gifts'." Doc raised his eyebrows a couple of times to let you know he thought he was pulling one over on them, whoever "them" were.

Jacob was just about to unleash a barrage of questions to see if he could find out what the hours ahead might hold when a woman walking toward him caught his attention. *I know that lady, but how do I know her?... Come on brain, talk to me... Should I know her name?*

"Hello Mr. Hamilton." The woman stretched out her hand in anticipation of receiving a greeting in return, "You don't remember me, do you." A sly smile revealed her knowledge of having one up on her acquaintance. "I'm Susie Johnson. I gave you Pastor Herman's name and phone number at the hospital last week."

"The nurse! Yes, yes, now I remember. I was a bit befuddled that night with a huge headache, so please forgive me for not remembering right away."

"Nothing to forgive, you had a lot on your mind."

"I suppose I did...but now that I've met you again, I want to thank you for helping me. I don't know what I would have done had I not called Herman." Jacob hesitated as his mind began to remember the night in the hospital more clearly. "You seemed a little nervous when you gave me his phone number; I didn't get you in any trouble, did I?"

"No, not at all, I guess you could say I got away with it. We're supposed to be pretty spiritually generic when we deal with patients. I don't know if I would have gotten in trouble or not, but I didn't want to put it to the test."

"I'm thankful that you followed God's leading. There's no question in my mind He worked through you to help me that night."

"Susie, you better get ready, here they come." Doc shifted in his chair as though he was bracing himself for an onslaught of some kind. Jacob didn't have to wonder what was happening for long, before he could move a couple dozen kids bumped their way into forming a line right where he stood. One little boy, about ten years old, looked straight up at Jacob and exclaimed, "I'm sorry mister, I didn't mean to step on your foot." Jacob saw excitement, which he had at first mistaken for rudeness. Once in line, the kids patiently awaited their turn.

Doc peered into ears, noses, mouths, manipulated necks with his fingers, and asked questions; then passed each child off to Susie who handed out fruits and vegetables. She produced tooth paste and tooth brushes from somewhere behind the table, which only certain children received. Jacob noticed the line growing longer, but the new additions were mostly adults. Some young women were holding babies and toddlers.

Jacob felt a firm grip on his left shoulder. "Are you available? I've got another job for you if you're willing." Herman was speaking to his friend, but his attention was held by the scene playing out in front of them. "Doc believes in preventive care. Most of these people never see a doctor unless they get sick. Then they go to Urgent Care, which is usually overburdened. Follow-up care seldom happens. An ounce of prevention is worth a pound of cure, you know...

"We're blessed that Doc is so willing to give his time in this way. He retired ten years ago and spent half of that time doing overseas mission work. Then God laid it on his heart to do mission work right here... We're praying hard for a dentist... Come on, I want to show you something."

The two men walked past the tantalizing smells of coffee brewing, bacon frying, and eggs being scrambled. Jacob was sure he smelled hash-browns and fried onions just before the smell of fresh cut oranges reached his nostrils. Soon they were descending a stairway that Jacob hadn't known existed.

The appetizing aroma of breakfast was quickly swallowed up by the smell of sweaty, filthy clothes. A man in front of them carried a stuffed garbage bag over his shoulder. The stench became so strong that Jacob stopped to allow distance between him and the putrid source. Herman was in a one way conversation with the man, pointing as if giving directions; then waited at the bottom of the stairs for his friend to join him.

"I'm sorry. I hope that wasn't too obvious."

"I'm sure he's used to it... He's new. I haven't seen him here before."

"My goodness, what do you have going on down here?" Jacob scanned the former dime store basement. To the left was a spacious area containing two rows of washers and dryers, at least a dozen of each, as well as tables obviously set up for folding clothes. To the right was a long wall with one opening that divided that part of the basement in half, an apparent hallway into which the putrid smelling man had entered. Above the wall opening hung a sign that simply read "SHOWERS". Smaller signs were affixed to the wall on each side of the opening; to the right, "MEN", and to the left, "WOMEN".

"Last year we realized that one of the needs of homeless people is cleanliness. Many of them want to get back on their feet and to do that they need a job. Most employers don't get past the smell or the filthy clothes of a homeless applicant. Also, Doc pointed out to us that personal hygiene is another form of preventive medicine... Of course, there are some who have chosen to be homeless and would rather panhandle than get a job, but even they appreciate a shower and clean clothes. There are also people who have places to stay, but have no access to washers and dryers other than a laundromat, and that costs money."

Jacob felt shame well up in his chest and confessed, "I'm embarrassed about what I considered ministry, even up to last week." Jacob was admitting his guilt to God as much as he was speaking to Herman. He knew his "ministry" of the past was centered on what he could get from God, not on what he could give to others.

"Oh, Jacob...God has no thought of who you were, only who you are." Placing his arm around his friend's shoulder, Herman pulled Jacob close to his side, "Come on, I want to show you what you can do."

The two men walked over to a table loaded with detergent. "Sally, who usually is here to do this, called saying she got a flat tire on her way in. She'll be here to relieve you in a bit. All you have to do is give instruction to those who need it." Herman ran Jacob through the process, showing him how to use the machines and how much soap to put in per load. "This place will be humming soon. Come upstairs when Sally gets here, and we'll sit down and have breakfast."

Before Herman reached the stairs people were invading the serenity of this underground chamber. Jacob found little need to help anyone with instructions; that is until the man with the putrid smell reappeared from the hallway leading to the showers. Being prompted by the Holy Spirit to get into the trenches, Jacob grabbed a bottle of detergent from the table and headed toward his opportunity for ministry.

"Hello, my name is Jacob," he awkwardly extended his hand as though it was piercing some kind of invisible barrier.

The man stood there and, having both hands occupied with belongings, purposely looked past Jacob to avoid eye contact. Making no effort to receive what was being offered he grunted, "Loner."

Jacob wondered what to do with his hand, its retraction turning out to be as awkward as its extension. "Do you need help with the washing machine?"

Eye contact finally came, conveying a message between two minds. Jacob conceded the stupidity of his question and led Loner to the last available machine. "Throw your clothes in, put one full squirt of detergent into this little compartment, turn the knob to normal, and press this button." *"Lord, if this is ministry, please give me a better attitude."*

Loner let the garbage bag fall to the floor on his left side; his right hand dropped a yet unnoticed duffle bag...right on Jacob's foot. Another message was being sent as Loner stood staring at the washer, *"You can leave now."*

Jacob backed away, looking down as he pulled his foot out from under the bag. His eyes jumped from the bag to Loner, then back down to the bag. *That's my duffle bag!* Ministry was no longer in Jacob's heart. *Is he the guy that hit me? Is he the guy that stole all my things?*

Anger quickly gripped the spirit of the man who, over the past five days, had been shown nothing but kindness, grace, and mercy. Jacob became even more agitated as he watched Loner empty the contents of the bag into the washing machine. *My t-shirts, my jeans, my SOCKS!... Calm down, Jacob, maybe he found the bag after the thief dumped it.*

"Hi Jacob, I'm Sally," the greeting fell on deaf ears. Sally gently placed her hand on Jacob's forearm, "Are you all right, Jacob?" Tension was noticeable on the face of the man she was there to relieve.

"Huh?...oh, yes...yes, I'm fine... I'm sorry" Jacob was so preoccupied with who he considered a thief that he only managed a glance toward Sally. Several thoughts were running through his mind. The first was to confront Loner and make him fess up. The second was to call the police and turn the *"bum"* in. He decided on the third, *I'll head up stairs, have breakfast, and think this through before I do something I'll regret.*

Herman, having seen Sally come in, was ready for his friend. Piping hot scrambled eggs, bacon, and hash-browns smothered in cheddar cheese sat on the table next to a bowl of fruit and a pitcher of orange juice. Marni sat next to her dad, excited to tell Jacob that he was coming with her next.

Jacob nearly stumbled into his chair, still obsessed with the basement encounter. *It's him. It's got to be him.*

The look on Jacob's face attracted Herman's concern, "Something wrong?"

"The guy that robbed me, hit me over the head and robbed me," Jacob raised his eyes to Herman's, "he's in the basement washing MY clothes."

"Are you sure it's him?"

"As sure as I can be. He has my duffle bag and my clothes. I don't know...maybe the thief looked through the bag, didn't find anything worth stealing and left it. Maybe this guy found...I don't know, but he looks the type."

"The type?"

"You know... He looks like he'd be the kind of guy that would hit somebody over the head and steal his things."

Marni looked up from her breakfast, made sure her daddy saw that she swallowed her food, and asked, "Did you tell him Jesus loves Him? If he knew, maybe he would say he was sorry and give you your things back."

Jacob was jolted from his "righteous" anger. The simplicity of Marni's words forced a fourth option to be considered...forgiveness.

"Marni, what was your memory verse for yesterday? Can you say it?"

"'For if you forgive men for their transgressions, your heavenly Father will also forgive you.' Matthew 6:14"

"Thanks honey." Herman sat silent, speaking through his expression, *"You have an opportunity to minister here."*

Jacob received the mental message in the same manner it was given and remained that way while he ate. Marni took Jacob by the hand after breakfast and led him to a room off to the side of the sanctuary. A sign above the door of this sizable area proclaimed; "Permit the children to come to Me".

"This is where the party is!"

Marni was right. There were balloons, hanging crepe paper, Happy Birthday signs, and a large cake sitting on a short table.

"This week it's Jodi's birthday. She's eight!" Marni let go of Jacob's hand and planted herself on a chair by the table. Her already radiant anticipation became brighter with each child that walked into the room.

Before Happy Birthday was sung and the cake cut, eleven children gathered around a shabbily dressed eight-year-old with a dirty face and placed a hand on her head, shoulders, or arms. With bowed heads the children were led in a prayer by a soft-spoken woman in her thirties: "We love You, Jesus, and we know how much You love Jodi. Bless her heart on this special day with knowledge that You have a path for her to walk, one that will lead her to the gate of life. Instill in her a desire to seek after Your righteousness and make known to her the joy of new life only found in You."

Jacob's demeanor was still dulled from his encounter with Loner, but the bitterness in his heart was no match for the infectious joy of eleven children celebrating the life of their friend. By the end of the party a servant's heart had returned to the man who entered the room as a brooding victim.

Later that day, after all the clean up was done and the sanctuary was once again readied for a service of worship and teaching, Jacob sat alone before his Lord. *Jesus, thank you for what You've shown me today,* he thought back on all the different ways people had been ministered to. The sight of people from the flock sitting across the breakfast table with people from the street, talking - sharing - listening, preached to his soul. He lost track of the times he saw Bibles opened and heads bowed over folded hands in the midst of one-on-one encounters.

I saw people's feet getting washed today, Lord, in a dozen different ways... Jesus, I really blew it with Loner. Please give me another opportunity to share Your love with him.

TRUTH

Chapter
21

Monday morning began with another man's-meal at Big Daddy's. Breakfast was billed to be every bit as hearty as the lunch Jacob had enjoyed a few days earlier. This gathering of seven men around a table set for eight had been assembled by Herman for Natasha's move.

"Jacob, let me make some introductions. You already know Fred; he's going to drive the U-Haul, Nate, John, Boxcar Eddy, and Tinny. Nate and John are fairly new to our fellowship, they have young families and have had a hard time finding work, but they're willing to work." Herman's emphasis bore witness to what he knew of their strong work ethic.

"This is the second summer that Boxcar Eddy and Tinny have spent in Duluth, they'll be heading south right after this job. We'll miss them. They've done a number of repairs around the church this year." Herman leaned over to speak into Jacob's ear as though he was going to tell a secret, although he whispered loud enough for those at the table to hear, "They're hobos."

Jacob looked sideways at Herman, then across the table at the two men. "Real hobos?"

"Real as flesh and blood," boasted Tinny in a high raspy voice that didn't seem to care who heard. "We got saved just 'bout the same time as the sky pilot there. We knew the kid in Denver. Couple years ago we heard he started a meetin' place up here so we figured we'd join his flock for the summer months. Glad we did too, he can sure make ya think when he wants to."

Jacob couldn't help but grin. "I didn't know there were still hobos around."

"There's a few of us here and there, although there's kind of a resurgence going on, but they ain't the real articles; bunch of pretenders is all. Boxcar and me, we've been jumpin' cow crates since we was kids."

"You weren't in church this weekend." Jacob was certain that if these two characters had been there he would have noticed them, or at least heard Tinny.

"We headed north last week to do some jammin' with some bluegrass boys. Boxcar here is a mean fiddle player, aaaaaand...I've been known to pick a tune or two on the banjo now and then." Tinny lifted his suspenders with his thumbs and let them go with a look on his face that could easily have been mistaken for pride. "The preacher busted us out of our bags this morning to tell us he had a job waitin' on us. We can always use a few nickel-notes. We'll be doggin' it to warmer weather as soon as we're done."

Jacob was left joyfully speechless. *This is going to be one fun day with these guys.*

Meanwhile Herman kept glancing toward the door, expecting someone else. "I asked Loner on Saturday if he wanted to make some money. He said he did, but maybe he changed his mind."

"Loner? You know him?" It was becoming obvious that Tinny was the spokesman for the pair of hobos.

"Met Saturday for the first time, he showed up to take a shower and wash some clothes. I had to coax him into eating breakfast, he didn't seem very hungry. As a matter of fact, he looked like he wasn't well. I tried to get him to see Doc, but he said no. You guys acquainted with him?"

"We first run into him in Chicagee last spring. I think he padded the hoof to get up here, that's probably why it took him so long. He's a yegg."

"A yegg?" Up to this point it had seemed Herman understood everything Tinny was saying, although Jacob had been lost a number of times, but this term even puzzled the "sky pilot".

"A yegg...a thief."

The revelation served as confirmation to Jacob, but instead of anger boiling up again, a sense of sorrow filled his heart for a man so lost.

"We know first hand, don't we Boxcar. He's proud of it, sees himself as a pro. We spoke the gospel to him in Chicagee, but I think it went in one ear and fell right out the other. I don't think he'll show. He's got easier ways of makin' road-stake."

"Fellas..." Herman gave a nod toward the door. Fourteen eyes brought a halt to Loner's approach. The thief's eyes stared straight into Jacob's until, unexpectedly, they were forced down by a flow of compassion.

"Loner, come and join us," Herman stood; his hand openly gesturing to the unoccupied chair.

Loner began to move forward again, cautiously, now not willing to look anyone in the eye.

Breakfast filled the stomachs of those seated around the table, all except for one that is. The thief refused to even order. Jacob agreed with Herman's assessment from Saturday, Loner did not look well.

The day was blessed with the season's first sign of Indian Summer. Warmth from the morning sun fought off the chill of late fall. Fred headed for the U-Haul with Boxcar and Tinny in tow. Nate and John hurried to their car to stick close to Fred so as not to get lost during the drive to the farm. Loner stood motionless, eyes fixed to the ground.

"Why don't you ride with me, Loner?" Jacob's invitation sounded cheerfully genuine. Loner's hesitation to open the passenger's door to the 1980 blue and white Chevy pick-up truck only heightened Jacob's compassion. "It's OK...you're safe."

Herman leaned with both hands on the driver's door of the pick-up as Jacob rolled down his window. "You guys have a good day. Between the U-Haul and your truck, I'm sure you'll be able to take everything in one trip. Natasha will be waiting for you at the farm. God bless." With a wave from all parties, the small caravan headed north.

Two tongue-tied men inwardly wondered how to begin the conversation already playing out in their heads. Loner finally broke the ice, "Why didn't you call the cops?"

Noise from the truck tires running over the rough street gave way to the comparable quiet sound of driving on new pavement, a moment in time, providing for the softness of a ministering answer, "Because...of who I've been."

"The cops looking for you?" In that instant Loner thought he might be sitting in the presence of a fellow thief instead of the kind of man he hoped Jacob to be.

"No...by worldly standards my thievery was legal, but I'm as guilty as any man who has ever held up a bank at gun point." A glance over at Loner told Jacob the message wasn't getting through. "I convinced people to give me money through deception. I told them things they wanted to hear, then took advantage of their faith in me."

"You're not a thief, you're a con man." The disgust in Loner's voice gave notice that thieves didn't think too highly of con men.

"Sin is sin, one's not any better than the other."

The revelation seemed to penetrate Loner's understanding. Being a thief was apparently acceptable in his mind, but to think himself on the same level as a con man visibly repulsed him.

Jacob decided to probe into Loner's motivation for being there. "If you knew that I knew...why did you show up this morning?"

Silence threatened to drag into the end of the conversation. Finally, in answer to Jacob's prayers, Loner began to open up. "I've got cancer... I saw a doctor in Chicago, there's really no hope... He wanted to do some things, but I saw no reason to. I had a life once... I was married and had a decent job. I managed a C-store in Oklahoma City. We never had time to have kids...my wife dropped dead of a brain aneurysm. Just like that, out of nowhere, she was gone... I started drinking at casinos just to be around people. Then I started gambling. Before I knew it, I was embezzling money from the store to stay ahead of the debt... I ended up spending three years in prison. When I got out I had nowhere to go, so I just lived on the street. Over the past ten years I've learned how to survive, but now...now I don't know how to survive this."

Jacob was shocked at how fast Loner spilled his guts. *Please, Jesus, give me words to say. Give me words that will bring his heart to You.* ... "'For God so loved the world, that He gave His only begotten Son, that whoever believes in Him should not perish, but have eternal life.' John 3:16, the most quoted verse in the Bible, and it's for you, Loner. Just like it was for me last week; after years of living a life of deception, after years of putting myself above all others, after years of being a con man...it was for me. Come to the Giver of Life, tell Him how sorry you are for the things you've done, and receive the gift of salvation and the offer of eternal life. Jesus has paid the price for your sins."

Loner stared at the floorboard of the pick-up truck. Just a week earlier he had hit Jacob over the head and left him a penniless heap on the ground; now this same man was freely telling him about something much more valuable than anything he gained by force, something that Jacob himself only recently found through loss.

Tears came slowly at first as the full gospel, which was shared with Loner by two hobos in "Chicagee", replayed in his mind. Then an uncontrollable flow exposed a vulnerable heart normally hidden from the outside world.

Jacob prayed silently as the spirit of the man next to him collapsed under the weight of sin. Then, the most beautiful sound of new life reached his ears..."Jesus." The thief had been redeemed.

The joy of salvation, so fresh in Jacob's heart, was now shared with the most unlikely of brothers. "Loner, what's your real name?"

... "Daniel."

"Daniel...you belong to the family of God now... You're not a loner anymore."

~

The move took only six hours. The men worked hard and stayed focused on the task at hand. Natasha was grateful and compensated each man beyond their expectations. To John, Nate, and Jacob, she offered employment for the remainder of the week. There were many chores to do around the farm before she would sign it over to the church. One of those chores was to deliver Jess' three "babies" to the buyer in Minneapolis. Selling the cars was bittersweet, especially the '59 Chevrolet. This was the car that Jess had proposed to Natasha in. But the knowledge that the money gained from the sale would provide for the care of human babies that might otherwise not know life outside the womb more than replaced the agony of separation.

Boxcar and Tinny were overjoyed at the news of Daniel's new birth. They were blessed to hear from Daniel himself how their witness to him in Chicago had ultimately led to his salvation. A bond was formed throughout the day, and by nightfall the three were boarding a Greyhound for warmer climate.

Jacob marveled at the handiwork of God as he watched two hobos and a forgiven thief board the bus together. *I may never see these men again. Boxcar and Tinny, what a pair. A week ago I would not have considered men like them to be ministers of the gospel. And yet, here they are, embracing a new babe in Christ, being entrusted by God with the task of discipleship, and promising to stay by Daniel's side as cancer demands more and more from each of them. Their obedience to the call of the Master unearths the stinking roots of what I used to consider ministry. And then there's Daniel, the "type" of man I would not have offered an ounce of grace...before receiving grace from God myself. A man I would not have gotten past the smell of...now...my brother in Christ.*

Lord, keep the scales falling. Give me spiritual sight beyond what my physical eyes can see.

Chapter
22

Friday afternoon capped off a solid week of work. The manual labor at the hobby farm flexed muscles Jacob had forgotten he possessed. Natasha's fair compensation would provide him with the opportunity to pay back the eighty dollars Herman had loaned him when he first arrived, plus buy gas for the truck and pick up a few groceries for meals at the church. But the first thing he decided to do was to return a portion of his wages to the farm. In the past he had never allowed himself or his church to get caught up in the abortion battle, "too controversial", but a skinny-armed little seven-year-old had changed all that.

Jacob anxiously waited for his carpooling buddies to gather their things so they could head back to town. He looked forward to the evening ahead, kicking off with Martha's home-cooked meal before heading to church for the Friday night service. He thought of how blessed he was to be, *Smack dab in the middle of God's will for my life.* He felt completely at home, even though home was the back room of a dime store sanctuary.

~

"So, I heard your week went well. Natasha has been very pleased with the work you guys have been doing for her. Seth, would you please pass the beans."

"We got a lot done, but my heart sure broke for Natasha. She spent most of this afternoon sitting on the porch swing. You could almost see the memories passing through her mind. I think it's going to be hard for her tomorrow morning when we drive away in Jess' cars. I got them ready today for the trip, which put me in his garage for quite a while. Every time I looked out she was staring in my direction... I'm sure she was wishing she could turn back the clock and run to her man and tell him she loved him." Jacob's words spoke of Natasha and Jess, but the heart grieved for the death of another union. He remembered looking back at the woman lost in thought, wondering what would have been, what could have been, had he loved Jenny in the way God designed. *Father, I am so sorry for rejecting the gift You gave me...for choking the life out of the seed You planted in us...*

Martha interrupted Jacob's thoughts, "Natasha does have regrets, she's shared them with us many times, but God had infinite knowledge that Jess would lay down his earthly life to show Natasha the way to eternal life. He has planted that knowledge in the depth of her soul and regrets are dying in the light of such unselfish love. I see in her, more than anyone I know, the reality of eternal life. She doesn't long for yesterday, yesterday is a vapor that dissipates when reached for; she yearns for the everlasting present only found in her Savior. I'm sure Natasha was thinking about Jess as she stared at you in his garage, but I don't think she was wishing he was back with her; she was more likely looking forward to the day when she will be where he is, in the presence of Jesus."

Jacob poked at a pork chop, his mind now preoccupied with the thought of actually being in the presence of Jesus. *If I was there right now, would I want to come back to this?* He looked around the table at the family he had grown to love. *Even this?* He was so grateful for his salvation, but he hadn't really given much thought to eternity, not in a way that would help him understand that this life held no comparison to the joys of Heaven.

Jacob realized for the first time that he himself had been grieving the loss of Jess from the moment he heard of his death, even though he had never met the man. The story had moved him so deeply that he had played out scenarios in his mind that might have produced a better outcome. *There is no better outcome. Jess is where we all want to be, in the very presence of our King, and Natasha has come to know her Savior.* The ache to see Jenny and Alicia come to salvation grew ever stronger.

~

Rolling meadows of the Rivers' Hobby Farm wore a majestic crown of frost as the morning sun peeked through white trees, giving the illusion of diamond bearing branches ripe for the harvest. Jacob shivered. Not even the hooded sweatshirt and winter jacket he had borrowed from Herman could keep the heat from escaping his body. Arrangements had been made with Natasha the night before that would allow Jacob to head out early; meeting up with Nate, John, and Fred at the buyer's house at noon. He thought he should stop by the Victorian mansion to make sure the heat was on as long as he was driving to Minneapolis. The place would have to be sold and he didn't want to contend with frozen water pipes.

Jacob entered the garage and headed for the '59 Chevrolet. He had looked through the restoration pictures of this beauty the morning before. The painstaking work that went into the process of bringing this car from a prior rust-filled state of neglect to its current state of "perfection" bore witness to the love of the master-restorer. He thought of what a great object lesson this car could be in a marriage counseling session.

The heavy garage door opened with a push of a button, the restored car door shut with the sound of solidity. Jacob ran his hands over the top of the steering wheel and then visually examined the interior, not a blemish was to be found. The object lesson of marriage gave way to the transformation of a human soul: once decayed by sin, now sanctified, washed clean by the blood of Jesus, and presented to the Father. Jess had restored this car to the manufacturer's original intent. Jacob couldn't help but smile as he envisioned Jess having been restored from the devastation of the fall of man to perfection by the very hand of his Creator.

The '59 was a present day example of a driver's expectations in days gone by. Long, low, sleek, heavy with a wide stance; the ride it offered felt stable and secure as it hugged the highway. The interior was spacious and the windows provided a panoramic view. Jacob began to notice the looks from people in cars passing by, especially older people. A longing to be transported back to a simpler time spilled from their eyes.

A quiet, still peace seeped into the passenger's compartment, separating Jacob from all that lay beyond. Suddenly, scripture passed through his mind as though it was being read to him. "And do not be conformed to this world, but be transformed by the renewing of your mind, that you may prove what the will of God is, that which is good and acceptable and perfect."

"I know that verse... Why did I think of that now?" Jacob pulled off the freeway at the next exit ramp and reached for his Bible laying next to him on the bench seat, "Where is it, Lord, show me where it is." He flipped pages through Galatians... "No, it's not Galatians. Ephesians?...no... It's one of Paul's letters, I know that much... Some Bible scholar I am. Romans! YES! Here it is, Romans 12:2." He read the verse again and then continued on.

"For through the grace given to me I say to every man among you not to think more highly of himself than he ought to think; but to think so as to have sound judgment, as God has allotted to each a measure of faith. For just as we have many members in one body and all the members do not have the same function, so we, who are many, are one body in Christ, and individually members of one another. And since we have gifts that differ according to the grace given to us, let each exercise them accordingly: if prophecy, according to the proportion of his faith; if service, in his serving; or he who teaches, in his teaching; or he who exhorts, in his exhortation; he who gives, with his liberality; he who leads, with diligence; he who shows mercy, with cheerfulness. Let love be without hypocrisy. Abhor what is evil; cling to what is good. Be devoted to one another in brotherly love; give preference to one another in honor; not lagging behind in diligence, fervent in spirit, serving the Lord; rejoicing in hope, persevering in tribulation, devoted to prayer, contributing to the needs of the saints, practicing hospitality. Bless those who persecute you; bless and curse not. Rejoice with those who rejoice, and weep with those who weep. Be of the same mind toward one another; do not be haughty in mind, but associate with the lowly. Do not be wise in your own estimation."

Jacob let his Bible fall to his lap. The revelation from scripture opened his mind, "You've taught me the truth of this over the last two weeks. Some of it You've allowed me to see in action, other parts You've ground into the fabric of my soul. Oh, Father, why do You love me so much?"

The answer came to Jacob's heart, the Spirit of God bringing understanding. *I'm your church, but You don't want people to see me...You want them to see You, just like I've seen You in Herman and Martha...Marni...in Doctor Mark and Susie Johnson...and in two throwback hobos. I've seen You touch people's lives through gifts You've given others... I've seen Your church like I've never seen it before.*

"Oh, Father, keep changing me; don't allow anything to remain as it was. I know You have work for me to do."

~

The spire topping the two story rounded corner rooms of the Victorian mansion could be seen well before the rest of the house came into view. Jacob's spirit churned as the tentacles of a past life reached out with a devious welcome. He didn't expect to feel so vulnerable. He pulled to the side of the road to pray for God's protection against former lusts that once had a stranglehold on his heart. Even though on guard, a voice penetrated his mind. *Look what you gave up to live in a one-room halfway house. You don't even have a closet because you have nothing to wear. Wait till you lay your eyes on the Mercedes again, you'll wish you had that to drive instead of a rusty old truck with holes in the floorboard.*

"Lord Jesus, I know what You have done to me, and I know why You have done it. I see the destruction of the path I was on. I understand how the pleasures of this world had formed scales over my eyes. I didn't see Your truth because I WANTED to believe the lie. I eagerly sought out worldly possessions and human affirmation. I justified my desires by entangling others in my web of deceit. Philosophies of man strengthened my resolve to say no to Your Holy Spirit.

"Thank you, Lord Jesus, for revealing Your truth to me. Thank you for showing me the foolishness of my arrogance and the wisdom of Your sound judgment. Thank you for opening my eyes to what we as Your church should really look like. Thank you for transforming me from one who has walked in the world to one who yearns to walk in Your will."

Jacob shifted into low gear, gradually let out the clutch, and moved forward into his past. "You have no hold on me. I belong to my King!"

Turning into the driveway cut Jacob's breath short. He hadn't expected to see Jennifer's car. His first thought was to run into the house, find Jenny, and joyously blurt out that he had given his life to Jesus. Satan egged him on with thoughts of conquest, but Jacob would have none of it. He would not walk in his former arrogance; he would walk in the sound judgment of the God he now served. *I've been a pastor almost my entire adult life. I walked in what I thought was ministry with my wife for most of that time, and just now I'm searching for a way to share with her the saving grace of Christ.*

Jesus, I find it ironic that I'm sitting here in Jess' car in the same situation he was in; wondering how to share You with my wife without scaring her off. My life really hasn't been any different than Jess', has it. We both selfishly served worldly gods. I just disguised mine in 'Christianese'. Thank you for Jess' witness of unselfish love. I know there is no time to waste when You have provided an opportunity to share Your gospel. Don't let me get in the way by trying to sell myself as a new man in order to win Jenny back. Keep my heart pure, concerned only for her salvation. Give me the words that will bring her to...or at least plant the seed that will bring her to You.

The back door was unlocked. Jacob stepped into the entryway and closed the door behind him, making more noise than he intended.

"Is that you, Jack? I thought we were going to meet at the restaurant." Jennifer hurried into the kitchen with her attention on the bracelet she was attempting to clasp. When she looked up, the coldness of the Hamilton home-life returned to the mansion. "I didn't think you'd stay away for long. Leave an address so my attorney will know where to serve the papers." She gave up on the bracelet and began to walk past the husband she hated.

"Jenny."

The soft voice used to speak the nickname only Jacob called her had not been heard by this abandoned wife in years. For a fleeting moment, Jennifer's escape plan faltered. Having been stopped in her tracks, she slowly shook her head from side to side,

"No... No...we are not going back there." She turned to face the man who had won her heart in their youth, the man who promised to protect and cherish that heart until "death do they part" only to turn out to be the one person in the world who could shatter it and walk on the broken pieces. "I'll not be a part of your ultra-ego anymore. I'm starting a new life and I don't want you in it. All I want from you is what I can get of the assets." Jennifer drooled over the idea of extracting revenge, "You better get an attorney, or I'll pick you clean."

The venom dripping from Jennifer's voice shook Jacob to his core. Even with all the angry words she had struck him with on the night she left, he had not heard this kind of hate. He prayed for a tone that would convey his heart toward the earthly possessions she threatened to take from him. "I don't want any of it... I only came back here to make sure the heat was on so the pipes wouldn't freeze. If you're going to be living here I won't worry about it. You can have the house and the bank accounts...they mean nothing to me anymore."

The steely stare from the hardened woman searched for the con man. She was long past grasping for hope, long past being willing to forgive. "I don't know what you're up to, but I'm sure you'll come out smelling like a rose. You always do."

Jacob knew there was no sense in trying to force a conversation. He wrote down Herman's name, phone number, and home address on the scratchpad by the kitchen phone, "I'm staying in Duluth. You can reach me through this man... Jenny," he prayed under his breath that the next words out of his mouth would begin to crack the wall he had forced her to build to guarantee her own survival. "I've asked Jesus into my life. He's shown me how wrong I've been about everything... I'm so sorry for what I've done to you and Alicia. There are things in my heart that I want to pour out to both of you, but I can't blame you if you don't want to listen. Now that I know you're here, I'll write you a letter...then you can decide whether or not you will hear what Jesus has done to me. Even if you decide not to read it, will you please pass it on to Alicia?"

Jennifer continued to stare, but this stare seemed to question rather than judge. Jacob realized a verbal response would not be coming so he dropped his head and left his wife in the care of his loving Lord.

Thank you, Jesus, for her silence...she didn't say no to the letter.

~

Jacob awoke at seven; showered, shaved, dressed, and then returned to his room to pray for Jenny and Alicia. He prayed that the hunger for God's truth that had exposed the emptiness in his own life would seize the spirits of his wife and daughter. He fell face down on the floor with arms stretched out, *Father, I need Your strength in order to remain steadfast in my prayers for Jenny and Alicia. Cause the ache in my soul for their salvation to be agonizingly sharp so that it forces me to my knees daily.*

Jacob was grateful as he joined others for the early Sunday morning service, grateful that God had provided the opportunity to make contact with Jenny. He now prayed for an opportunity to do the same with Alicia.

In stillness, amongst fellow believers sitting before the throne of God, Jacob began to recognize the call God was placing on his life. *I was so lost, Lord. I became lost because I was willing to abandon Your word in exchange for my pleasures. Two weeks ago I walked away from a lie in search of Your truth. What I found was the Creator of all things, the King of all kings, the Lord of all lords, and the Savior of my soul... You simply want me to shout that from the mountaintops...* Jacob smiled at the thought of how simplistic the call of God really is; *receive His truth and tell everyone you know.*

I can grasp the simplicity of the call, Lord...but walking in it is another matter. You've shown me what it takes; diligent attention to Your word, perseverance in trials, a heart of a servant, hope, love, devotion to prayer...but I'm weak, Lord, I'm so weak. Please continue to teach me, I know I'll gain strength through Your knowledge.

A small hand squirmed its way under Jacob's in search of a squeeze. He followed the skinny little arm upward until his eyes rested on the toothless grin of the seven-year-old seated next to him. *Give me a heart like hers, Lord Jesus, and please...put me in the trenches.*

~

Monday's icy temperatures caused Jacob's truck to moan in its struggle to rouse from slumber. The crisp late morning air had a different affect on the man behind the wheel; it awakened a desire to know what would come next. Anxious to enter into real ministry, Jacob almost begged God to use him. His spirit settled some as he waited for the defroster to clear the windshield. The peek-holes at the bottom of the glass gradually grew larger, revealing more and more of the world before him. Understanding came with every inch of receding frost. *You're right, Lord, I have to be patient. I can't walk in Your will if I venture out blindly.*

Jacob's day had been planned out the night before. His morning had been spent cleaning the church, followed by an early lunch from the kitchen before heading to the Women's Center. The afternoon would be consumed by a four-hour prayer vigil he had committed to at Martha's urging. He was not at all hesitant to stand against the atrocity of abortion, God had set his heart straight on that issue, but making such a visible public stand would be a stretching experience for this former pastor who had avoided controversy at all cost.

Jacob's spirit was drenched in an unfamiliar heaviness; Alicia had been on his mind all morning. Not even his fervent prayers while on his knees cleaning the toilets eased the load. Something was wrong and he prayed that God would allow him to minister to his daughter.

The drive to the Women's Center took eight minutes, not long enough to settle the nervousness in Jacob's stomach. He ignored a parking spot directly across the street from the Center to have the opportunity to drive around the block one more time. *Give me strength this morning, Jesus. Strange how I can preach in front of thousands of people in an auditorium, and now I'm afraid to stand in silent prayer on the street.*

Two men and three women were already huddled together; there were no signs, no outward appearances of their purpose. Some people who passed by glanced with curiosity, others ignored the group altogether. One or two people stopped and conversed with whoever lifted their head to respond to the inquisition. Jacob knew he couldn't sit in his truck forever, "OK, Lord, here I go. Take my mind off of me and put it on the moms walking into that building."

Real ministry was uncomfortable at first; Jacob's palms were sweaty inside his gloves, but once his focus changed his prayers became specific. He was no longer the center of his own attention as his heart began to drink in the reality of what was going on behind the walls he faced. This was abortion day, the women and young girls walking in today had already made their appointments.

A solid hour of prayer passed quickly. Alicia once again weighed heavily on Jacob's mind. His eyes, opened by the Spirit of God, lifted slowly toward the Women's Center as fear plunged like a dagger into his heart. The daughter that he had longed to see, the one that he had begged God for another opportunity to be a father to, the baby he had "aborted" on the day of her birth, gingerly emerged from the building.

Alicia's eyes met the eyes of her father and spoke in agony of what she had done. The one person in the world she didn't want to know was standing twenty feet away, staring into her soul.

Jacob slipped his hands from the grasp of the others, stepped from the prayer circle, and began a walk that seemed in slow motion. The desire to hold his little girl close overwhelmed him. *Father, speak to her. Let her know I love her.* Finally, he stood face to face with a scared young woman frantic to escape, but forced to surrender by the inability to run. In silence he reached out and gathered into his arms a rigid body, limbs pressed tightly against each side. With a tender touch, Jacob invited his daughter to rest her head on his shoulder.

The unfamiliar but long desired warmth of her father's embrace began to slowly melt Alicia's frozen spirit. Lost, and abandoned by all she thought would save her, she now found herself in the place her search for acceptance had begun; the very place she had wanted to be for as long as she could remember.

Life's experiences caused Alicia to fight hard against the hunger for belief. *I can't trust you. You don't love me. You only want to use me again.* Jacob's arms squeezed tighter as Alicia's head fell deeper into his shoulder. He began to feel the warmth of her tears on his bare neck as he tenderly cradled the back of her head with his hand. *Father, show her Your love. Open her heart to Your truth. Teach me how to minister to her. Lord, make me the father I should have been so many years ago.*

Words began to form in Alicia's mind; words that, in the past, she had wanted to scream out. *Say them. SAY THEM!... He doesn't want to hear them. He doesn't want to be bothered.* The battle raged until the foreboding emptiness in her soul forced them to the surface in a desperate cry, "Help me, daddy. Please help me."

Part III
Restored

Chapter

23

Her nightmare showed no fear of morning's light as a silent scream lingered long after she awoke. Alicia had never felt so cold. Her hand slowly slid across her belly; the "problem" was gone.

Life out from under the legalistic canopy of her father's tent had been intoxicating; drugs - alcohol - sex all provided opportunities for self expression while knowledge gained from intellectual minds who proclaimed God's death settled into the void of His forced absence. A four year war, waged to gain freedom, had been won... *But if this is freedom, why do I feel so enslaved?*

Alicia had traveled north in order to discretely discard a troublesome embryo, after which she fully intended to drive back to Minneapolis and pick up life where it had left off. The last thing she expected was to come face to face with her father praying in front of the abortion clinic. *What made me fall into his arms? Why did I spend the night?* The thought that her dad just might love her after all, passed through her mind. *Oh, daddy, I need some time to think. If you see who I've become you'll reject me all over again.* Alicia got dressed, took a scrap of paper and a pen from her purse, and sat down to write:

> Dad, I'm not ready. Please forgive me for
> running off. I'll let you know where I am
> when I get myself together.
> Alicia

She quietly closed the door of the halfway house, tiptoed past her father who was sleeping on the dime-store sanctuary floor, and slipped once more into hiding.

~

Six months had passed since Jacob's encounter with Alicia. His daughter's silence caused time to drag on, but the winter had not been wasted. Jacob helped with the conversion of the River's Hobby Farm into "Jess' Child"; the name chosen by Natasha to honor her late husband and their aborted baby. The elders who oversaw the fledgling ministry had offered Jacob an opportunity for fulltime employment. Pastor Herman encouraged his friend to accept the job, "It will provide stability while God continues to strengthen you for what lies ahead." Jacob hadn't needed much encouragement; he was not ready to leave the safe harbor God had provided for him. Herman's family had become his family, and the people at Duluth Christian Fellowship had become his brothers and sisters in Christ.

Jess' nostalgic garage was converted into a caretaker's apartment, and Jacob moved what few possessions he had from the halfway house to his new home. He quickly became a father figure to girls who had never known a father's love. The irony weighed heavy on his heart; *Lord, if I could only show this love to Alicia.*

Jennifer was also never far from Jacob's mind. He continually prayed for her salvation with an ache as strong as the first day God had placed it in his heart. He considered himself "more married" today than in all the years he had lived with Jenny; finally understanding how to love his wife through Christ. He'd written and sent the promised letter, but had received no reply.

~

Jacob's morning began in Natasha's garden where yellow daffodils had emerged from winter's cold grip. He stared at a tulip begging to burst; a sliver of red hinting at the beauty to come. Lost in thought, his friend's approach went unnoticed.

"Morning, Jacob."

"Oh...good morning, Herman; you kind of snuck up on me there."

"I didn't mean to. You seemed a bit enamored by that tulip."

"I guess I was. I am more and more astounded every day by the beauty of God's creation... What brings you out here this morning?"

"A couple things...and this is one of them." Herman held up a letter. "I didn't see yesterday's mail until this morning. I was a little excited when I saw a hand addressed letter. I haven't received a personal letter from someone in a long time; e-mail you know. I got even more excited when I saw that it wasn't addressed to me... It's from Alicia."

"Alicia?" Jacob jumped up from the garden bench and snatched the letter from Herman's hand. "I'm sorry. I didn't mean to be rude, but…"

"I know. I'll leave you alone for a while. I'll be in the house. I'm driving Shelly and her baby to their new apartment. Would you be willing to come with? I can bring you back; Natasha and I are going to sit down with Aria later this morning."

"Sure, let me know when you're ready to leave."

Herman slipped his hands in his pockets, turned and looked at the old farm house. With a shake of his head and a smile directed at the handiwork of God, he said, "I don't think Natasha ever had in mind becoming a mom to seven girls and grandma to seven babies when she offered this place for ministry."

Natasha had been a reluctant recruit in the very ministry she birthed. Giving God the farm and bank account came easy, but when He asked for her hands and heart she drew back. *"Not me, God…please, not me. How can You trust me to hold a baby in my arms when I've worked my entire adult life to kill them? Oh, Jesus…how can I hold them close and look into their eyes?"*

Herman gave a light knock on the old wooden screen door, a door Natasha insisted remain during renovation. "Jess loved the sound of this door slamming shut," she had said. "To him it was the most welcoming sound an old farm house could have."

"Come in Pastor, I'm just heating some milk for little Jamie. I get to feed her this morning before they head out. I'm going to miss that little girl."

"I doubt that, she and her mom will be living in town two blocks from your house. I bet they'll be over for tea before they're even settled."

"Maybe you're right. They're still going to need support, and I know just the 'grandma' that will give it to them."

"I brought the apartment lease that Shelly needs to sign; will they be ready to leave soon?"

"Right after Jamie's fed. I stayed here last night to help Shelly get things together. She's a wonderful mom." Tears began to well up in Natasha's eyes.

"Are you OK?"

Herman's gentle tone caused Natasha to pause and drop her head. Nodding, she answered, "Yes...but I find myself crying a lot."

"Something we can pray about?"

"No, they're good tears. I look around this place and see playpens where my most valued antiques used to be; toys cover the floor of Jess' den. I thought my life was over when Jess died... I cry because I can't figure out why God would take someone like me and..." Tears now trickled down her cheek. "My life is so full. I don't deserve one ounce of the grace God has shown me. My tears are tears of gratefulness. I don't want them to ever stop flowing..."

Shelly's entrance interrupted the tender moment with delightful anticipation. "Where do you want me to sign, Pastor?"

Herman placed the signed document under his arm, grabbed two suitcases and headed to his van. He tried to read the look on Jacob's face as they convened at the back of the vehicle.

"She wants to see me. She's invited me to come and stay for the weekend."

"That's great news!"

Jacob didn't look like he had received great news, even though it was what he had longed for. "How am I going to tell her about Jesus?... She knows what a con man I've been. How can I expect her to believe anything I say?... I have no credibility."

"It's not your credibility that will bear witness to Alicia. What will witness to her is the life changing power of the Holy Spirit, made evident in the new creation her dad has become. Don't jump ahead of the Spirit of God; wait on Him for the words to speak."

Chapter

24

The old Chevy pick-up truck was dependable, but it didn't offer much in the line of comfort. Jacob was glad the trip to Minneapolis would only take two and a half hours. The constant bang of the hard tires against the patched pavement was beginning to get to him. *I should probably fix that hole in the floorboard, maybe this old buggy would quiet down some.*

Jacob's mind drifted back to the three days of prayer which prompted his heart to be patient. *Listen to her. Don't lay your expectations on her. Don't tell her what you want her to do or be. Hear her out so you know how to pray for her.* He counted on God's strength to overcome his propensity for control. His mind drifted back further to counseling sessions with Herman. *Lord, he knew when to be silent and when to speak Your truth. Please grant me that sensitivity during my time with Alicia.*

Arrangements had been made to meet at "The Malt Shop" for supper. A twelve year old heart had once been shattered at this very restaurant by a father who had no appetite for nurturing. Alicia returned many times in later years with other male figures in an attempt to reclaim the pieces that had been left on the floor.

"Hi dad", Alicia greeted her father at the door with a cautious hope the environment would jog a memory. "They have great burgers and malts here, and I know how you love a good malt."

"It's so good to see you, Alicia." Jacob slipped an arm around his daughter's shoulders and gave a squeeze. "How are you doing?"

"Great, dad, really great; I've got a lot to tell you." Alicia seemed over bubbly, even to herself. *Get it together, Alicia, don't let your nerves project a façade. Be real with him.*

"Hi, just the two of you?"

"Yes." Jacob immersed himself in blissful thought. *Yes, just the two of us, me and my daughter.*

"Can we sit over there?" Alicia pointed to the familiar table, grateful that it was available.

The two of them chatted between bites of burgers and sips of malts. Alicia was bursting inside to share the news with her dad that she was sure would change their relationship forever. *How do I start? Do I just blurt it out?* "Dad..."

The awkward pause worried Jacob. *Is she going to tell me something I don't want to hear? Is she getting married? Is she moving away?*

"...I want you to come someplace with me tomorrow night. Would you be willing to do that?"

"Well...sure, where are we going?"

"To church."

Jacob's spirit did a back-flip. *Did she say church, Lord?* "Church? You've been going to church?"

"Yes... I know while in college I said I didn't believe in God, but things have changed. I look at things so differently now." Alicia thought back on the lies she had swallowed; the discovery that God was manmade - that there was no truth - the euphoria of believing she had the right to do whatever felt good. She didn't think about the abortion, though, at least she would not admit she was thinking about the abortion.

"How did it happen? How did your thinking change?" Jacob hungered to hear from his daughter's lips that the Holy Spirit had transformed her heart.

"Some friends invited me to come to church with them. I don't know what made me go really, but I'm very glad I did. It's different, but I enjoy it so much. I've never felt so...so accepted in my life. I actually look forward to being there. We meet on Saturday evenings, but I have to warn you that sometimes the service goes on for hours."

Jacob was aware his expression betrayed his attempt to hide the concern welling up inside; there was no mention of Jesus, repentance, or salvation. *Jesus, please keep me from saying anything that will begin building a new wall between us.* "Sounds exciting." He knew the subject had to change before he began asking questions he was sure she would not want to answer.

Jacob's mind slipped the bonds of time; all of a sudden Alicia didn't look so grown up. "You might not remember, but we've been here before. I took you here when you were twelve. I wish I could say it was my idea, but it wasn't. Your mom saw how detached I was... I was not a good father to you. I lived a self-centered life. I'm not only sorry for not being the father I should have been...I'm ashamed... I also never allowed you to be my daughter. When I think of how lonely you must have been..."

Alicia was caught off guard. Even though these were words she longed to hear, she never expected them to flow from her dad so freely. *What has happened to him?*

"I've prayed and prayed that God would allow me to correct mistakes I've made... I didn't like the answer I got." Jacob reached across the table with an open hand. Slowly, Alicia's hand disappeared within his tender grasp. "As much as I would love for us to go back to that night...when we sat at this very table...when I turned away from my little girl's eyes as they searched for a way into my heart...we can't. I can't undo what's been done. I can't correct the mistakes I've made. I can only ask you to forgive me and pray that you will allow me to be a part of your life from this time forward."

Tears ran down both cheeks as Alicia turned her head and looked at the floor. She marveled as she witnessed the pieces of her twelve year old heart defy gravity. *My daddy does love me... He does!*

~

Como Park Conservatory was on Alicia's docket for Saturday morning. The Victorian style glass greenhouse, where a weary soul could bathe in the restful scents of floral balm no matter what the season, had become a favorite hideaway. This morning the beautiful surroundings would be employed for a different purpose. Alicia did desire to spend time with her dad, but a hunger for acceptance overpowered the need for complete honesty in the bond she hoped to form. She was certain that once they were in church her father's questions would be answered. An afternoon walk on the shores of Lake Harriet would successfully accomplish her goal of killing time.

~

Church began at 7 p.m., at least that's what the sign said. 7:20 produced no hints the gathering was anywhere near ready to come together as one body. Several lines had formed in front of a well equipped coffee-bar. Many people had already purchased their brew and took seats on one of the numerous couches, wing back chairs, recliners, and even bean bags. The scene reminded Jacob of a gigantic family-room in someone's basement. *Could this be the sanctuary?*

Jacob scanned the room to see if he could notice anyone who might appear to be the pastor. His spirit became agitated when he noticed a young lady sitting on the floor, legs crossed, eyes closed, open palmed hands slightly raised; *Yoga? Oh Father, what has Alicia stumbled into?*

A swivel stool occupied a place in the center of the room. A man wearing jeans and a t-shirt, declaring "Love Like Jesus", excused himself from a conversation in order to take up residence on the pedestal. "Welcome. You are all welcome. This is a place of acceptance. Whatever stage you are at in your spiritual journey, you fit in here because we are all emerging. We invite you to join in on the conversation of life. We want to hear what your vision for life is and what your dreams are. We are a community of people who love God in the way of Jesus…"

Jacob's spirit was grieved. *This is not good, Lord. I don't know what this is all about, but the spirit of this place is grating against my spirit.* He turned his head to look at Alicia, praying she wouldn't see the despair of his heart. Her full focus was on the facilitator, for he had now invited others to join in on this "emerging conversation".

The service meandered on for more than three hours with emphasis on building community. Jacob surmised this was being accomplished through the offers of inner healing, spiritual cleansing, or walking the outdoor labyrinth. The name of Jesus had been invoked many times throughout the service as an example of how to live and love; no mention of the cross or resurrection. Finding ways to come together on common ground while embracing differences, in order to build the global church, was a favorite topic of discussion.

The drive back to Alicia's apartment was awkward. The last thing Jacob wanted to do was damage this fragile new relationship with his daughter. *Be careful, Jacob, don't say anything that will hinder the work of the Holy Spirit.*

"Wasn't it great, dad? I feel so much peace in that place. I rejected God most of my life. I never knew how much He loved EVERYBODY."

Jacob discerned a shallow understanding of God's love. "He loves us so much that He sent His son to die for us." The declaration went unanswered.

"I'm glad you came tonight... Are you going to stay in Duluth or will you come back to the Cities?"

Jacob pondered the question. Was she saying she would like to have him closer? "I...I don't think I'll be in Duluth forever... Right now God has placed me in the care of some people who have been very helpful in showing me how wrong I've been. More importantly, He's used them to show me where His truth is found. I've fallen in love with His word."

Alicia sat silent. She had never known her dad to admit he was wrong on anything. Now, twice in the last twenty-four hours he has confessed to being wrong. Alicia threw out a question drenched in hope, "Are you going to try and see mom?"

Jacob's heart sank. The separation from his wife was the fruit of his own sin. "I want to see her... I've written her a letter, but I've not heard from her."

Neither spoke for the rest of the drive home. Jacob parked his truck in front of Alicia's apartment, turned off the ignition, and twisted in his seat so that he could face his daughter. "Alicia... what has happened between your mom and me has been mostly my fault. Please know that I will never again abandon her. My heart is hers. No matter what happens, no matter where she is at, I will honor the covenant of marriage I entered into with her. She is my wife, and I will be true to her and will pray for her for as long as we both live."

Alicia looked at her father to see if the con man had returned. What she saw instead was a man making a promise birthed from a spirit of brokenness. *You're for real, aren't you, dad. Something has happened to you that I don't understand...but I want to.*

~

Jacob was unaware of seeds planted over the weekend. His hope had included a miraculous moment in which the Holy Spirit would open Alicia's eyes to His truth. Instead, he felt she appeared to have begun walking down a path that may be just as dangerous as rejecting God outright. *What is this emerging conversation all about, Lord? Where did it come from? It sure seems to have Alicia's attention.*

Chapter

25

Each day without divorce papers was an encouragement to Jacob. Jennifer had not responded to his letter in writing, but he was praying that her silence was a response in another form. *Lord, I begin this day by asking You to draw Jenny to Your truth. As much as I desire to restore our marriage, I know the most important thing is for Jenny to be restored to You. I place her in the care and love of Your Holy Spirit.*

~

"Good Morning, Herman."

"Good Morning, Jacob. How was your weekend?"

"Confusing." Herman's office had become an open invitation for conversation with his trusted friend. "Alicia took me to church, but it was like no church I've ever been to. Do you know anything about the emerging conversation?"

"I've heard of it, but haven't spent any time checking it out. Actually, I haven't found the time to check it out. Is Alicia involved in it?"

"I don't know if I'd call it involved...it's more like she's taken in."

Herman placed his pen in his notebook, closed the pages, and moved it off to the side of his desk, "Concern is written all over your face, brother."

"I am concerned... When she first invited me to come to church with her I just about jumped out of my chair. Not long into our conversation, though...well...something just didn't seem right. When I was at the church it was even worse. I can't put my finger on it, but something's just not right. Everything was casual, you know, coffee-bar, dress; and then they met in a big open room filled with couches and recliners. My first thought was 'Seeker-Friendly'. Shoot, I know about Seeker-Friendly. I used a lot of that movement's market-oriented-methods at my church. But this goes beyond that somehow. It almost felt like there was a sinister undercurrent of some sort."

"A spiritual battle going on maybe?"

"Maybe... There was a girl there doing Yoga and they had a labyrinth outside. I've not seen those things in a church before. But what irritated my spirit the most was the 'conversation'. It was loving and condemning at the same time. They talked a lot about caring for people and accepting people for who they were. Then in the next breath they talked about people who are close-minded to this kind of conversation; they weren't very loving in their thoughts about them."

"What do you need?"

Jacob knew the question was all-encompassing and it blessed him to his core. "I need some time on your computer. I want to do some research on this emerging conversation to know what I'm dealing with."

"You got it. You can have some right now if you want. I'll be making hospital visits and then running up to the county jail. My office is yours until I get back."

"Thanks, Herman, I'm really anxious to check this out."

~

Herman's absence provided four solid hours of research. He found Jacob submerged in notes upon his return. "So what did you find?" Herman sat down in the chair usually occupied by Jacob in their meetings, spiritually delighted in the obvious role reversal.

Jacob turned away from the computer screen and leaned back in the pastor's chair. An ominous tone drenched his reply, "I found the sweet venom of love."

"The what?"

"To one who doesn't know the truth of God's word, this stuff sounds pretty good." Jacob exhaled, then with a slight shake of his head drew a breath and confessed a past tactic. "I depended on the scriptural ignorance of my flock. It's easy to manipulate an unguarded mind. This church is depending on that same ignorance to sell their perverted definition of Christianity..."

Herman waited patiently, knowing Jacob was sorting his thoughts as he spoke.

"I never preached the true gospel. The true gospel tells of the 'fall' and points out our sin so that we understand our need for the Savior. A generic gospel was much more acceptable. My gospel was that God loves us so much that He wants us to be happy and to have every 'good' thing. This church's gospel is that God shows His love through tolerance. They put a premium on affirming people where they're at in their 'journey'. They would rather learn from each other's differences than from the word of God."

"What about the emerging conversation, did you learn anything about that?"

"They just...talk. Everybody has different ideas and they get together...and talk; in churches, bars, on blogs, wherever. The conversation is mostly about what the church should be versus what it is. Embracing the mystery of God seems to take precedence over obtaining any knowledge of God. It's as if they're aware that Biblical truth will result in division so they question everything. The desire for unity trumps the desire for truth...

"You know, reading through this stuff, I could almost see the serpent slithering his way in and out of their conversations, spewing his 'sweet venom of love'. They call it accepting each other's differences in order to build community, but it's really an unwillingness to stand on God's word."

"You're worried about Alicia."

"Yes... In college she was set free when she learned that God was dead, now she's set free by a god who's tolerant of who you are. Nothing has changed...except where she's searching."

~

Jacob stood outside of his caretaker's apartment and watched the sun slowly sink beneath the horizon; blackness now hid the distinction of his surroundings. *It's easier to believe what we want in the dark, isn't it Lord. If we don't let Your light expose the truth we can justify anything, believe anything, make up anything.* With a heavy heart he thought on 2 Timothy 4:3, *For a time will come when they will not endure sound doctrine; but wanting to have their ears tickled, they will accumulate for themselves teachers in accordance to their own desires...*

Oh, Jesus, Alicia is trying to find a god who fits into her thinking. She's not looking for truth; she's looking for acceptance.

Show her how empty her desires are. Jacob understood the deep ache of emptiness and the desire for anything to take it away. He had grabbed at a number of different answers to life before he sought out God's truth. His search had been done in secret, not wanting the sheep of his fold to know how lost their shepherd was. In the end, he understood that only surrender would lead to victory.

TRUTH

Chapter
26

Jennifer grimaced. What she believed were broken ribs almost caused her to forget about her beaten and swollen face. Jack had not turned out to be the man who could fill her emptiness. She carefully inched her way to the side of the bed and sat up. She looked around and thought about how this room had once been a place of escape...now it was a prison. There were no bars on the windows and no lock on the door, her confinement was a result of what she could not find outside the walls; a reason to live.

Jack was gone, moved on to his next prey. He had entered Jennifer's life in one of her moments of weakness, recognizing her willingness to explore beyond the bonds of a broken marriage. He was patient in his hunt, following the scent of a wandering heart, knowing it would be hungry for empathy.

Jennifer was more than willing to fall into the arms of a man with a blank slate. She didn't want to know who he was; he listened, he cared, and that's all that mattered. Now the game had been played; the hunter had his trophy, and the hunted...*might as well be dead.*

~

Jacob smiled at little Charlie. The infant's grasp was beginning to make his finger go to sleep. "I suppose you'll want to throw a ball around later this morning, huh?" Charlie just stared. "Well, maybe we'll teach you to walk first." Jacob's love for children was fully awakened in this new life. He freely provided his services to baby-sit for any of the moms who needed a break. There were times when he found himself pushing a three seated stroller filled to capacity; a bag stuffed with juice bottles, diapers, and baby wipes hanging from the handle.

"Jacob!" Natasha shouted with alarm out the back door of the farmhouse. "Jacob, Alicia's on the phone!" Her voice instilled fear in Jacob's heart.

"What is it? What's wrong?"

Natasha grabbed Charlie from Jacob's arms and handed him the phone. "I don't know, but she's hysterical!"

"Alicia... Alicia... Calm down, honey! Please tell me what's wrong."

"It's mom!" Alicia screamed between convulsions. "I...I think she's dead!"

"Wh...what...where are you!"

"I'm at the house." Sobs were interrupting every word. "She's on the floor in a pool of blood. Oh Daddy!... There's a gun on the floor!"

Jacob fell to his knees and began to pray, "Jesus, please don't let her be dead!"

Charlie began to scream, frightened by Jacob's reaction. Natasha dropped to her knees next to Jacob, put her free arm around his shoulder, and prayed. There was no need for Jacob to tell her what was happening; she could hear Alicia's frantic voice.

"Did you call an ambulance?"

"YES! BUT I DON'T KNOW IF SHE'S BREATHING!"

Jennifer was laying face down. Alicia was too scared to touch her mom. "I can hear the sirens, dad! They must be coming!"

"OK, go down stairs and show them the way. Stay on the phone with me! Don't hang up!" Jacob could hear his daughter running down the hardwood floor hallway and then down the stairs. The arrival of the paramedics did nothing to calm his fears.

"There're policemen here too, dad!"

The bedroom was now full of activity. The paramedics worked at a hurried pace. "I have a pulse."

"SHE'S ALIVE, DAD!"

"Thank you, Jesus! Thank you, Jesus!"

Natasha jumped from her knees and grabbed her car keys from the hook by the back door. "Here, take my car and get down there, and here's my cell phone so you can stay in touch with Alicia." Jacob hesitated as Natasha forced the keys and phone into his hand. "Go!... GO!"

~

The drive to the Cities had been agonizing. Jacob was thankful for a full tank of gas so he didn't have to stop. He called Herman between conversations with Alicia to let him know what was happening, but Herman already knew and was not far behind in his van.

Alicia dropped into her dad's arms when he arrived in the waiting room, her body trembling with fear. Her face felt hot and wet against his neck.

"I'm here, honey. I'm here."

"Daddy, I couldn't help her... I didn't know what to do."

"You did the right thing, honey. You got help. That was the right thing to do."

"When they turned her over...she looked so bad. Her face was all beat up, and her chest was full of blood. I don't know what happened to her. Somebody must have done this to her." Alicia broke down again and Jacob held his daughter tightly.

Blood all over her chest? Jacob hadn't dared ask Alicia on the phone where Jennifer had been shot. He assumed it was a head wound, a suicide attempt. Now wasn't the time to ask questions. He would wait until he could talk to the doctor or the police.

"Jacob, I got here as fast as I could."

"You didn't have to come, Herman, but, man, I sure am glad you did. This is Alicia."

"Hello, Alicia. I've been praying for all three of you. Do you know anything yet?"

"All I know is that she's in surgery." Jacob's eyes suddenly looked past Herman and focused on the face of a man in scrubs walking his way. He tried, but was unable to read the expression looking back at him.

"Mr. Hamilton?"

"Yes?" Jacob's reply begged to know if Jennifer was alive.

"And are you Alicia?"

"Yes. Please, please tell me my mom's alive."

The doctor gave a reassuring half smile and nodded his head, "She's alive. I'm doctor Capple. I'm the surgeon who did the operation. Please come with me."

Four people entered the small conference room. "Doctor, this is my pastor, Herman Groves."

"Hello, Pastor Groves." Dr. Capple looked at Alicia, "Your mom," then at Jacob, "and your wife is going to be OK. The bullet took a path that miraculously did very little damage. It missed the major arteries and bypassed the lung and heart. The gun was a small caliber pistol which was a good thing. If it had been any other gun...the outcome might have been very different."

Jacob immediately thought of his .22 caliber pistol he kept in the desk drawer in his office.

The door to the conference room opened and a police officer stepped in. Doctor Capple glanced up and then continued, "Mr. Hamilton, your wife's face showed signs of a beating. She also has three broken ribs. Do you know anything about this?"

Jacob's stomach began to churn. The thought of someone hitting Jenny sickened him. He looked at Alicia as she bent over in the chair holding her midsection. She began to cry uncontrollably, "Who would do this? WHO?"

"I don't know anything. We're separated, and I've been living in Duluth. I rushed down here as soon as Alicia called me." Jacob turned to the police officer, "What do you know? Did somebody try to kill her?"

"The shooting has every sign of an attempted suicide."

Alicia screamed, "NO! NO! I DON"T WANT TO HEAR THIS!"

Herman put his arm under Alicia's, "Let's go out to the waiting room and let your dad talk to the officer." Alicia put up no resistance.

When the door shut, Jacob turned his attention back to the officer, "If she was beaten by someone, why do you think she wasn't shot by someone?"

Dr. Capple explained, "The injuries to her face and ribs are at least two days old. She was shot this morning."

"Mr. Hamilton, can you confirm your whereabouts the last three days?" Suspicion did not seem to be in the officer's voice, but the question stirred an uneasy feeling deep inside Jacob.

"I was in Duluth working, and yes, I can prove my whereabouts."

"Was your wife in a relationship with someone else?"

This question hit Jacob harder than the first. He knew his failure to be the husband Jenny needed had helped to drive her to this moment. Tears began to run down his cheeks, "Yes...she left me for someone else last fall."

"Do you know his name?"

"Jack." For the first time Jacob felt hatred toward this man who had now violated Jenny in more ways than one.

"Do you know his last name...where he lives...anything about him?"

Jacob's voice was weak, "No." *How could I have been such a fool? How could I have left Jenny with no protection? How could I have pushed her out of my life and not cared where she landed... What kind of man am I?*

~

Jacob groaned as he shifted in the waiting room chair. His neck ached, his shoulder ached and his left leg was numb from the position it had been in for the past three hours.

"Mr. Hamilton." The voice sounded so muffled that Jacob wasn't sure it was real. "Mr. Hamilton, your wife is awake."

Jacob opened his eyes to see a nurse leaning down to speak to him. "Awake? Can I see her?"

"Not yet. The doctor wanted me to let you know that she is awake and alert. She's going to be fine physically, but he wants to be careful about visitors due to the situation. Dr. Martin needs to speak to her first."

"A psychiatrist?" Jacob couldn't help but notice the look of concern that washed over Herman's face as he sat up on the couch.

"Yes. And then, when she's ready, the police need to question her."

"Sounds like it will be quite a while until we get to see her... Look, I know she might not want to see me, but Alicia has just got to see her mom."

"Why don't you folks go to the cafeteria and grab some breakfast. Doctor Martin will come and talk to you as soon as he can."

Breakfast proved to be only a short interruption in a long wait. Dr. Martin finally escorted Jacob, Alicia and Herman to the conference room at 3 pm.

"I spoke with Jennifer for about forty-five minutes this morning. Police detective Joe Sandler spoke with her at noon. Officer Sandler and I then met to discuss what we've learned." Dr. Martin spoke methodically.

"Jennifer admits to attempting suicide." The clinical tone from the doctor unnerved Jacob. "She informed both Officer Sandler and me that her other injuries are a result of a fall down the stairs. At this point we have no proof otherwise. She also refuses any sort of treatment and, therefore, I cannot be of any help to her. Dr.

Capple will be down soon to talk to you." The doctor stood and abruptly left the room.

Alicia stared at the door with her mouth open. "What is wrong with that man? We didn't even have time to ask him questions."

A smile crossed Jacob's lips, "I think your mom is OK. She once told me she would never let a psychiatrist mess with her mind... I wonder what she said to him."

Dr. Capple relayed great medical news; Jennifer's recovery time would be short. She would most likely be able to leave the hospital within a few days. He was more concerned about her state of mind. "We can't ignore the fact that she tried to end her life. Mr. Hamilton, I understand she lives alone in the house you jointly own."

"Yes."

"I don't think it's a good idea for her to be alone when she goes home."

"Dad, I can move back home and be with her."

"Yes...yes you could. But what if she won't let you? Let's see how she responds to us the next couple of days, and then we'll see if she'll allow us back into her life."

"I think that's wise." Dr. Capple showed genuine concern. "Right now she has told me that she doesn't want to see either of you. We need to give her some time. It's hard to look loved ones in the eyes when you survive a suicide attempt."

Herman was being very careful to know his place in these conferences he was allowed to be a part of. "Dr. Capple, tomorrow morning when you check on Jennifer, will you ask her if she would be willing to talk to me?"

The doctor looked at Jacob as if to get permission.

"Herman, are you going to spend another night down here? You have so much to do at home and at the church."

"Martha and the elders have got things covered. Maybe she'll be willing to talk to me. We can pray all night that God will soften her heart."

~

"And you were dead in your trespasses and sin, in which you formally walked according to the course of this world, according to the prince of the power of the air, of the spirit that is now working in the sons of disobedience. Among them we too all formerly lived in the lusts of our flesh, indulging the desires of the flesh and of the mind, and were by nature children of wrath, even as the rest. But God, being rich in His mercy, because of His great love with which He loved us, even when we were dead in our transgressions, made us alive together with Christ (by grace you have been saved), and raised us up with Him, and seated us with Him in the heavenly places, in Christ Jesus, in order that in the ages to come He might show the surpassing riches of His grace in kindness toward us in Christ Jesus."

Herman folded his hands and placed them on top of his open Bible. "Father, I know that you love Jennifer. This passage in Ephesians tells us she is no different than any other person who has walked in this world. We have all been dead in our sin. We have all lived and indulged in the lusts of our flesh. She is not unique amongst sinners. She is simply lost...as I was...until You found me. Father, speak to her tonight. Call her by name and draw her to You." Herman slipped into the motel room bed, pulled the covers to his chin and began to pray that Jennifer would be willing to see him in the morning.

Chapter

27

"Good morning, honey."

"Good morning, dad."

Jacob sat down at the table in Alicia's small kitchen. "Did you sleep?"

"Not much. I wish I would have stayed at the hospital. Maybe mom would have been willing to see me... Dad...do you think mom really fell down the stairs?"

"Not likely."

"Well if Jack beat her up, he could've come back and tried to kill her." Alicia's hand shook as she poured her dad a cup of coffee.

Jacob gently placed his hand on her forearm, "We're going to have to get used to the idea that your mom tried to end her life. We can't be any help to her if we don't face the facts ourselves."

"But why, dad, why? I saw her last week and she seemed fine. She wasn't unhappy. What could have made her do it?"

"Only she knows. I think the last thing we should do is try to make her tell us. We're going to have to be there for her, love her, and if she'll talk, we need to listen."

Alicia set the coffee pot on the table and sat down. She stared at the man across from her, hardly recognizing him as her dad. She loved the weekend she had spent with him, but he was so out of character from the dad she grew up with. And now, here he was, showing love to her mom in a way she didn't think him capable.

The words fell from her heart, "What's happened to you, dad? You're not the dad I've known."

This was the moment Jacob had prayed for. God was giving him the opportunity to introduce his daughter to his Savior. *Please give me the words, Lord.* Jacob's voice was soft - tender, "I'm not the same. I'm a brand new creation. I know what a con man I was. I know how self-centered I was. I knew it long before I ever admitted it to myself. Even though I was a pastor and had everything you think a man would want...I was empty. There was an ache in my soul that wouldn't leave. When I left the church that Sunday morning, I begged God to show me His truth...because I was so tired...so very tired of pretending."

Alicia spoke in a half whisper, "You found His truth, didn't you, dad."

"Yes." Jacob began to share with Alicia all that had transpired since he stepped down as pastor of The Victorious Church. Every detail was scrutinized by a hungry heart that desperately wanted answers. Two hours later the floodgate opened.

"What do I do, dad...what do I do? I've bounced around to so many 'truths'. I've given my heart so many times. Nothing lasts...nothing." Alicia wiped her tear-soaked cheeks with her sweatshirt sleeve, "...I'm afraid your love won't last."

"It's not my love you see. My love is selfish. It's Christ's love you see working through me, and His love is eternal."

"But could He really love me...after everything I've done." This was not a question; it was an ownership of sin. "I killed my baby, dad... I killed my baby..." Alicia buried her head in her arms and sobbed.

Jacob scooted his chair next to Alicia and wrapped his arm around her shoulder, pulling her close. "Jesus paid the price through His death on the cross for our sin. There is only one beyond His forgiveness and that's rejecting His truth." The Holy Spirit spoke to Jacob's heart not to share any further; the newly planted seed needed time to take root.

~

Dr. Capple led Jacob, Alicia and Herman into the now familiar conference room. "Physically, Jennifer is doing great this morning. Let's see, this is Wednesday, I would like to keep her here until Friday morning to make sure everything is OK. That will give you time to figure out how you will handle things when you take her home." The doctor's expression darkened, "Have you been to the house?"

"No." Jacob had avoided even the thought of walking into the Victorian mansion.

"You know you have to make sure that everything is cleaned up before she leaves here."

"The police gave me the name of a company that will clean the room. I talked to them last night. They told me it would all be done by noon today."

"Be sure to check it out so there are no surprises."

"I will."

Herman moved forward in his chair, "Will Jennifer see me?"

"At first she declined, but when I asked her again right before I left the room she said she would. Perhaps you should do it right away before she changes her mind again."

"Thank you, doctor. Jacob, I think we should pray before I go in there."

"Do you mind if I join you?"

Jacob and Herman both looked at Dr. Capple with wide eyes.

"I accepted Jesus as my Savior over thirty years ago. I've been praying for Jennifer since she first arrived."

Alicia watched three highly educated, professional, strong men drop to their knees. Pastor Herman prayed that God would soften Jennifer's heart and that she would be receptive to the good news of the gospel. Dr. Capple thanked God for miraculously guiding the bullet's path, allowing Jennifer more time to respond to the gospel. Jacob entered the room in his heart marked "Jenny" and prayed for the salvation of his wife.

Unable to hold back tears, a new creation in Christ knelt next to her father, "Jesus, I don't know if I have the right to come to You to ask anything, but please...keep my mom from ever trying to hurt herself again."

~

Herman gently knocked on the door to room 216. A quiet raspy voice said, "Come in."

"Hi Jennifer, I'm Herman Groves. Thank you for being willing to see me."

Jennifer's countenance was hard, her jaw clenched. She turned her face away and stared out the window. "You're Jacob's friend," the statement was angry.

"I am."

"Tell him to go back to Duluth... I don't need him here."

"Is that why you were willing to see me, to pass on a message to Jacob? You could have had Dr. Capple do that."

Jennifer turned back to take another look at this man whose voice was relaxed and gentle. "No...that's not why I wanted to talk to you."

"You want to know about Alicia."

"Hm...perceptive...I bet you bring your wife flowers."

"I do."

"You can sit down if you want."

"Thank you... Alicia is scared."

Once again Jennifer turned away to stare out the window. "Did she find me?"

"Yes." Herman could see Jennifer's eyes squeeze shut as a tear ran down her right cheek. "She loves you." The tear became a stream.

"...It's hard to remember that somebody loves you when you hate yourself so much."

"She's not the only one who loves you."

"Jacob? Huh...he doesn't love people. He loves what he can get from people."

"Jesus."

The stare out the window became a glare directed straight at Herman, "I tried Jesus, and all I got was stepped on."

"You got stepped on by Jacob, a Jacob who at the time knew nothing about the transforming power of the Holy Spirit."

"It's just another con."

"Somehow, I don't think you really believe that." Herman prayed that the Holy Spirit would guide his words. "Jennifer...I didn't ask to see you so I could defend Jacob. You tried to end your life. You came to a place where you could see no hope for what you believed your life should be. You were angry that the life you wanted turned out to be a living hell...

"I wanted to see you to tell you that your Creator is calling you to His arms. He knows your sin. He sent His Son to die for your sin. His greatest desire is to hear you say, 'I'm sorry, Father. Can I come home?' And when you do, you can be assured He will say yes because of what Colossians 1: 13-14 tells us; 'For He delivered us from the domain of darkness, and transferred us to the kingdom of His beloved Son, in whom we have redemption, the forgiveness of sin.' God loves you, Jennifer. Your hope should never have been in Jacob, it should never have been in yourself. Your hope is in Jesus."

Chapter

28

Jacob unlocked the back door. Oppression was thick. His mind flew back to the first day he had passed through this entrance. The realtor guaranteed the house offered "everything a home owner could possibly want." The mansion didn't live up to its billing, and now the emptiness was foreboding.

The kitchen and back staircase looked in good shape, no telltale signs of the horde of people who had been a part of saving Jennifer's life. The bedroom also showed no evidence of what had transpired three days earlier. *The bed's made. Did Jenny do that before...* Jacob couldn't finish the thought. He looked around the room. The only thing out of the ordinary was the smell. *They must have used some strong disinfectant or something.* He opened two windows.

Jacob looked out on a back yard patio that had only held the promise of family barbecues. His heart was heavy; he knew the likelihood of seeing Jennifer was slim to none. She would be released from the hospital, and if allowed, Alicia would take her home. He would drive back to Duluth without having any contact with his wife. *She has good reason not to trust me. Lord, get Alicia in to see her this afternoon. She needs to know how much we love her.* Jacob quickly realized his prayer was more like a demand. *I'm sorry, Jesus, I trust You.*

~

The doorknob to room 216 was just inches away. *What will she look like? What will I say?* Fear stirred in the pit of Alicia's stomach until it threatened to rise up through her throat. She withdrew her hand and spun around to lean against the wall. *Jesus, will You help me with this? I need to be strong for my mom. She doesn't need a crybaby.*

Herman turned the corner and headed down the hallway toward Jennifer's room. Alicia's anxiety seemed to shout at him. "Hi Alicia, are you OK?"

"No... I'm scared to go in there."

Herman placed his hand on Alicia's shoulder and gently guided her away from the door. "Your mom is scared too. It's going to be hard for her to face you."

"I know...but I just don't want to say anything stupid or do something that will upset her."

"Your mom's not as blind as you think. She knows she hurt you."

"Hurt me? If I had been there for her she wouldn't have felt so alone."

"She made choices that didn't turn out well, the responsibility for those choices are hers. She doesn't blame you. The important thing right now is not to be afraid to say I love you... Are you still mad at her?"

"I'm not mad at her. Why would I be mad at her?"

"Because she tried to take your mom away."

Herman's words were more than Alicia could defend against. Now in the waiting room, she collapsed onto a chair and buried her face in her arms. The tears provided relief after trying so hard not to cry. "I didn't want to be mad at her, but...she scared me...and I'm still scared. What if she tries it again? What if I find her again and this time it's too late?"

"Do you want some more time before you go in and see her?"

Alicia's tearful face turned determined, "No...no. She needs me and I'm going to be there for her. Jesus can help me...can't He?"

"Yes, He can help you. Let's pray about that right now. Jesus, Paul wrote in 2 Corinthians 12:9; 'And He said to me, "My grace is sufficient for you, for power is perfected in weakness." Most gladly, therefore, I will rather boast about my weaknesses, that the power of Christ may dwell in me.' Lord, Alicia has confessed her weakness and now needs Your power to face the difficult task before her. I pray that You demonstrate to her the truth of Your word and instill in her Your peace that surpasses all comprehension. Amen."

"Jesus, if You can help me, I'll take all the strength and peace and power I can get. Amen."

~

Jennifer was standing at the window, looking out on the world she had tried to escape. She heard the door open. *How am I going to turn and face her? I've always been the one she counted on, the one she leaned on. I've taken that away from her. Now she'll look at me and wonder...*

"Mom..."

Jennifer slowly turned, looking down. The light from the window behind her darkened her face. She felt small. She was unable to lift her eyes off the floor. Her voice was barely audible. "I'm sorry, Alicia, I'm so very sorry."

ᴧa walked across the room, carefully put her arms around ᴧ mother and pulled her close. "I love you, mom."

~

Jennifer cracked open the door and gave a light push; the bedroom offered no welcome, only a reminder of entrapment. She had to will her feet forward, never expecting to enter this prison again. *What have I accomplished by being so stupid? Here I am, back in the same place...with more wounds.*

"Are you going to be OK, mom? I'll go put some lunch together."

"Yah...I'll be fine." Jennifer walked over and sat down on the edge of the bed, "I think I need to catch my breath."

The bedroom seemed different to Jennifer, as if she was in a foreign land. She laid back and tried to rest, but after only a few minutes she found herself sitting again. *I don't belong here. I don't want to be in this room. I don't want to be in this house. What DO I want?* The cold emptiness that had invited her to pull the trigger began to stretch its icy fingers around her soul once again. "No! NO!"

Alicia dropped the jar of raspberry jam on the tiled kitchen floor, "MOM!"

Jennifer was on her knees in the hallway by the time her daughter reached her. In frantic gasps she pleaded with Alicia, "I can't stay here! We've got to go someplace else! Can we go to your apartment? PLEASE?"

Alicia fell next to her mom and wrapped her in her arms, "Yes, yes... It's going to be OK, mom. It's going to be OK."

~

Herman had returned to Duluth; Jacob decided he needed to stay until Jennifer and Alicia were settled. Alicia would need support, and he prayed that God would allow him to see Jennifer before he left. The phone call from Alicia explaining the change of plans set him scrambling to get his things together and leave the apartment before his wife and daughter arrived. He shut the door on Natasha's car mere seconds before Alicia and Jennifer parked in front of the apartment building.

Jacob watched from the parking lot as Alicia helped her mom exit the passenger side of the car. Jennifer's face looked bruised even from a distance. Her vivacious step was gone. He hardly recognized the form of the once envied wife of a "prosperous pastor". *Oh, Jesus, I pray this is the bottom. Holy Spirit, speak loudly to her so that she doesn't need to fall any further before she can hear Your voice.*

~

Two weeks of cramped existence in Alicia's small apartment encouraged both women to seek out a new home. Jennifer, whose strength was returning, searched for possibilities on the Internet while Alicia checked out what was found after work. But today was Saturday and the two roommates were going to hit the streets together for the first time since their search began.

"Are you getting tired, mom? It's been a long morning."

"I'm more hungry than tired"

"How about we check out the house for rent on fiftieth and then stop at the Malt Shop for lunch?"

The house on fiftieth turned out to be the one. The 1950's story and a half bungalow was large enough for both to spread out a little, yet small enough to feel like home.

"I love the front porch, and the porch swing is great!" Alicia was hoping her mom would show some excitement.

"Yes, this will work...this will be fine." Jennifer paid the deposit along with the first and last month's rent. A smile finally cracked her hardened expression. Two and a half weeks earlier she sat on the side of her bed, battered and bruised, hating life to the point of trying to end it. Now, she looked over at her roommate, *I'm renting a house with my daughter.* Her smile turned into a grin as they walked out the door.

The Malt shop was a short distance from the bungalow. "This is a celebration meal, mom, do you want to split a burger? They're pretty good size here."

"You order what you want and I'll take half of it. You probably know what's good. I know you've come to this place a lot."

Lunchtime was full of girl chit-chat; talk about decorating the new house and the potential for "Teas" with girlfriends. Alicia was excited to see her mom enjoying herself. "I'm really glad we'll be living together, mom... I've missed being with you. I know we've seen each other off and on, but it hasn't been the same since I left for college."

Jennifer's mood turned reflective, "Girls grow up and begin their own lives. That's the way it's supposed to be."

"I know, but when I left for college I was running, I wanted out in the worst way... I abandoned you, mom, and I'm sorry."

"You didn't abandon me."

"Yes I did. I was so angry at dad. I thought only about myself. When I cut him off from my life, I cut you off too. I know I called so you wouldn't worry, but...I never really told you the truth. I'd pretend I was happy. Deep down inside, I was full of hate...hate for dad."

"You shouldn't hate your dad, he's not evil he's just...full of himself. There are people who think the world revolves around them, and he's the king of that world."

"People can change, can't they, mom?"

"Sure, I watched your father change. He was different when I met him, so interested in helping people. But when he planted the church something happened. People turned into numbers, indicators of success. His passion to help was exchanged for a passion to build. That's when he began to shut me out. I became just another tool in his belt; the dutiful wife who supported her handsome charismatic husband."

Alicia thought about interrupting, telling her mom what had happened to the father she no longer hated, but the moment was not yet ripe.

"It wasn't entirely his fault. I began to see the perks. We played the role at home as much as we did at church. We didn't grow apart like most people do, we literally traded relational intimacy for the 'riches of the kingdom'... For a time it seemed like the trade-off was worth while, a testimony to my own greedy heart I suppose." Jennifer looked at Alicia through teary eyes, "I watched as he shut you out... I watched as he used you. I made token efforts to try and get him involved in your life, but I didn't force the issue.

I was compliant until I got so lonely...by that time there was nothing between us.

"I'm sorry, Alicia. I'm sorry I let your dad walk on you like he walked on me. I don't think I will ever be able to forgive him for taking my hopes and dreams for our family and turning them into stage props for his kingdom"

Alicia looked down at the empty floor and whispered, "I have."

Jennifer wasn't sure she heard right, "Did you say...you have?"

I didn't mean for her to hear that, Jesus. I don't know if I'm ready to tell her what's happened to me, let alone what's happened to dad. What do I do? What do I say?

"Are you all right, sweetie? You look like you're a million miles away."

Alicia's response was timid. "I...I have things to tell you mom...but I don't know if I'm ready. I've done so many stupid things... I have so many secrets. I've chased after things I believed would give me answers to life. I've been involved with people...men...that I thought could somehow save me from whatever it was I was running from. In the end, I found what I was looking for in the last place I wanted to look...and it happened in a way I never expected it to happen."

Jennifer's attention was averted from her tirade against the 'king of self'. *Secrets? Stupid things? Men?* "What are you talking about, sweetheart?"

"Not here, mom; when we're alone and we can talk freely. But I want you to know something... Dad is not who he used to be, and I don't hate him anymore. I love him in a way I never believed possible...and he loves me... For the first time in my life, I really have a dad."

Jennifer watched with amazement as a peaceful smile spread across Alicia's face.

Chapter
29

Summer was in full bloom. Jacob was making a practice of beginning his mornings in prayer seated on the bench in Natasha's garden. Jennifer was at the heart of the majority of his prayers. Phone conversations with Alicia had kept him apprised of his wife's progress since his return to Jess' Child. The conversations also served to build on the brand new relationship he now enjoyed with his daughter. Alicia was hungry and peppered her dad with questions that continually caused him to dive deeper into scripture.

The ring tone of Jacob's new cell phone was a welcome melody. "Good Morning Alicia!"

"Hi Dad, I've got some great news for you!" Alicia sounded so excited that Jacob knew he would not have the opportunity to ask what the news was before she would blurt it out. "Mom and I are coming to see you!"

He was stunned to the point of silence.

"Dad?... Are you there, dad?"

"Yes...I'm here."

"We've been talking a lot, and I've told her about what's happened to you and to me and..."

"Whoa, slow down a little. What have you told her about you and me?"

"I've told her just about everything! About you coming to know Jesus and about me coming to know Jesus!"

"You've got to take a breath, honey. You sound like your going to hyperventilate."

"I'm sorry. I'm just so excited!"

"I can hear that. Maybe you better start at the beginning and fill me in on how this has all come about, but do it slowly."

"OK... I'll calm down." Alicia attempted to slow her breathing. "After we moved in together we decided we would end our days over a cup of tea, getting to know each other again. We both discovered how little we knew about each other's lives. Four years apart ended up being a lifetime of experiences, both good and bad. I told her everything... I told her...about my baby..."

Jacob now listened to hear if Alicia was breathing at all. "Are you OK, honey?"

"Yes...it was so hard to tell mom the truth of what I had done. It's not just the abortion; it's everything that led up to it. It was my selfish desire to be accepted by somebody...anybody...that made me not care about what happened next. I didn't think much about consequences my whole time at college...as long as I was satisfied in the moment... The truth is I was never satisfied in the moment. There was always something gnawing at me, something that kept saying, 'No, this doesn't do it. This isn't it.' Then that 'something' seemed to egg me on to the next thing, the next philosophy, or the next guy..."

Jacob silently asked God to forgive him for his part in Alicia's search for truth. *Lord, if I had only been the father You meant me to be, she might have been spared much of her pain.*

"Anyway, mom told me how empty she had been, and still is. She said she didn't see that emptiness in me and asked if I had been so empty, why wasn't I empty now? The door was open, dad. She wanted to know. I couldn't tell her how I came to know Jesus without telling her how you came to know Jesus."

"How did she respond to you?"

"She was quiet. As a matter of fact she didn't say another word. After she finished her tea, she got up and went to bed. I was afraid I had really turned her off. I went to bed and prayed that God would help her understand how much He loves her. In the morning she asked me if I would drive to Duluth with her on Saturday. She says she wants to talk to you about getting everything out of the house and putting it on the market. But that's not why she wants to see you."

"Why do you think she wants to see me?"

"To see if what I told her is true."

"Oh, Alicia, I can't try and sell her on what a new man I am in order to try and win her back. It can't be like that."

"Give me some credit, dad. She doesn't want to see if you're a new man, she wants to see if you're still empty."

"What are you talking about?"

"She never experienced my emptiness. She never saw me lying in bed crying my eyes out. She never saw my blank stares out the window. She never felt the coldness of my heart leading up to the abortion. I can tell her I was empty, but that doesn't mean she believes it. She lived with you, dad. Do you think for one minute that you fooled her? You were the most spiritually bankrupt, selfish person she has ever known... She's not really coming to see you; she's coming to see if there's hope for her."

Jacob cringed at the insight of his daughter. How foolish he had been to believe that he could hide the darkness of his soul. *Oh, Father, as clearly as Jenny has seen my corruptness, let her now see Your love.*

~

Alicia's face paled as the beauty of the city and river below came into view. The last time she had entered Duluth she was on a mission to rid herself of a "complication". *Jesus, I know that You've forgiven me...but I still hurt...I still hurt.*

"Why couldn't your dad drive into town and meet us? I don't know if I feel all that comfortable going to some pregnancy shelter. I hope he's not trying to pull something."

"Actually, it was my idea." Alicia was timid in her confession. "Meeting there doesn't have anything to do with you or dad; there's someone there I want to...to talk to...someone dad has told me about. I think she can help me understand some things."

Jennifer felt slighted, but only for a moment. *Why should I feel bad if she can't come to me for answers; I don't have any for her, I don't have any for myself.*

The turn onto the long straight dirt driveway of the old hobby farm immediately put an end to expectations of an institutionalized setting. Alicia harbored feelings of regret as she realized she had not even asked her dad about his work. All her questions had been rooted in self. Jennifer's mind had conjured up a brick clinical-looking building; certainly not a warm appearing farmhouse with lush lawns and beautiful gardens.

Jennifer's jaw tightened at what she saw next; Jacob on a porch swing with baby and baby bottle in hand. "I knew he'd be up to something. This has got to be one of the best cons he's ever come up with."

"Cons? Mom, I don't think..."

"Oh, come on Alicia, don't you see what he's up to?"

"Mom, we're an hour early, we weren't even supposed to be here until after lunch."

"A good con man plans for every possibility."

Alicia's heart pounded at a possibility she had not planned for; that the day could be a disaster.

Jacob's surprise at the early arrival would have been apparent to any unbiased onlooker. He quickly made his way across the porch to the front door, called out as he stuck his head in the living room, and handed the baby off to the approaching mom. A flustered inventory of his appearance made him realize the smell of baby spit-up would only draw attention to the stain on his shirt.

Jennifer's mind was reeling as she exited the car. *I cannot think of one time he EVER gave a bottle to Alicia. It's a little late for the daddy act now.*

Alicia ran to embrace her dad as he stepped off the porch. "I'm sorry we're early."

"That's alright. Have you ladies had lunch?"

Alicia didn't get time to answer; she was cut off by the coldness of her mother's response. "We aren't going to stay long. Where can we talk so we can get this over with?"

"Hello! I'm so glad you girls have come!" Natasha rushed out the front door as though she was there to greet long lost friends.

Stopping next to Jacob, she wiped her hands on the apron she was wearing, and said, "So, Jacob, this is Alicia."

Jennifer stared. *Who is this?* Natasha's outward beauty had been increased by the inward joy of her salvation. *Jacob couldn't be...no, he wouldn't be...she's older than him.* Jennifer could hardly believe the thought even passed through her mind.

Natasha stretched out her arm, and Alicia stepped forward and fell into a welcome hug. Jennifer felt uneasy as the woman now walked toward her with her hand extended. "It's a privilege to meet you, Jennifer. We are all ready to sit down for lunch. It would be a blessing if you and Alicia would join us."

Jennifer's hand grudgingly lifted to meet Natasha's. The warmth of the invitation almost left a defiant heart defenseless. At the very least, it planted a seed of curiosity about this new life Jacob had come to know.

The kitchen was, at first glance, chaotic. Several young moms were settling fussy infants into baby seats that sat in front of them on the table, while two others were cradling babies in one arm and setting the table with their free hand. Within seconds, though, all seemed to be calm as the members of the household and their two guests bowed their heads to give thanks.

"Father, You are our provider, and we thank You for this food. We know that it is to nourish us so that our lives can nourish others. Amen." Jacob lifted his eyes and smiled at Natasha, offering thanks for her role in bringing Jenny to the table.

Lunch passed quickly, and the only man at the table came close to tears knowing that his wife and daughter were seated with him. Soon they were alone as the new moms left the kitchen to tend to babies' demands, and Natasha had gotten up to answer the phone. "Alicia, I know you want to talk to Natasha. Why don't you help her with the dishes while your mom and I step outside."

"Sure, dad."

Jacob turned to Jennifer, "Will you walk with me?"

A husband and wife who had not spoken beyond necessity in years now found themselves walking side by side through a lush meadow where knee high grass and colorful wildflowers infused the warm air with the smells of summer.

Jennifer was first to speak, "I don't know when the last time was that I had your undivided attention."

"It's been a while, and I'm sorry for that." Jacob prayed to say only the right things, knowing Jennifer's heart held no trust.

"What do you do around here? What's your job? Do you sit on the front porch every morning feeding babies?" The questions were drenched in sarcasm.

Jacob looked sideways at Jennifer and then down at the stain, realizing he still hadn't changed his shirt. "I feed babies sometimes, when I get the opportunity. By title, I'm the caretaker. I do whatever needs doing. Sometimes that's fixing a leaky faucet, or a leaky roof. Sometimes, it's changing a dirty diaper."

"You change dirty diapers?" Jennifer couldn't help but laugh out loud at the thought of the egotistical, name-it-and-claim-it pastor changing a dirty diaper.

"It is pretty funny, isn't it."

Jennifer abruptly stopped and sat down on a rock. Jacob turned and walked back a few steps to where she was.

"What are you really doing here, Jacob? What's the angle? I know what Alicia has told me, but it just doesn't add up. I know you too well. Why haven't you touched the money in the bank account? Why haven't you wanted to sell the house to get what's coming to you out of it? And what's with this...caretaker thing? You like being in charge. You like being the head man. You like having people serve YOU.

"I read your letter, but I don't buy it. Sometimes I think me walking out on you was the first time you didn't get what you wanted, and this whole scheme is to get me to come back to you. Then maybe you'll dump me, so you can say I didn't dump you." Jennifer watched her husband's eyes closely, looking for any sign of having hit a nerve.

Jacob bent over and began to pick wildflowers. With an array of color in hand, he spoke softly. "I never liked flowers much, that is until my eyes were opened to the beauty they hold. Now there are times I sit and stare at a flower, in awe of the genius of the One who created it. Sometimes I wonder how I could describe one of these beauties to those who are blind. What would I say? How would I say it? How could I make them understand the intricacies...the colors? I've come to the conclusion that I can't. I can only share what I see...and pray for sight." Jacob reached out his hand to offer Jennifer the bouquet and gently said, "I have seen the beauty of Christ's sacrifice for my redemption... It's as simple as that... Come on; let me show you around Jess' Child."

~

"My dad says you have quite a story." Alicia took the rinsed dish from Natasha's hand and placed it in the dishwasher.

"I'm not proud of my story."

"Oh...I didn't mean it like that... I..."

"I know. I think everyone who has come to know God's truth looks back and wonders about the time wasted, the mistakes made, the pain caused..."

Moments passed before Alicia tried again. "He hasn't really told me your story; he just thought that maybe...well, maybe you would be a good person for me to talk to."

Natasha handed Alicia the last plate, wiped her hands on her apron, and poured a cup of coffee, "Would you like one?"

"Sure." Both women settled back down at the kitchen table. "He said you might be able to help me... I had an abortion."

"Yes, I know."

"I convinced myself that it wasn't a baby... The problem was that I HAD to convince myself."

Natasha reached an open hand across the table and waited for Alicia to accept the invitation. Squeezing her hand gently, she said, "And now, all you want to do is hold that baby in your arms and beg for forgiveness."

Alicia's chin dropped onto her chest. First tears began to run down her cheeks; then sobs fought to find escape between breaths. Within seconds, her body was shaking uncontrollably.

Natasha stayed put, holding tightly onto Alicia's hand. After several minutes had passed, she began to share her heart. "My abortion was just the beginning. Through the years I worked hard to convince other women that what was inside of them was not a baby. The Women's Center...where you had your abortion...is there today because I was one of those who pushed, and pushed, and pushed for its existence.

"In the book of Romans, at the end of chapter one, Paul talks about people who didn't see fit to acknowledge God; he says God gave them over to a depraved mind. He then lists things that filled their hearts; unrighteousness, wickedness, greed, malice, envy...murder... The first time I read that I fell on my knees and begged God to forgive me, but he wasn't done convicting me. Verse 32 says, '...and, although they knew the ordinance of God, that those who practice such things are worthy of death, they not only do the same, but also give hearty approval to those who practice them.' I gave approval to other women...even helped them do what I had done. I had so much blood on my hands that I didn't believe God could ever forgive me. But He did forgive me...

"I repented, turned away from my sin and clung to the promise of Romans 6:22-23; 'But now having been freed from sin and enslaved to God, you derive your benefit, resulting in sanctification, and the outcome, eternal life. For the wages of sin is death, but the free gift of God is eternal life in Christ Jesus our Lord.' My sins had been paid for, and I was set free...yet...I hurt so much.

"I cried myself to sleep night after night because admitting my sin was also admitting that what was inside of me...was a baby...my baby." Natasha reached over the table to receive a second trembling hand, "I have been forgiven, but sometimes I think God has allowed the hurt to remain for a purpose. I don't pretend to understand all His ways...I just know that He has His way.

"I look at my life before I came to know Jesus; He has changed everything about me. I am not the person I was. The old Natasha did not feel this pain. She felt guilt, which she successfully crammed in a corner of her soul and ignored. The pain comes from knowing that another human-being was involved, a helpless human-being; one that needed to benefit from my love rather than become a casualty of my selfishness." Natasha squeezed Alicia's hands tighter, "We hurt because we are beginning to love others as ourselves. It's a good hurt, one that will change how we live our lives. As for the past, we leave it in God's hands...and trust."

Alicia lifted her head, slipped one hand from Natasha's, and wiped tears from her eyes. "I have been so selfish. In my mind the world has always revolved around me. I didn't give a thought to who my baby was. All I thought about was how this THING was going to affect my life. Once I convinced myself it wasn't a baby, it was out of the equation.

"I think I looked at my parents the same way, like they were objects instead of human-beings. The first thing I thought when I found my mom on the floor in a pool of blood was, 'How could she do this to me?' It never crossed my mind that she was as empty as I was. And I never thought that my dad might be empty; I just believed he was the cause of my emptiness."

Natasha released Alicia's other hand and took a sip of coffee. Setting the cup back down, she said, "You are seeing God's truth, Alicia. I am willing to sit down in conversation with you anytime you would like. Maybe I've learned some things that, when shared, will help you. But...the best help I can give is to advise you to be in

God's word every day. Allow the Holy Spirit to continually open your eyes to the truth of scripture."

"You sound like my dad. It's the same advice he gave me, and it has opened up a relationship with him that I never believed I could have. We talk almost every day about what I've read. He's helped me so much."

Natasha gave a slight grin, "You may be the one who will help your mom in the same way."

"Oh, I don't know... I..."

"Do you think your mom would be here, on a walk with your dad, if she hadn't seen something in you that made her heart yearn? She's searching, and you have been the lighthouse that has pointed her toward Jesus."

Tears once again began to roll down Alicia's cheeks, but not selfish tears; these were tears from a servant's heart. *Thank You, Jesus.*

Chapter

30

Jennifer was quiet, staring out the side window, watching the trees go by at seventy miles an hour. Nothing had been settled about the sale of the Victorian mansion, it was hardly mentioned. She had concentrated on her real reason for the trip, and now she was confused.

Alicia was bursting at the seams with all she wanted to say about the day in Duluth; the best day the Hamilton family had spent together in her life. Still, she allowed fifty miles to go by before she gathered the nerve to break the silence. "I didn't expect Jess' Child to be such a beautiful place."

Jennifer's response did not come quickly. She finally turned away from the window and looked straight ahead, "We still have a couple of hours to go, don't we?"

"Yah, maybe a little less."

"...Your dad is different, I'll give you that."

"More than you know, mom. I don't even recognize him from the dad I grew up with."

"How can somebody change that much in such a short time?"

"You can't do it on your own."

"Jesus, right?"

"I know, it always sounded pretty lame to me too. But here I am; a brand new creation."

"I used to think I was a Christian... I was playing a game. I think it had more to do with how I felt than what I believed. When I didn't feel anymore..."

"I don't know if I ever even thought I was a Christian. When I was a kid I was just following the rules, doing what I was supposed to do. I was looking for answers in dad instead of in God. The youth group stuff at church was just...fun. Maybe everybody assumed I was a Christian because I was the pastor's daughter. Nobody ever took me aside and told me I was a sinner in need of redemption. I had no Biblical foundation to stand on when I left for college, only rules that I was more than happy to leave behind."

"I always thought your dad was the problem; what delusion I lived under. I let you down, Alicia... I'm sorry."

"How could you teach me, mom, when you didn't know yourself? I don't blame you. I don't even blame dad. We were all lost, in need of being found... I've been found by my Savior, and I will never be lost again."

"What do you mean, you've been found? I thought YOU found God?"

"My Bible is on the back seat, grab it and open it up to Matthew 18."

Jennifer reached back and took hold of a book she had read many times. She had gone through the entire Bible four times with the women's group at The Victorious Church, and yet she hadn't a clue what she would find in Matthew 18.

"I think it's verses 12-14. Read them out loud."

"What is this, Sunday School?"

Alicia couldn't help but grin. Not only had this been a great day, but now her mom was going to read to her from the Bible. *You are something else, Jesus!*

"What do you think? If any man has a hundred sheep, and one of them has gone astray, does he not leave the ninety-nine on the mountains and go and search for the one that is straying? And if it turns out that he finds it, truly I say to you, he rejoices over it more than over the ninety-nine which have not gone astray. Thus it is not the will of your Father who is in heaven that one of these little ones perish."

"See, He's been searching for me the whole time I've been lost, and He found me! Isn't that great, mom!"

A tear dropped on verse 14, and Jennifer turned her head to once again stare out the window.

~

The lost lamb returned to the Victorian mansion on Monday morning to pick up her Bible. Turning the key in the front door lock was the easy part, stepping across the threshold demanded more courage. The first step seemed an invitation to fear; the second, a proclamation not to be conquered by fear. Jennifer quickly climbed the stairs to the second floor, entered her bedroom and walked directly to the end table next to the bed, retrieving her Bible from its drawer. No more than three minutes passed from the time she had parked in the driveway to the moment she had returned to her car. Her morning mission had been accomplished, and she believed she had won the first battle in a recently declared war.

Jennifer's new home with Alicia provided a comfortable porch swing for daily reading and nightly discussions. The two women set aside girl talk and focused on matters that spoke to the soul. The mom was on the edge while the daughter continually prayed for God to gently push. Saturday night brought another unexpected invitation to Alicia.

"Would you like to drive up north with me again tomorrow morning?"

"To go see dad again?" Alicia's surprise was joyfully voiced.

"I'm really curious about this church he's going to. I thought we could leave in time to make the service."

"Oh, mom, you know I want to!"

~

Alicia's GPS directed the two visitors right to the door of Duluth Christian Fellowship. "Let's sneak in the back and find a seat." Jennifer's hope would not be realized.

"Dad!"

Jacob stood just inside the door welcoming people. His surprise and joy were unchecked as he hugged Alicia with one arm and placed his free hand on Jennifer's shoulder. "What are you doing here? No, no, that's not what I mean. I'm so glad to see you both." He looked behind him and asked a man standing near, "Mark, will you greet people?" He then returned his attention to the two people he loved more than anyone else in the world and said, "Please, come and sit with me."

Jacob led his family up front to take seats with Pastor Herman's family. He couldn't help but again marvel at the handiwork of God as he took his regular seat next to Marni. On his left sat his own daughter with Jennifer next to her. When the service began two girls, unaware of the other's actions, reached over and gently placed their hand on Jacob's knee. Jacob, grinning from ear to ear, placed a hand on top of each and praised his Savior for His loving-kindness.

Martha Groves was the first to approach for an introduction when the service ended. "This is my daughter, Alicia, and..." Before Jacob could go any further, Alicia introduced her mother in an effort to save her dad from awkwardness in knowing how to introduce Jennifer. But awkward introductions were not a concern for a little girl who was just trying to get things straight in her mind.

"Is this your daddy?" Marni clung tightly to Jacob's hand.

"Yes it is. He's my daddy." Alicia took hold of Jacob's other hand and smiled as she looked into her father's eyes.

"And this is your mom?"

"Yes."

Marni let go of Jacob's hand and reached out to Jennifer. "Are you Mr. Hamilton's wife?"

Jennifer was first caught off guard by the little girl's artificial legs; then she was caught off guard by her question. Only a week ago the last thing Jennifer wanted to be was Jacob's wife. Now she was put on the spot with a question she didn't want to answer, by a little girl she didn't want to refuse. Receiving her hand she said, "I...I am," figuring this to be the easiest reply to avoid any explanation.

But the innocence of a child has no bounds. Marni tugged on Jennifer's hand to draw her next to Jacob. Then she placed the wife's hand into the hand of her husband and stepped back, smiling at the Hamilton family standing in front of her. Without another word, she turned and headed off to find a friend.

The warmth of Jacob's hand caused Jennifer to linger. This moment that should have seemed awkward instead seemed almost natural. But slowly, Jennifer retracted her hand from the light grip that desired to tighten.

"It is so good to meet both of you." Martha greeted the ladies with genuine love. "Would you join us for dinner? Jacob eats with us every Sunday after church. It would be a joy if you could join us too."

A pleading look from Alicia convinced her mom there was no way out. "I suppose we could. Thank you."

Martha's attention was quickly stolen away by others, leaving the Hamilton's alone with one another. "I can't believe you're here again. I mean, I'm happy you're here again, but I'm very surprised."

"I am too." Jennifer was sheepish. "I was curious about this church. After my conversation in the hospital with your pastor...that sounds really funny, 'your pastor'. You haven't had a pastor since before we were married. You were always the pastor... Anyway, after talking with him and then to you last week, I just had to see what this place is all about."

"And...did you come to any conclusions?"

Jennifer's eyes began to tear up, "Please, don't ask me now."

Jacob knew better than to press. With a twinkle in his eye he softened the moment, "Come on girls, let's go to the kitchen and see if there's a cookie to be had."

~

Jennifer and Alicia were treated to a normal Sunday afternoon dinner at the Groves'; conversations about family adventures, updates of individual endeavors, and laughter, lots of laughter. This was a family life unknown to the two who had spent the majority of their lives under Jacob's roof. In short order it became a family life neither wanted to leave. Late afternoon provided time for the adults to visit without the children. Even later, Jennifer and Martha had time to talk over a cup of coffee back at the kitchen table.

"How are you doing, Jennifer?"

"You mean after...you know about the suicide attempt."

"Yes."

"I suppose everyone Jacob's involved with up here knows. Maybe the whole church knows."

"Actually, very few people know. The ones who do know only know so they can pray for you."

Jennifer was surprised at how easy it was to talk with Martha. "Maybe being a pastor's wife you can understand. There were so many expectations...so many unrealistic expectations. Don't they know we're just human like they are?"

"Who are they?"

"You know, the people, the people who look at you thinking you've got all the answers. The ones who think you should have the perfect marriage; should never have a bad thought or never have a hair out of place."

"Look at me."

Jennifer looked up.

"Do I have a hair out of place?"

"You do." Jennifer began to chuckle, "You actually have a lot of them out of place."

"They were more than likely out of place in church this morning, too. Didn't you notice?"

"No, I didn't. You're not wearing makeup either."

"HUH! Make up! Who's got time for makeup? I'm happy just to know the kids have clean faces before we leave for church." Martha could see a light come on. "Whose expectations were you really trying to live up to, Jennifer?"

"Hmm...I never saw it like that before. They were mine...and Jacob's, but mostly mine. I suppose I had expectations for both of us that neither one of us could live up to."

"Having unrealistic expectations is not good, but it isn't really the problem, is it. Expectations are 'fill', something we think will fill the emptiness. Even the emptiness isn't the problem. Emptiness is only a fruit of the problem.

"We were created to worship God and to have fellowship with Him, but we're separated from Him because of our sin. When we're separated, we're broken; we're not what we were created to be. We can look for all kinds of ways to fix the problem, but there's nothing we can do. There is only one fix, and Jesus accomplished that on the cross."

"You make it sound so simple."

"It is simple. God created Adam to be in His presence. When Adam sinned he forfeited his and our relationship with God because sin cannot be in His presence. Jesus shed His blood on the cross to cover that sin, and He has offered that covering to us.

Our sin is the problem. It is the root cause of our emptiness. It's what keeps us from the presence of God."

"But what do I do? Do I just say the words...say 'the prayer'?"

"Saying the prayer means nothing if you don't first understand your need for the Savior. Tell me what you think God sees when He looks at you."

Jennifer sat silent for some time. Then, in a weak broken voice, she began, "He sees someone who tried to destroy the gift of life He gave. He sees someone who stole what rightfully belonged to her husband and sold it dirt cheap to another." Tears now began to flow. "He sees someone who cared more about herself than she ever did about her daughter. He sees...He sees..." No more words would fit between the sobs. Jennifer buried her head in her arms in shame.

Martha moved to Jennifer's side of the table, sat down and wrapped her arms around her shoulders. "Now the words will mean something. Now the prayer is real."

Between spasmodic breaths Jennifer repented. "I'm sorry, Jesus. I don't deserve what You've done for me. Please forgive me...please forgive me."

Martha softly stroked Jennifer's hair. "Now...God sees one redeemed by the blood of His Son."

~

During the next three months Mr. and Mrs. Hamilton submitted to the counseling care of Pastor and Mrs. Groves. The restoration of their marriage would be given the time and attention needed, nothing would be rushed. Jacob remained at

Jess' Child while Jennifer continued to live with their daughter. Love bloomed as summer gave way to fall.

Jacob looked forward to every weekend visit from his wife and daughter. Jennifer would bunk at Herman and Martha's while Alicia spent her weekends at Jess' Child, helping Natasha minister to new moms. But this weekend visit would be different. This weekend, Jennifer would come home to her husband.

Jacob watched the entrance to the driveway as his wife's car approached. There was coolness to the breeze. His sport coat was not standing up to the task, and a shiver ran through his body. When the car came to a stop Jacob opened Jennifer's door and welcomed her into his arms. The cool breeze was defeated by the warmth of her embrace.

"We're going to get there just in time, I'll put your suitcase inside and we can head out. Did you drop Alicia off at the church?"

"Yes."

"You look beautiful."

"And you look VERY handsome."

The drive to town down the country road on this cool fall day was lavished in praise. Jacob and Jennifer prayed and sang songs to their Lord.

Alicia met her mom and dad at the front door of Duluth Christian Fellowship. She handed her mother a beautiful bouquet of flowers and gave them both a hug. Jacob smiled at Marni and, as the music started, bent down to give her a kiss on the forehead. "You look absolutely stunning this morning, young lady." Marni simply said, "Thank you", turned and began walking down the isle, tossing red rose pedals onto the white carpet runner.

The front half of the sanctuary was filled with brothers and sisters from church; the Groves family and Natasha seated in the front row. Moms and babies from Jess' Child filled the last rows occupied, ready for a quick exit if necessary. Two hobos, decked out in tuxedoes and bowties, stood off to the right facing the congregation. With fiddle and banjo in hand, they awaited their turn to bless their friend in this ceremony to renew wedding vows.

Jacob looked at his daughter and lovingly squeezed the hand of his bride. He was overcome with joy. His family was whole.

~~~~~~~~~~

"It's leaning to the right, dad, move it to the left...my left."

"Is that better?"

"A little bit more...there. Perfect!"

"Oh look, it's snowing." Jennifer stood at the front window of the caretaker's apartment, a home she now had shared with her husband since their vow renewal. "I was beginning to worry that we wouldn't see any snow for Christmas."

Jacob took Alicia by the hand and joined his wife at the window. The giant flakes landed softly on the ground. "This is our first Christmas together."

"Dad, we've had a lot of Christmases together."

"No...we've shared a lot of holidays, but never Christmas. This year we truly know what the birth of Jesus means to this world. This year we are celebrating the birth of OUR Savior." Dad, mom, and daughter stood together and watched as a lifeless landscape was transformed by the purity of fresh fallen snow.

Several minutes passed before Jacob broke the silence. "Let's sit down to a cup of hot chocolate; I have something I want to talk to both of you about."

The ladies curled up on the couch with their cocoa. Jacob returned clutching a warm mug and settled into the space left for him between the two women he loved most in the world. "Our lives have changed so much, just look at what God has done to us. Deep inside, I think we all know there will be more change to come. Alicia, having you here on staff at Jess' Child is truly a blessing to your mom and me. I can see how you have fallen in love with this ministry and how well you and Natasha work with the moms and babies."

"I do love this place. I love ministering to these girls. I love having the freedom to tell them about Jesus. I feel more at home in that old farm house than in any place I have ever lived. I also love our church. No offense, dad, but for the first time in my life I have a church family."

"No offense taken, honey, I feel the same way."

Jennifer slipped her hand into Jacob's. "You don't think we'll be staying here, do you."

"I don't know when it will happen, but I know God has other work for us to do. Right now I am perfectly at peace being here, but my heart is to be a shepherd of a flock. God has used Herman to show me how a real shepherd tends his sheep, and I think He's shown me for a purpose... I just want us to be prepared for when change comes. I don't think it will happen tomorrow, but it will happen; which brings me to something I think we need to do as part of that preparation.

"We live pretty simple lives here. Jenny, you asked me once why I haven't touched any of the money that's in our bank account, and now there's much more in the account from the sale of the house. I never really answered you, although I shared this with Herman when God first laid it on my heart. That money doesn't belong to us. It was gain from manipulation. People gave that money for ministry, and an egotistical pastor believed he was 'the ministry' they were giving to." Jacob paused and prayed that His wife's heart was ready. "I think we need to make a complete break from the past. The excessive salary I took from the Victorious Church was sinful, and I want to be rid of any temptation connected with that money." He set his hot chocolate on the small table in front of him, leaned back, and slipped his arms around both of his girls. Encouraging them toward him as if forming a huddle, he whispered, "What if we give all of it to Jess' Child as a Christmas gift?"

Alicia immediately grinned from ear-to-ear and said, "I love my new daddy."

Jennifer was quiet, and Jacob feared he might have asked too much, too soon. But within moments Jennifer pressed against her husband's shoulder and kissed him on the cheek. "I know the emptiness of earthly treasures. Just show me where to sign." She then looked down at her hands. The right hand was the first to be stripped, then the left; leaving only the simple wedding band that had been returned to her finger just a couple of months earlier. Next to go were the diamond studded earrings from her pierced ears. Without a word, she stood and disappeared into the bedroom. She returned holding a jewelry box. "I've felt a conviction about this stuff for some time, it won't be hard to say goodbye to them."

Tears trickled down Jacob's cheeks. He understood the agonizing process of transformation; he understood the overwhelming freedom of surrender. *Father, thank you, for loving Jenny so much.*

"What about my car, Jacob? That was purchased with the same money."

"I know."

"If we sell it...we'll have nothing to drive."

Jacob raised his eyebrows and spoke through a sheepish grin, "Weeeeell...we'll still have my truck."

Jennifer thought of the embarrassment of past rides in that four wheeled rust bucket. "Couldn't we take part of the money we get from selling the car and buy something more suited to our needs?"

Jacob gently caressed Jennifer's hand, "If we're going to trust God, let's trust Him in everything. He knows what we'll need to accomplish the plans He has for us." Jacob nudged his wife and daughter close once again, "What a wonderful Christmas this is going to be...for us...and for Jess' Child."

Alicia laid her head on her daddy's chest. "Dad, will you do something for me that I've wanted you to do ever since I was a little girl?"

"Sure, if I can."

"Read me the Christmas story."

Jacob smiled, gave his daughter a loving squeeze, picked up his Bible, and turned to Luke 2. "Now it came about in those days that a decree went out from Caesar Augustus, that a census be taken of all the inhabited earth..."